Gravely Dead

A Midcoast Maine Mystery

Gravely Dead

A Midcoast Maine Mystery

Lawrence Rotch

This is a work of fiction. Names, characters, places, and incidents are the product of the author's imagination or are used fictitiously. Any resemblance to actual or persons, living or dead, is entirely coincidental.

ISBN 978-1-4357-1365-9

Prolog

Myra Huggard's weather-beaten Colonial had sat by the water's edge for nearly two centuries, and the passing years swayed its back as though time itself was trying to press the structure back into the ground. The still January night spirited away what little heat remained in the building, causing a roof beam to shift in the cold with a heavy thud.

Myra's eyes fluttered open and her arthritic fingers picked at the blankets, trying to bring them closer against the icy air. The old woman listened for another sound, but all she could hear was the beating of her heart.

The Russians were back. Myra knew they were Russians because she had seen them one evening as they prowled around her back yard in their furry Russian hats and black coats. They had looked like bears in the uncertain light. Or maybe like a pair of deer, her eyes not being so good anymore.

Myra took Evan's ancient, double-barreled shotgun to the heathens one night when she caught them poking at her abandoned chicken coop. She stood in the doorway and yelled at them to go away, but they just stared back, eyes glittering in the moonlight, until their silence made her so mad that she took a shot at one. She would have fired the other barrel too if the recoil hadn't knocked her off balance and stove in her shoulder so bad it took weeks to straighten out. Later, Myra wondered if they had known what she was saying, being Russians and all. In the end, she figured the shotgun spoke their language well enough.

Tonight was different. Tonight, they were inside. She took grim satisfaction in knowing the da ŋg foreigners wouldn't find what they were looking for.

Unless they were looking for her.

An occasional creak marked their progress as they crept around downstairs. Or maybe it was just the house shifting in the night. Cathy said she imagined things.

Myra fumbled in the darkness for the bedside lamp, but the damn thing wasn't where it belonged, and she knocked it onto the floor with a crash. They would know she was awake now, and that made her afraid, because the shotgun was downstairs, propped in a corner beside the front door. She would have to remember to put it under her bed at night from now on.

If there was a now on. Myra's ninety-four years and failing health didn't promise much of a future in any event, but she had survived this long by confronting adversity head-on, not by giving in to negative thoughts, like some she knew.

It occurred to her that she could even keep the shotgun under the covers. She smiled grimly at the idea of blasting the Russians to bits from the warmth of her bed, with scraps of comforter flying in all directions. That would give them a surprise.

The noises seemed to be coming from the kitchen, and Myra decided she might be able to sneak downstairs in the dark and grab the shotgun from the front hall. Bruised shoulder or not, she'd to put a stop to their prowling once and for all.

The old woman swung her legs slowly, painfully, out from under the covers and into the frigid air of the room. Sitting on the edge of the bed, she eased her feet into the fleece-lined L. L. Bean slippers that Cathy had given her for Christmas. Myra thought fondly of Cathy for a moment as her feet enjoyed the cozy warmth of the slippers.

The fondness faded when she remembered what Cathy had said

about the Russians.

"You know perfectly well there aren't any Russians sneaking around here," Cathy had told her. "It was just an old movie. Why would they come prowling around anyhow? Besides, they're our friends now."

"Not any more," Myra retorted. "I took a shot at one last week."

Cathy gave her a worried look. "Gosh, not the shotgun again. You'll hurt someone if you aren't careful."

"Dang right, and they'll holler in Russian when I put the lead to them. Just wait and see."

"Don't ask me to buy you any ammunition," Cathy replied tartly.

Myra frowned at this, trying to remember how many shells were left in the box.

Myra hunched on the edge of the bed a while longer, until the dizziness of sitting up had passed. Cathy's slippers were warming her feet, but the rest of her was beginning to freeze.

Cathy would believe in the Russians now. In fact, if worse came to worse, she'd have to deal with them. Myra had given her careful instructions about what to do if things went wrong, and she hoped the girl was up to the job, what with being so damned honest and prissy.

It was reassuring that Sarah Cassidy would be here in a few months. The fact that she hadn't clapped eyes on Sarah in almost forty years didn't enter into Myra's thinking. The girl had shown she knew how to keep a secret, and she was sensible enough to stop Cathy from being too much of a wuss. Besides, Sarah was from Boston, where there must be lots of Russians, and she would know how to deal with them.

Another noise from downstairs made Myra wonder if the events that she had set in motion would cause trouble for Cathy or Sarah. Normally, the old woman wasn't burdened with feelings of guilt, preferring to put the blame for her actions where it belonged—on the other person. Even so, the Russians, with their strange ways, made her nervous.

Myra's dressing gown lay on the covers. She worked her arms into the sleeves and shuffled along the edge of the bed, using the mattress for support. Launching herself from the corner of the bedstead, she staggered across the narrow room, guided by the faint, cold glow of moonlight filtering through the window curtains. Myra opened the door cautiously and crossed the hall. Breathing heavily, she paused at the top of the stairs, her hand on the newel post.

The staircase dropped precipitously to face the front door across a small, cramped hallway. To the left lay the parlor, where Myra had wintered over hens and started pullets, years ago when she still had a flock. A door at the right led to the dining room and beyond it, the kitchen.

A faint, quivering red glow outlined the dining room door. What could that be? Then it hit her. Of course, the Russians would have candles so they could see.

Or perhaps she had forgotten to close the firebox door to the kitchen stove when she filled it with wood last evening. It was getting harder and harder to remember these things, though she didn't admit it to anyone for fear they'd shut her up somewhere, like they did to poor Hazel Gartley. It hadn't taken that devilish nursing home six months to steal all Hazel's money and kill her off.

Myra stood and breathed a while longer. The last two months had made her keenly aware of the grey area that lay between being alive and being dead. She had seen Hazel pass through that strange land, a place where people—like that sniveling Gerry Gartley—made decisions "for her own good," without listening to what Hazel wanted. Myra wasn't going to let that happen to her.

The edges of the stair treads looked like a row of writhing orange snakes in the flickering candlelight. She blinked a few times to clear her eyes, but the snakes were still there.

Myra hated snakes. Trying not to step on them, she started down slowly, her hand clutching the banister. Suddenly, she was pushed from behind. Or perhaps she just lost her balance.

She felt herself pin-wheeling down the stairs, bones snapping like dry twigs. The momentum threw her across the narrow hall, fetching her up against the front door.

There was no pain yet, but her legs wouldn't move, and her left arm was crumpled under her. Myra's head was jammed up against the door, where an icy draft swept through the door sill's crack and sliced into her face.

The butt of the shotgun was inches from her nose, but her right arm wouldn't work properly. With her last strength, Myra made her fingers climb up the stock and lock around the trigger. The gun went off with a roar, dropping a blizzard of plaster onto her motionless body. Overhead, flames roared through the house.

Chapter 1

E arly March sunshine streamed through the windows, warming the back of Sarah Cassidy's neck as she stood and contemplated her handiwork. She had just finished sawing five inches off the legs of her reproduction Chippendale dining room chairs, and she realized the truth of what she'd heard: it really was hard to get the lengths just right so the chairs would be steady. She'd need pieces of cardboard to even the legs up. A power saw might have worked better.

The sun that baked Sarah's neck brought a ruddy glow to the slender board that balanced on her highly polished dining room table. Even placed catty-corner, the board was almost too long to fit in the room and it lay there, ends drooping precariously over the table's edge. Sarah admired the flawless mahogany, thinking that it had better be flawless, considering what the lumber supplier in nearby Boston had charged for it.

Her prize couldn't negotiate the hallway, so she had been obliged to carry it around the back yard through two inches of slushy snow and slide it in the dining room window. Something else for the neighbors to gossip about.

She looked at the chairs again. They were a bit dwarfish now, but no matter, their backs were the perfect height to prop up the overhanging ends of her board. She carefully positioned the chairs under the board, slipping bits of cardboard under some of the legs.

Next came the old, disused encyclopedia from Claude's study.

She carried several volumes at a time, stacking as many as she could on each chair to weigh it down.

Panting a little, since lugging thirty musty volumes around the house was a chore, Sarah paused in front of the hall mirror. Dark, shoulder-length hair framed an unmistakably Irish face that evoked, as her mother used to say, peat smoke and leprechauns. She tucked a stray wisp into place and gave her reflection a critical look. Not bad, despite the strands of gray. Her figure had held up pretty well too, all things considered, and one could take her to be well under her true age of fifty-five. If the lighting was right.

"You'll do, Sarah Cassidy," she murmured, pleased that she could say that now and believe it. Most of the time. It was even becoming second-nature to think of herself as Cassidy again, after all those years of being Johnson.

She returned to her work.

Her father's big, handmade tool box sat on the sideboard. The box, with its drawers, compartments and special holders for the various tools, had fascinated Sarah when she was a little girl. She rooted out two heavy iron clamps. Using two pieces of scrap wood to protect her precious board, she clamped it to the table top.

The lower jaws of the clamps were bare and they dug into the underside of the table with a satisfying, dent-making, crunch as she tightened them.

Until recently, Sarah hadn't realized, perhaps hadn't been willing to realize, how much she disliked the dining room set. Or, more accurately, how much she disliked the lavish dinners she placed on the table for Claude's hard-drinking business associates. At any rate, those days were over.

She gave the clamps an extra twist.

Next came her father's heavy plane. The senior Cassidy had been a carpenter who specialized in cabinetry, and Sarah often watched him work when she was a child, helping with some of the simpler jobs when she was a little older.

Still, the plane was intimidating. She had practiced on a cheap piece of pine from the local Home Depot until she was able to make long curls of wood roll out of the plane, shaping the board the way she wanted. Even so, she paused over the mahogany.

"You've got to start sometime," she said at last, descending on the board. A thin ribbon of wood fell to the floor. She figured there would be a lot more of them over the next few days.

Muffy Willet stared at Sarah with disbelief. "Why in the world do you want to go to Maine?"

They were sitting in what the real estate agent had called "The Breakfast Nook." That was twenty-nine years ago, when the Reproduction Colonial, like Sarah's marriage, had been new, exciting, and full of promise. Sarah still loved to gaze out the bay window to the deck, perennial bed, and lawn.

Stan's Lawn Service normally came out in the spring to spread their magic potions, thereby ensuring plenty of lush grass for them to mow all summer. She didn't let Stan's eager minions lay a glove on her flower bed, however.

"I went to summer camp in Maine when I was a kid."

"That was a lot of years ago, dear," Muffy pronounced.

"Thanks for the reminder. Anyway, I've kept in touch with the Merlews, who ran the camp, and they offered me an apartment in their house for the summer."

"They must be older than Methuselah by now. Are they still running it?"

"No," Sarah replied, "they retired and sold the camp years ago. It's long gone."

"Are they the ones who gave you that old boat in the garage?"

The boat in question was named *Owl*, a Herreshoff 12 ½, seventy years old and in need of serious repair. *Owl* was about sixteen feet long, with comfortable seats and the reassuring feel of a much larger vessel.

"Yes. It's been sitting in their barn for years."

When first introduced to *Owl*, Sarah was told the boat's seaworthy behavior was largely due to the 750 pounds of lead in her keel that helped the vessel "stand up to the wind." Needless to say, Sarah had known perfectly well that lead sank in water, and she had fretted over this until learning about the flotation tank in *Owl's* bow that made the boat unsinkable.

Designed in 1914, more than four hundred of the vessels were built in cedar and oak over a period of thirty years, plus numerous modern fiberglass versions. Many sailing afficionados consider the "12" to be one of the finest, most seaworthy sailboats of its size, and Sarah had been smitten from the moment, more than forty years ago, when she first laid eyes on *Owl's* comfortable cockpit, graceful curves, and wineglass-shaped stern.

"I learned to sail in that boat," Sarah added.

Erica Strom, a tall Nordic type, and one of the camp counselors, had taught Sarah the secrets of capturing the wind in *Owl's* sail, and introduced her to the joy of feeling the boat come alive under her hand. Sarah took to it like a duck to water and ended up teaching sailing herself when she became a counselor after Erica left.

Sarah's friend gave her a worried look.

"God knows you've gone through a rough patch with Claude," Muffy said, "but running off to Maine and living with a bunch of strangers isn't the answer. Don't you think you should be here with people who care about you at a time like this?"

"I just need to get away and think for a while. Someplace where I won't keep seeing Claude running around in his Porsche with some under-age bimbo."

"Yes, but way up there?"

"It's not as though Maine is a foreign country, for heaven's sake."

"Some little village in the middle of nowhere? It might as well be. What's the place called? Bryant Cove?"

"Burnt Cove, and it's not that small anymore."

A week of work had produced an ankle-deep pile of mahogany shavings in the dining room, and one of them had escaped, lying curled up in a delicate brown spiral on the kitchen floor. Muffy was staring at it, apparently trying to figure out what this alien thing was, but too polite to ask. For Muffy's sake, Sarah was glad she'd kept the dining room door closed.

"Why don't you pop down to New York and stay with your sister for a while, if you want to get away?" Muffy said, still furrowing her brow over the shaving. "You could take in a Broadway show, enjoy the city. Or visit the kids. At least you'd be with family and not all alone in the wilderness"

"It's just for the summer."

"I wish you two could patch things up," Muffy said.

"Have you seen him driving around with Lolita?"

"Lurlene," Muffy corrected reflexively. "It's just male menopause, you know. A puppy-dog kind of fling. He'll be back in a few months with his tail between his legs."

Sarah tried not to think about the image Muffy had conjured up. "He's barely willing to admit we're divorced, in spite of all the court appearances, legal paperwork, decrees, and settlements. And he's a lawyer, for god's sake," she said. "It's scary."

"It's just that he cares about you so much."

"He has a strange way of showing it," Sarah said. "Have you seen him when he's angry? Don't you remember what happened when my brother was in Boston last year and Claude saw us eating lunch together?"

"Claude just didn't recognize him in time."

Her ex-husband hadn't always been so jealous, and Sarah couldn't figure out how things went wrong, or if she had contributed in some way.

In the end, he found Lurlene, somehow blaming his infidelity on Sarah for being too old, too inattentive, too boring. Sarah gave herself a mental shake. She wasn't going down that road again.

"He is working on his anger problem," Muffy said.

"He has to. It was either that or jail."

Chapter 2

Sarah got off the expressway at Brunswick, picking up Route 1 partly for the scenery, and partly so she could travel at a slower pace with the unaccustomed weight of *Owl* on the trailer behind her Ford Explorer. Tourist traffic was still manageable in early May, so she had time to enjoy the sights.

Many of those sights were changed from her youth, some for the better. The Androscoggin River was cleaner than she remembered, with a fresh salt-air tang instead of the open-sewer aroma of her childhood. Most of the changes, however, had to do with the proliferation of gas stations, motels, antique shops, and the various other conveniences required by a thriving tourist industry.

The bridge over the Kennebec River in Bath, and the smaller bridge over the Sheepscot in Wiscasset were both new, though the views were familiar—except that the derelict coasting schooners in Wiscasset had rotted away.

Sarah continued up Route 1, through Damariscotta and Waldoboro, where she was pleased to see Moody's Diner was still going strong.

The sign for Burnt Cove was small and set well back from the pavement, almost as though the town didn't want to be found. The road itself was further hidden by a combination Irving gas station and convenience store. The last time she had been here, Dinger's used-car lot occupied the opposite corner, a patch of dirt with a few tired heaps parked haphazardly, and a tiny shack of an office where

Will Dinger used to sit reading girly magazines as he waited for customers. The young entrepreneur must have done well, for the place was now Dinger's Auto Mall with dozens of cars surrounding a cinder block building whose showroom windows covered more acreage than Will Dinger's original lot. Sarah slowed to negotiate the sharp turn onto Merrifield road, the most direct route to Burnt Cove.

Maine's coastline slopes from the southwest up to the northeast in a series of peninsulas that reach like rocky fingers, in a more or less southerly direction, into the sea. Merrifield Road ran along the east side of one of these fingers, and Sarah caught glimpses of the Kwiguigum River as it grew from a tidal brook at Route 1 to a broad sound at Burnt Cove village, half way down the peninsula.

To the confusion of unsuspecting tourists, Merrifield road became Squirrel Point road in the village of Burnt Cove. The town itself sat at the intersection of these byways and the Cross Point road, which bisected the peninsula. Passing through town, Sarah continued south on Squirrel Point road.

She thought about her hosts as she neared their house. The Merlews had been in their late thirties when Sarah started going to the Migawoc Camp for Girls, and they ran the place like a big, extended family—perhaps because Kate and Sam never had children of their own. Sarah figured they were both pushing eighty.

She crept slowly up the Merlews' driveway, the trailer lurching as it swung off the pavement.

It felt like she was passing through a time portal, with everything looking different and yet the same. The Colonial, set back from the road, looked just as she remembered it. A one-storey kitchen wing jutted out from the back, while beyond the kitchen, in the tradition of New England connected architecture, lay the woodshed, followed by a small apartment that had once been used by Kate's mother. The apartment would be Sarah's temporary home. The aroma of wood smoke greeted her nostrils.

The Merlews bustled out the door and stood gaping at her for a moment longer than was comfortable. Finally, Kate, her gray hair done up in a French twist, hurried forward to embrace Sarah.

"Good heavens," Kate exclaimed, "I never would have recognized you if it weren't for *Owl* back there."

"I'm glad Lester got her down to you all right," Sam added.

"We're ripping the barn apart, so you'll have to leave the boat outside," Kate said.

Sam was staring at *Owl*. "Looks like you fixed her all up," he said. "I hope you didn't find any nasty surprises, like rot or whatever."

"Actually, she still needs some work. There are a couple of broken ribs that I don't know how to fix."

"Been sitting in the barn for years, collecting dust. Probably not good for her," Sam replied.

"Come on in and warm up for a while. Sam can show you the apartment later," Kate said.

The big Glenwood cookstove had created a sultry atmosphere in the Merlew's kitchen. The worn, oak-topped table was as Sarah remembered it, but the Victorian-era cabinets had been replaced and the wooden counter-tops were now Formica.

Sarah watched Kate fill three mugs from a Mister Coffee, another jarring sign of change. An old percolator used to live on the stove, where it sat all day, turning the breakfast coffee into something that Sam referred to as "roofing tar" when he drank it in the afternoon. She studied Kate, much as she had examined the scenery on the way up, looking for familiar signs. The old woman had the same compact build, round face, and sparkling blue eyes, but, not surprisingly, there was a frailty in her expression and actions that hadn't been there forty years ago. An array of pill bottles lined the shelf over the coffee maker.

"I hope you're going to enjoy it here," Kate said.

"You can stay as long as you want," Sam added. "No one is using the apartment, and there's no point in letting it go to waste."

Kate put steaming mugs on the table. "Things aren't the way they used to be," she said, as though reading Sarah's mind.

"It's a lot more built up than I remembered."

"A ton of new houses in the last few years," Sam agreed. "You should see the new places out where the camp used to be."

"Sam's chairman of the town planning board, so he knows all about those new houses," Kate added.

"The planning board? That sounds like a lot of work," Sarah commented.

"Darn right it is, and thankless too," Kate replied tartly. She sat down across the table with her coffee mug and regarded Sarah. "It's been a long time."

"Thanks again for inviting me up for the summer. It's just what I needed."

Kate stirred her coffee. "I hope so. You certainly loved sailing."

"It's funny," Sarah said, "but I didn't realize Myra owned *Owl.* I thought it belonged to the camp."

Kate's spoon twitched as she stirred. "Remember the playing field next to Myra where we had the archery targets? She bought *Owl* for the kids to use when she and Evan sold us that lot. She rented the boat to us for a dollar a year, plus upkeep. God knows why."

"I never thought of her as being generous. I never thought she liked the camp kids either."

"She was a vicious old woman," Kate said, her face flushed. "*Owl* was a fluke."

"But why give the boat to me?"

"She liked you," Kate said. Sam shifted in his chair.

"I wonder if it had anything to do with Evan," Sarah blurted out, before she could catch herself.

Surprise and consternation flitted across Kate's face. "Myra never felt guilty about anything in her entire life," she snapped.

"Now mother," Sam pleaded, "she wasn't all bad."

Kate glared at her husband. "The woman was a vampire. You know perfectly well she extorted money from anyone she could sink her fangs into."

"I don't know any such thing, and you shouldn't go around spreading talk like that."

Kate turned to Sarah. "She was murdered, you know. Not

surprising, if you ask me."

Sam heaved an exasperated sigh. "We wrote you that Myra's house burned down back in January. She probably overloaded the wood stove and forgot to close the firebox door. It was mighty cold that night. They found her body in the front hall, a bunch of bones broken. She must have fallen down the stairs trying to get out."

"Pushed, more likely. What was she doing with the shotgun? And why had it been fired?" Kate demanded.

"The heat did that," Sam said, as though reciting a well-worn argument. "The police decided it was an accident, so that's what it was. She shouldn't have been living there all alone anyway, what with her mind going and not being able to get around very well."

"If it was an accident, then what happened to Cathy Leduc?" Kate went on relentlessly.

"The police are looking into that. She'll probably turn up on her own," Sam replied, sounding peevish. "Cathy dropped in on Myra a lot towards the end to help out," he said to Sarah.

"Anyway, Myra's gone, and good riddance," Kate said as she fiddled with the plastic pill dispenser in front of her. "But the town won't be the same without her."

"It'll be a lot more peaceful for the planning board," Sam commented. "Myra sued the town twice over Oak Hill. Lord, she could turn a planning board meeting upside down in five minutes flat."

Kate scowled. "Cathy helped her—drove Myra over to that lawyer's office, and persuaded him to work for free."

"Jamison Kincaid," Sam added. "He handles most of the real estate transactions around here."

"They were frivolous lawsuits," Kate said disapprovingly. "The court threw them out in the end. Typical Myra, stirring up trouble, just for the hell of it."

"Myra didn't care much for Oak Hill," Sam commented.

"What's Oak Hill?" Sarah asked.

"It's a development going in behind the Baptist church," Kate said. "You'll see the signs when you go into town."

"Only two lots have been approved so far," Sam added. "The other ten are still pending."

"They act like all the lots were approved, putting in that big paved road," Kate said. "It wasn't just Oak Hill that had Myra going, either. She didn't like it one little bit when we started splitting the camp into house lots and selling them."

Sam helped Sarah carry her luggage into the apartment and showed her around. The living space consisted of a sitting area with a sofabed, chairs, and a coffee table. A kitchenette occupied one corner, with a short length of counter separating it from the rest of the room. A small bedroom and a bath were located on the wall that backed up to the woodshed. The apartment was sunny, comfortable, and just what Sarah was looking for.

"You're awfully kind to let me stay here," Sarah said again. "I hope it's not too much of an inconvenience."

" Now. It'll be nice to have someone here. Give Kate something new to think about."

"She looks a little frail. Is she all right?"

Sam pointed to a thermostat on the wall as though he hadn't heard. "You've got your own furnace, so you're completely independent out here. We fixed it up for Kate's mother, haven't used it much since she died."

"We eat at six," he added, "and Kate said you were welcome to join us, give you a chance to settle in without having to hunt up a meal right off."

"Thank you. I'd like that."

He turned to Sarah. "Kate's had some health problems the last few years. I imagine you saw all the pill bottles. They keep things under control, but Lord, it's expensive."

"What about insurance?"

"It helps some, but not enough. Thank God we've been able to sell the campground a little bit at a time to pay the bills. The field next to Myra that Kate was talking about? We sold it last year. It was the last of Migawoc. The last piece." He sighed. "The last piece we bought when we were building the camp up, and the last one we sold." He shook his head as though trying to clear it of the past. "Don't worry about us. We'll get by."

Sarah suddenly felt like an intruder in Sam and Kate's lives, stirring up painful memories. She changed the subject. "What about Cathy Leduc? The one who disappeared?"

"She moved here from Lewiston four or five years ago. Works as a receptionist for Doc Caldwell, out on Route 1. She got to know Myra as a patient, and she'd been keeping an eye on the old lady for a couple of years. Cathy went missing right after Myra died. The cops are looking into it, questioning her boyfriend, and all that."

He went to the door and paused, his hand on the knob. "You remember old Amos Gaites' boatyard across the sound, where we used to store *Owl?* His son is running it now. He might be willing to help you work on the boat."

Chapter 3

Gaites and Son Boats was located across Kwiguigam Sound from Burnt Cove, only two miles away by water. Of course the trip was more like thirty miles by road—up one peninsula to Route 1, and then down the next. The place consisted of a big, ramshackle boat shed and a couple of smaller buildings on a tidal cove roughly 100 yards across. A pot-holed dirt parking area separated the buildings from a timber pier at the water's edge.

Parlin Gaites, somewhere beyond the sixty-five-year landmark, and known as Pearly to his friends, was of medium height, with short gray hair hidden beneath a paint-stained Red Sox baseball cap. He had placed a mast on a pair of sawhorses beside the shed and was going over the varnished spruce with sandpaper. Pearly worked outdoors partly to enjoy the unseasonably warm morning, but also to escape Eldon Tupper, his ill-tempered employee, who was working noisily inside. Much of the racket was courtesy of a local country music radio station, while the rest came from various objects being thrown around. The noise level was a reliable indicator of Eldon's mood, and things were loud today. A pair of State Police detectives had been questioning Eldon again, and Pearly figured it would be a couple of days before the young man was fit to live with.

He looked up as a black Ford Explorer sporting Massachusetts plates lurched into the yard with a Herreshoff 12 in tow. He stared at the woman who dismounted from the SUV, and moved to intercept her before she encountered Eldon, who had taken to bashing something inside the shed as though he was a crazed blacksmith.

"I need to fix a couple of broken ribs on my boat, and I was wondering if you could tell me how," she said.

Pearly decided that his visitor might be the spitting image of an older Cathy Leduc, but she sure didn't waste as much time on small talk.

He glanced at the Herreshoff. "I can see the bulge from here. That's serious work." He walked over to get a closer look.

"I'll do it myself," the Cathy-look-alike said, "but I need someone to tell me how."

Pearly groaned inwardly.

"I've done some work on it already, the paint and a new shear plank."

Pearly had clambered onto the trailer's fender and was leaning over the rail trying to get an inside look at the broken frames. "New shear plank? Which side?"

"The one your leaning on."

He glanced at the varnished mahogany, paused, and looked again more closely. The plank in question was the topmost one and it was shaped like a piece of molding, a delicate wine-glass curve that echoed the shape of the hull itself. He ran his fingers over the mirror-smooth finish and looked up. "How'd you get the shape?"

"I used a plane and a chisel. And lots of sandpaper."

Pearly meditatively ran his fingers along the plank again. "Nice job."

"Thanks, but how do I fix my boat?"

Pearly pulled off the Red Sox cap and dragged the back of his arm over his brow. "We're bound up tight right now, so I couldn't get to your boat before the end of June."

"Just tell me what to do," she repeated.

"It would take longer to show someone how to do a job like that then it would be to do it myself."

Pearly winced as a series of crashes burst from the shed. Eldon was supposed to be painting the deck on Percival's boat, not wrestling bears, though Pearly figured his oversized employee would be a good match for a bear. In fact, he had been a hot prospect for the New England Patriots before a bad knee ended his dreams of fame and fortune.

Pearly stepped off the fender and edged further away from the shed door.

"The trouble with an old boat like that is you never know what else may be wrong: rot, bad fastenings. These jobs have a way of growing."

"Couldn't I put a fiberglass patch or something on it to get through the summer?" she said.

"A fiberglass patch?" Pearly replaced his cap. This was turning ugly. He looked over towards the pier, where a strip of paving, running beside the pilings to the water, served as a launching ramp. Three seagulls were perched on the ramp squabbling over an unidentifiable, long-dead lump of something. "I know someone who might help you. Guy named Oliver Wendell, lives up on the Hound Hill road, off Route 1. Designs and builds boats. He's John Wendell's son."

Pearly saw her blank look. "John Wendell, the yacht designer?" Pearly shrugged. "Better'n he seems, anyhow."

Sarah rattled out of Pearly's driveway onto the tarred road while *Owl* lurched along behind, a dead weight. She was beginning to think the boat should be named *Albatross* or *Disaster* instead of *Owl*. She'd hoped for a little encouragement, some advice that would get her out on the water in a few days. Instead, *Owl* was beginning to sound like a lost cause, or months of work at the very least. The boat was becoming a metaphor for her own life—worse than it looked.

Yes, she and *Owl* had a lot in common. They were both old, useless, beat up, bulging, rotting, on the verge of total collapse.

Sarah headed back up to Route 1, and down Merrifield road to Burnt Cove. She would get some groceries and spend the afternoon settling in, perhaps take a drive around Squirrel Point. Oliver

Wendell could wait until tomorrow when she had finished wallowing in her self-pity.

Burnt Cove consisted of a few dozen buildings clustered around a small, sheltered harbor. Like everything else here, the center of town was disconcertingly changed, yet unchanged, from her childhood. Many of the old buildings were still there, but freshly fixed up and surrounded by new ones.

The old Grange hall was now a gift shop. Tabler's market, on the other hand, looked the same except for pavement replacing dirt in the parking lot.

The archetypal Lobster Shack was still at the water's edge, hard by the town pier, where it looked like it had sat since the dawn of time. The place had been enlarged, though, and embellished with awnings and picnic tables.

The town pier had been rebuilt and its adjacent parking lot was paved now. A boat hauler, a big, low-slung trailer with hinged, hydraulically-powered arms to support a boat, was easing a forty-foot yawl down the ramp into the water. At least Sarah thought it was a yawl and not a ketch. She tried to remember Sam's teachings on these matters. She was sure they both had the big mast in front of the small one. Yes, she remembered, a yawl has the small mast in back of the rudder, while a ketch has it in front, just like Y comes after K in the alphabet. Sarah smiled to herself, pleased at being able to dredge up such nautical lore and careful not to think about other, more arcane boat types.

She stopped at Tabler's market on the way home and picked up a few groceries. Their choice of food had gone upscale. The meat, potatoes, beans, and Wonder bread of old had been augmented by racks of wine, exotic cheeses, and focaccia. The prices were more upscale as well.

Sarah drove past the Merlew's driveway and continued on towards Squirrel Point. Though she didn't plan to go that far right now, the road eventually led to the rambling, turn-of-the-century Squirrel

Point Hotel, where it made a hairpin turn and meandered back up the west side of the peninsula back to Route 1.

Migawoc Camp had once occupied almost twenty acres along the rocky shoreline of Kwiguigum Sound, a sizeable amount of waterfront by present standards. Migawoc's land was covered with mansions now, most of them huge.

Myra's small, run-down Colonial had sat at the far edge of the camp, which was how Sarah came to know her in the first place. Driving slowly, Sarah found Myra's battered mailbox and the short, dirt driveway. Not wanting to maneuver her trailer into Myra's cramped drive, she parked across the road, next to a "Land For Sale" sign.

Myra's yard was smaller than Sarah remembered. There was a modest vegetable garden, untended since fall, beside the house. Next to the garden, a small hen house rotted amid a jungle of brush. A derelict Studebaker, whose faded pea-green paint was spotted with rust, sat nearby. A stand of poplar saplings surrounded the vehicle like the bars of a jail cell, and one had managed to grow through a crack between the front bumper and the body as though trying to prevent the car's escape.

Nothing was left of Myra's home but a pile of burnt wood that filled the cellar hole. A few charred beams reached drunkenly into the air as though caught while trying to escape the flames, and a shattered chimney jutted out of the wreckage. The smell of damp ashes, overlaid with a faint aroma of decay, hung in the air.

Beyond the blackened foundation stones, a scraggly patch of lawn reached down to a line of trees, with the water just visible through the branches. Most people would have cut down the trees to open up a view across Kwiguigum Sound, but Myra had kept them, claiming they held back the fog.

To Sarah's left, through a thick stand of brush and softwood, lay Migawoc's former archery and playing field. The screech of a power saw echoed through the trees.

Sarah remembered when she and Marlee Sue Ruggles had first met Myra Huggard. The girls were both thirteen, Sarah from South

Boston, her friend from New Orleans.

Marlee Sue, with her wealthy southern background, and Sarah with her working-class Boston-Irish upbringing, had both felt out of place in a Maine summer camp at first, and they instinctively banded together from the start.

The day they met Myra, the two city-girls had wandered beyond the archery field and gotten lost in a nearly impenetrable strip of fir and spruce. Eventually, they emerged behind Myra's chicken coop where their arrival stirred its occupants into a frenzy of squawking that brought Myra out to investigate. She was in her fifties then, a tall, boney, worn, hard-faced woman, her gray hair in an unkempt bun.

"Why are you brats stirring up my hens?" Myra demanded.

"We're lost," Sarah replied, noticing that Myra had a black eye.

"*Lost?* I suppose you're from the dang camp. I've had trouble with you kids before, now git." She glared down at them and made shooing gestures with her hand as though they were a pair of oversized chickens.

"But we don't know which way to go," Marlee Sue said, in her lilting southern accent.

"I don't care where you go, just get off my land before I take a shotgun to you." Myra glared some more and swore under her breath. "Come on," she said impatiently. Without waiting for a response, she pushed her way into the woods.

If Myra Huggard thought that she had permanently disposed of her visitors, she was sadly mistaken.

A silver-gray Volvo sedan purred into the driveway, jolting Sarah back to the present. Her apprehension at being caught here was relieved by the appearance of the man who emerged from the car. He looked about her age, with a round, friendly face, high forehead, and thinning blonde hair done in an artful comb-over. Overall, he had the appearance of a man who had known hard manual labor in his youth, but had gone soft in middle-age.

"Brian Curtis," he said, extending his hand and giving her a dazzling smile. "I'm the real estate agent in town, and saw your car out front."

He, and half the town, she supposed.

"Sarah Cassidy," she replied, entranced by the smile.

"Looking the place over?"

"No, but I knew Myra and decided to stop by."

Brian's expression sharpened. "You knew Myra?"

"I went to Migawoc when I was a girl," Sarah explained.

He glanced at the cellar hole. "Terrible accident. You heard what happened?"

"Yes, the Merlews told me."

"You staying with the Merlews?"

"Just for the summer."

"Well good," Brian said gallantly. "And if you decide to buy the place, let me know."

He looked at his watch. "I'm late for an appointment, but maybe I'll catch you later."

Sarah watched the Volvo glide away, then turned to the Studebaker and the rotting hen house. Things had changed.

Speaking of change, what had become of Marlee Sue? Sarah had lost touch with her long ago, but she pictured her young companion lounging on the veranda of a classic southern mansion while she sipped a mint julep and chatted with a handsome Southern Gentleman whose name began with Colonel.

A southerly wind had sprung up and brought with it cold, damp ocean air. The glimpse of water Sarah could see through the trees had a steely gray look that made her shiver, reminding her that coastal Maine in early May was a lot cooler than Massachusetts.

Sarah decided to explore the shoreline another day.

She emerged from the driveway and started across the road to the Ford. Suddenly, she was engulfed by the roar of an engine, the flash of a red fender, the blast of a horn. She leaped for the ditch, felt a blow, and tumbled through the air as the trees whirled around her.

A Chickadee sang its spring song in the trees overhead, while a cool wind hummed faintly through the spruce boughs. Dappled sunlight touched the ground where Sarah lay in the ditch and inventoried her aches and pains. Her right hip, wrist, and shoulder were sore. She moved her limbs cautiously. Nothing seemed to be broken, though her forearm was scraped. She lay shivering for a moment longer amid the smell of balsam, dampness and dead leaves. If she had been any slower . . .

Icy water began to soak through her clothes, and she eased into a standing position, staggered over to the Explorer like a woman twice her age, and leaned against the warmth of its hood. She looked again at the scrape on her forearm, half-heartedly brushed twigs and leaves from her hair and clothing, and wondered why the truck hadn't stopped. Did he panic?

On the other hand, the truck was accelerating when it swept around the corner, and the driver blew his horn and swerved across the road as though trying to hit her.

That's when she noticed a man watching. He stood some twenty feet away, beside a battered bicycle with a pair of five-gallon plastic buckets tied on either side of the rear wheels. Unkempt gray hair sprouted from under a grimy, knitted watch cap that looked like it had once been navy blue, untold years ago. A scruffy beard hid most of his face.

He stared at her through bloodshot eyes. "You don't live here," he announced.

Sarah looked at his grungy clothes. "No, do you?"

"I live on the planet's surface," he replied solemnly.

Sarah wondered if she was hallucinating, or if her hearing had failed, or if she was dealing a nutcase on a bicycle in addition to a homicidal maniac in a truck. Was the whole town like this?

"Did you see what happened?" she asked. "Do you know whose truck that was?"

"I see things that live in ditches."

By way of demonstration, he leaned over, picked an empty beer can from the underbrush, and tossed it into one of the buckets.

"Perhaps you aren't compatible with the space-time continuum," he added as he remounted his rickety machine and peddled off.

Sarah covered the short drive to her apartment in a daze. She barely glanced at the immense new house going up next Myra's place, or the second mansion that occupied the former location of Camp Migawoc's log dining hall.

She parked the car and trailer as far out of the way as possible and limped to her door with the bags of groceries, thankful that she hadn't bought anything heavy.

Once inside, she finished brushing the stray twigs out of her hair and weighed the relative merits of eating lunch before or after soaking her bruises in a hot tub.

She jumped at the telephone's unfamiliar ring and looked around. Where was the dang thing? By the third summons she had located it—a beige Princess phone on the kitchen counter.

"Hello?"

"Where have you been all day, for gosh sake?" Her ex-husband demanded peevishly.

"How did you get this number?"

"You didn't answer your cell. We have to talk."

"Talk to my lawyer. Don't tell me you've forgotten the restraining order already."

"That was in Massachusetts," he said.

"*What?*"

"What have you done to our house?"

"My house. Remember the papers we signed? And the judge? And all those lawyers?" she retorted.

"There are wood shavings and sawdust all over the place."

"What the hell were you doing in there?"

"And what did you do to our dining room set?" Claude said, ignoring her. "It looks you're planning a banquet for a bunch of pygmies. That set cost fourteen-hundred bucks."

"We got it at a half-price sale, remember? Besides, it's my dining room set now, so I can have as many pygmies for dinner as I want, and I bet they can't hold as much booze as your pals, which will save a pile of money."

Sarah paused to catch her breath. "Wait a minute. How did you get into my house?"

"Muffy let me in."

So much for changing the locks. She would have a serious talk with Muffy. "I didn't give her a key so you could go wandering around in there."

"I was just looking for some of my stuff."

"What stuff? There's nothing of yours in there."

"You're a hard woman, Sarah. We shared a lot of memories in that house. We raised our kids there, and now you're trashing it."

"If you can trash our marriage with Lolita, I can trash my dining room."

"You know perfectly well her name is Lurlene, and you can't blame it all on her."

"It's a good place to start."

"Nonsense," Claude replied in his most lawyer-like voice. "Remember what the marriage couns—"

"Goodbye, Claude."

"No, wait—"

Sarah hung up and leaned against the counter. Her hip ached. Her arm ached. Her shoulder ached, and now her head ached.

The phone rang. She put it in the refrigerator to muffle the sound, fitting the cord behind the orange juice carton. Claude on ice.

How did her life get to be such a mess?

Brian Curtis put off calling Doc Caldwell until evening, and he regretted mentioning the woman at Myra's place as soon as the words left his mouth.

"What was she doing up there? What's she up to?" Harry Caldwell's voice jumped out of the phone.

"What makes you think she's up to anything?"

"What makes you think she isn't?"

"Hell, Doc, if I had a nickel for every sightseer who poked around Myra's place—"

"She's not just anybody. You said she knew Myra from the old days. I don't like it. Did you get her name?"

Brian sighed. "Cassidy. Sarah Cassidy."

"*Darn.* And she's staying with the Merlews?"

"So what if she is?"

"Sam is the planning board chairman, that's what. Maybe Sam asked her up here because Myra told her something that would derail Oak Hill."

"Like what?"

"How do I know?" Caldwell said. "She's mentioned in Myra's will, though."

Brian paused. "Cassidy? How do you know that?"

"Somebody has to keep track of these things."

"I still think you're making a mountain out of a mole hill," Brian grumbled, though he wasn't so sure now.

"Myra added Cassidy to her will when she rewrote it last November, so they must have stayed in touch. I thought our troubles were over with Myra gone."

"I don't see how Cassidy can make trouble for Oak Hill," Brian said stubbornly.

"You want to take a chance on that? Well I don't. I've got a pile of money sunk in this, and so do you. You're single; ask her out. Use your charm. Find out what she's up to," Caldwell commanded.

Brian fumed. He was *dang* tired of people ordering him around like he was a lazy, stupid hayseed.

Sarah crawled out of bed Wednesday morning and soaked in the tub, as she had the evening before, until she looked like a prune and the aches subsided. Her hip was a deep purple and showed signs of more spectacular colors to come.

Fortified by a hefty dose of Tylenol and able to walk almost normally, Sarah set out in search of Oliver Wendell.

Yesterday afternoon's fog still clung, wet and cold, to Squirrel Point and Burnt Cove, but the ground rose and the haze thinned as she headed inland and crossed Route 1. Hound Hill road lifted her still further, into a watery sun. Through the trees, she could see fog filling the valleys below like a biblical flood.

The house was a typical Maine Colonial in a state of genteel decay. Also in typical Maine fashion, a large barn overshadowed the house. A hayfield separated the buildings from the road and a dozen ancient apple trees lined the dirt driveway. A derelict boat was rotting into the ground beside the barn, and Sarah could see the bow of another boat through the building's open sliding door.

She pulled into the yard, stopping abruptly when a black and white dog, possibly the hound of Hound Hill, bounded out of the barn. It barked and wagged circles around the Explorer, looking for a way to get in. Sarah watched from the safety of her seat. She wasn't big on dogs, but this specimen looked fairly safe, though unnecessarily boisterous. She was spared the need to find out more about the beast when a tall, spare man in sawdust-covered work shirt, blue jeans and painter's hat emerged from the barn's shadowy interior.

"Wes, come" he called. Wes responded by standing on his hind legs with his front paws on the driver's door and woofing through the partly open window.

"Wes, down." The man came over and hauled his panting, slobbering companion away from the Ford's door. "Now stay down before you scratch the paint."

Skeptical of assurances that the dog was harmless, Sarah got out warily. She didn't see any scratches in the paint, just dirty paw prints. "Hi, I'm looking for Oliver Wendell."

"Well, you found him."

Behind Wendell's lanky frame, she could see that the classic Maine barn had been converted into a workshop. A boat occupied the main floor, and the space that had once been stalls was now lined with workbenches and various tools. "I was down at Gaites' boatyard because I need some work on my boat, and he sent me to see you."

"Pearly Gaites sent you here?"

"I guess so. He had grey hair and a Red Sox cap."

"That's him."

He stared at her through sawdust-coated glasses for an uncomfortably long time. Sarah guessed he was in his mid-fifties. She tried to nudge the conversation along. "There are a couple of broken ribs, I mean frames, and he thought you might be able to tell me how to fix them."

Oliver glanced at the Herreshoff. "That's serious work." He walked over to get a closer look. "She's one of the newer boats. Must have been built in the late thirties, after they switched over to mahogany trim."

"I was going to fix it myself, but I need someone to tell me what to do."

"Unh, huh," he said unenthusiastically.

"I've done some work on it already, the paint and a new shear plank."

Like Pearly yesterday, Oliver had climbed onto the trailer's fender and was leaning over the rail, trying to get an inside look at the broken frames. "Which side?" he inquired.

"The one your leaning on."

Once again, like Pearly, Oliver did a satisfying double-take and ran his fingers over the varnished mahogany.

"I used a plane and a chisel. And lots of sandpaper," she said, feeling a sense of déjà vu.

"Nice job," he said.

"What about the frames?"

"I can see two that are broken," he said, craning his neck over the rail, "but there might be more."

"Why would they break like that?"

"Well, they're only about an inch square, and that's a pretty sharp bend at the turn of the bilge where they broke. This was cutting-edge yacht design a hundred years ago, and Herreshoff pushed the limits to make the boat as light as possible," he replied. "She may have hit something hard enough to crack the frames years ago, and they finally got dry and brittle enough to let go."

"The boat has been sitting in a barn for years."

"Doesn't help," he commented, getting down from the fender.

"How do I fix the frames?"

"Pearly didn't explain that?"

"No. Mostly he just wanted to get rid of me."

"Mmm." Oliver studied the planking.

The dog sniffed the right leg of her jeans. She hoped he wasn't about to mistake her for a fire plug. "What does 'mmm' mean?"

"Pearly has a lot on his plate right now." He turned to Sarah and said briskly, "Okay, here's what you do: First, you take off part of the deck, and some of the planks, so you can get at the broken frames to sister in new ones. Next, you cut new frames out of oak, steam them, and fit them in. Then you put it all back together. The devil is in the details, but that's the general idea."

"What do you mean by 'steam?'"

Oliver gave her pained look. "You put the frames in a steam box. Pearly has a long box made out of four boards, and he feeds steam from an old boiler into one end and has a lid on the other end. When they've been in there the right length of time—not too long and not too short—they'll be nice and limber so you can bend them."

"That doesn't sound too bad."

He gave Sarah a look of despair. "It may not *sound* bad, but you're talking about a seventy-year-old boat. There's no telling what you may find: rot, corrosion, more broken frames. Every screw in the hull may have to be replaced. Herreshoff built these to last twenty-five or thirty years, not seventy. You could have more of a hobby here than a boat."

Sarah turned away, brushed at her eyes irritably. "All I want to do is sail it this summer."

Oliver shifted his feet, clearly anxious to be somewhere else.

"There may be another way," he said. "If the rest of the fastenings are all right. And that's a big if."

"What?"

"You could laminate new frames out of thin strips that bend easily and glue the strips together with epoxy right in the boat. You wouldn't have to take anywhere near as much apart."

"Can you show me how to do that?"

"I've got a boat to finish."

"Just tell me what to do. You won't even know I'm here."

"Here? You're thinking of working here?"

"That would be easier, wouldn't it?"

"For you maybe," Oliver muttered. He looked at her suspiciously. "Do you have tools?"

"Of, course," she replied airily.

"Well . . ." Oliver rubbed the back of his neck. "Pearly sent you? I'll have to charge if it takes too much time."

"That's fine. Where do I start?"

"Take off the seat on that side so you can get at the frames." He nodded to a spot beside the barn door. "You can park the boat over there."

"How do I get the seat out?"

"How did you take the old shear plank off?"

"A hammer and a big screw driver."

He looked at her, horrified. "Y. kes. We can do better than that. Come on."

He strode towards the barn and Sarah followed, the dog trotting at her side and bumping into her leg with unwarranted familiarity. She began to wonder what she had gotten into.

Chapter 5

It was almost lunch time, and Oliver was leaning over the rail of a slender rowing boat, applying sandpaper to the inside of the boat's narrow stern when his uninvited guest appeared with a collection of boards in her arms. They seemed to be in one piece.

When he first looked at *Owl*, Oliver had run his hand along the new shear plank, his fingers finding only a few tiny imperfections in the shaping of the wood, nothing obvious to the eye. It was an impressive piece of workmanship.

She had needed some help at first, but she was good with her hands, and more important, seemed to have a natural gift with tools. Once underway, he hardly knew she was there. All in all, not as bad as he'd feared.

"Looks like you got it off in good shape," he said.

She came to a stop with her burden. "Can I put this in here somewhere out of the way?"

"It'll be safe in the corner over there."

"Thanks." She put the boards down and turned to admire the rowing boat. "It's beautiful."

"Mostly, it's late."

She ran her fingers tentatively over the hull. "I know I'm being a pest, and I'd like to make up for it somehow. I'm pretty good with sandpaper." She looked around. "Or I could sweep the floor, tidy things up . . ."

The scent of her perfume mingled with the aroma of cedar and paint that filled the shop. Oliver preferred to work alone and her presence made him uncomfortable in a variety of ways, not the least of which was the fact that she stirred up memories and emotions he had locked away when Arlene died.

On the other hand, maybe he was getting too set in his ways, and she seemed willing and able to help.

"Well, the inside of the hull needs to be sanded up in the bow," he said. "You can see where I couldn't reach with the power sander."

They worked for a while in silence, Sarah at the bow, Oliver at the stern. Wes lay in the sun by the doorway and watched these strange goings-on closely.

"You don't seem like a typical Massachusetts tourist," Oliver commented. "What brought you up here?"

"I spent summers at Camp Migawoc when I was a kid." She looked up. "Are you from Maine?"

"I grew up in Massachusetts. A little town called Wissonet on Buzzard's Bay."

"And your father is John Wendell, the yacht designer."

"Yes."

"I gather he must be well known," she added.

"One of the last of the big-name designers of the fifties and sixties." He glanced at her. "What brings you back after all these years?"

"I had the summer free and the Merlews invited me up. Did you design this boat? I like the shape."

"Graceful. I didn't design it, though. This is a Whitehall rowing boat. They were developed on the New York waterfront in the early 1800's. Some were quite big, but a Whitehall this size might have been used as a water taxi."

"A water taxi?"

"In the old days, you'd hire one if you needed to go someplace along the waterfront, or get out to a ship. They're still popular because they row easily and go well in choppy water."

"I suppose the streets weren't always safe in those days," she said, thinking about her experience with the red pickup. Of course that was just an accident.

"The waterfront could be tough in those days," he agreed.

Silence fell again, and she noticed him glancing in her direction every once in a while, checking on her work.

Finally, he asked, "Where did you get the Herreshoff?"

"It belonged to Myra Huggard. She gave it to me."

Oliver stared at her with awe. "Myra gave you a boat? You must be somebody special. She wasn't what I would call generous. And a boat—"

"I sailed *Owl* in camp, and taught sailing there too. I suppose she was putting her affairs in order and thought I'd like to have it."

Oliver nodded. "Myra probably didn't know it, but Herreshoff 12's have gotten pretty valuable. One in good shape can be worth twenty grand or more today. It's too bad. She could have used the cash. Of course, the boat could be pretty much worthless, if it's in bad shape."

Sarah stared across the room, her thoughts far away. "The girls at camp used to sing a kind of nursery rhyme whenever they walked past Myra's driveway. You know, 'Old Mother Huggard went to the cupboard to fetch—'" Sarah caught herself. "Most of it was obscene, but you get the idea. We did it to be mean. I feel guilty now."

"You were just kids, and she wasn't exactly a friendly person." Oliver returned to the sandpaper. "We'd better look the boat over before you put in too much work. Fixing one can turn into a lifetime job."

"You mean like checking the fastenings?"

"Yes. And rot. The transom tends to rot out on those."

"Can I ask you a question?" She said.

He shrugged.

"Why does everybody look at me like I'm from another planet?"

"Everybody? Like who?"

"Like you, for starters. And Pearly Gaites. And the Merlews. And some nutcase on a bicycle."

"It's just that you look a lot like someone who disappeared recently. At least from a distance. She's a lot younger, though, in her twenties."

"You mean Cathy Leduc?"

"You know about her?"

"Only that she was a friend of Myra and she disappeared right after Myra died, which sounds a little suspicious."

Oliver put down his sandpaper. "The word around town is that Cathy and Myra were arguing about something last winter, and it didn't help when Cathy disappeared a day or two after Myra died. Anyhow, some people think Cathy killed Myra and ran off."

"Could they have fought over the Oak Hill Development?"

Oliver gave her a surprised look. "I doubt it, but you never know what people will fight over in a small town. Cathy is a kind of an environmentalist, and she hates the development as much as Myra did, but Eldon Tupper is her boyfriend, and Eldon's brother is a builder who makes his living off developments."

"Did that make problems between Cathy and Eldon?"

Oliver looked as though he was about to tell her to mind her own business, but instead he replied, "Personally, I think Myra got careless with her wood stove, and Cathy took off for reasons of her own, maybe figuring people would blame her. I wouldn't say that in front of Eldon, though."

"What's Eldon like?"

"You'll know him when you meet him—works for Pearly. He's big, really big, and 'some ugly' right now, as the saying goes. The cops have been questioning him about where Cathy is and what happened to her."

"What about the guy on the bicycle?"

"Sounds like Ziggy Breener, the can-man. I don't know about Massachusetts, but lots of places around here have a can-man. Ziggy rides all over town picking up cans to collect the deposit. I didn't think he was back yet, though. Ziggy disappears in October and heads south for the winter. He won't tell anybody where."

"He goes south for the winter?"

"According to Ziggy, cans are like flowers; they bloom in the summer. I've been told he was an emergency-room doctor before he had a nervous breakdown of some kind and moved up here. He's got a shack out on Meadow road."

Oliver made a half-hearted effort to dust off his shirt. "That's enough for now. Let's look at that boat of yours."

A hammer and a wicked-looking icepick in his hand, Oliver ambled outside to where *Owl* sat. "With luck, this won't hurt a bit, old girl," he said.

Sarah wasn't sure if he was talking to her or *Owl*.

The Explorer made its way home in a more sprightly fashion without *Owl* behind it. Sarah felt more sprightly too, after Oliver pronounced the Herreshoff repairable, at least for another summer. Brian's Volvo swept by she neared the Merlew's drive. She waved, getting a big grin and a wave in return. Things were looking up.

Sarah's equanimity came to an abrupt end as she entered her apartment.

"Where were you? I've been cooling my heels for an hour."

Sarah gave a startled shriek. Claude was sprawled on her sofa, his feet resting on the tiny coffee table, Gucci loafers twitching impatiently.

"What are you doing here?" she demanded.

"You wouldn't talk on the phone yesterday, so I came here." He got up and handed her a pair of envelopes.

"What are these?" she asked, taking them warily.

"A peace offering."

"A peace offering?" She looked more closely. "They were mailed way back in January! Have you been sitting on them all year?"

"I've had a lot on my mind, thanks to you."

"Where do you get off stealing my mail!"

"Steal? That's harsh." He tried to look contrite. "I've been seeing the shrink, and going to that silly anger management class, just like your pet judge ordered, and I've learned how to control my temper, and I realize now where our relationship went wrong. We've made mistakes—I've made mistakes—and we've had our differences, but our relationship is bigger than that. We need each other to be whole." He gave her an almost desperate look. "I need you to be whole."

Claude paused, looking earnest and a bit confused by his own emotions. Sarah stared, open-mouthed. Could he really have turned over a new leaf? Did the shrink do that?

"Walking through our house," he went on, "made me see how much of our lives we've shared. It felt so empty without you—like my life." He made a helpless, flapping gesture with his hands as though unable to express himself. Sarah stood, speechless.

"Remember when we first moved in," he said, "and didn't have any furniture for the place, and we even had to buy new beds?"

"And a new sofa?" she said, smiling.

"And that awful rug the Willets gave us?"

"And how peeved they were when we got rid of it?"

"And the second-hand washer that exploded?"

"With half our clothes in it?" Sarah laughed. Those had been good times. "And remember when we bought the dining room set?"

"Yes," he said, momentarily distracted.

"And that beat-up old Volvo, so we'd have two cars for the garage?" she paused. "Wait. Where's the Porsche?"

"I hid it in the woods."

"And luscious Lolita?" she demanded, the spell broken. "Did you hide her in the woods?"

"I wish you wouldn't call her Lolita. It's insulting." He gave a dismissive shrug. "I dropped her off in Freeport. The important thing is I think we should try again—"

"*What!* Let me get this straight. You dropped off your baby bimbo to go shopping while you came here to con me?"

"Lurlene means nothing-"

"*Nothing?* How many other nothings have there been?"

"This isn't going the way I'd hoped," Claude whined.

"Out!"

"Think of all the good years we had. You can't just—"

"I'm calling 911!"

"Here? The nearest cop-shop must be an hour away. Face it, you're a city person. You don't belong out here in the woods." Suddenly his eyes narrowed.

"Darn , why didn't I see it before? You've got some hick boyfriend hidden away up here. I should have known."

"You're accusing *me* of infidelity? You're the one who's been fooling around!"

"How do I know you haven't too?" he demanded.

"Get out!" Sarah backed into the kitchenette, while she groped behind her for the phone.

"Hope I'm not interrupting anything." Sam Merlew appeared in the doorway, a double-barreled shotgun broken open over one arm. "Just wanted to let you know I'm hunting rats, so don't be surprised if you hear a shot."

Claude nearly fell backwards over the coffee table.

"It's just rat-shot," Sam said, "like sand. Couldn't kill a person with it." He pondered for a second. "Well, maybe close up."

"See what I mean?" Claude gasped at Sarah. "People hunt rats with *shotguns* up here."

"Have you seen any around?" Sam asked Sarah.

"This is my ex-husband," she croaked. "He's just leaving."

"Well, I won't stop you then." Sam positioned himself at the end of the counter, between Sarah and Claude. "Is that your little red car parked on the old tote road?"

Claude nodded.

"Hope it's all right," Sam said, looking earnest, and much dimmer than he really was. "Moose use that road, and red riles them up something terrific."

Claude blanched and fled.

Chapter 6

S arah was pleasantly surprised to see that Claude hadn't tampered with the letters. One had a return address of "C. Jamison Kincaid, Attorney," and was postmarked February 23. The other was postmarked January 7, a day after Myra died. The smiley-faced return address label said, "Cathy Leduc."

Claude probably took them from the mailbox out of spite, or curiosity because of the Maine postmarks.

He had disapproved of *Owl* from the moment she arrived on their doorstep in late October. The boat had been dirty, decrepit, and smelled like a Maine barn—a blight on the their back yard, in his opinion. Not even storing it in the garage had stopped the complaints. One more bone of contention in their disintegrating marriage.

She opened Cathy's letter first. Inside was a sticky-slip note attached to another envelope.

"Hi," the note said, "Myra wanted you to have this if she died before you got here. I need to talk to you when you get to Maine, because I know you're someone I can trust. Take care, Cathy."

Would Cathy write a note like this if she was about to run away? It seemed unlikely. Why hadn't she tried to make contact? What had happened to her?

The inner envelope bore the words "Sarah Cassidy" in a painstakingly written script. Sarah opened it and found three snapshots of her and Marlee Sue from their camping days, and a note.

She glanced at the photos hastily and then turned her attention to the note:

> "Sarah Cassidy,
>
> I know how much you loved being at the camp and the water so I am giving you my boat. I hope you will like it and think better of me for having it.
>
> I may never see you again and that is for the best, but please believe what happened to Evan wasn't your fault. It was drink that did him in.
>
> Some things cant be undone and we just have to put behind us. You did nothing to be sorry over. We must forgive and forget. 'Judgment is mine says the Lord.'
>
> I hope your life turns out good,
> Myra Huggard"

Sarah reread the note, thinking about the reference to Myra's dead husband, Evan. She had seen him in the late afternoon of the day Migawoc closed for the season, and he had died that night in a drunken accident. Was she saying there was a connection?

Myra's words knotted her stomach. What did she mean? The crotchety old woman would often say something with a hidden meaning, and then accuse the kids of stupidity when they didn't get it. Was this was another example of Myra's perverseness?

She glanced briefly at the pictures again. Maybe they were one of Myra's riddles too.

Myra Huggard was a riddle that Sarah had never solved. The thought was humbling and disturbing. Did she really understand anybody? Her choice of husband certainly hadn't worked out.

Though Sarah hadn't seen or heard from Myra in years, the note reminded her that the Huggards, both of them, had been lurking somewhere in the back of her mind all this time, and they were part of what had led her here.

Putting the photos aside for later, she opened Janison Kincaid's envelope. It was a brief letter informing her that he was executor of Myra Huggard's estate, and Sarah had received a "minor inheritance." Would she please get in touch with him at her earliest convenience?

It hadn't occurred to Sarah that Myra would have a will, but of course her land was certainly valuable. She wondered who Myra had left it to. *Owl* must be the "minor inheritance."

"Do moose really hate red?" Sarah asked.

Sam shrugged. "Who knows what a moose hates?"

Sarah sat at the Merlew's kitchen table sipping a mug of coffee. "And do you really hunt rats with a shotgun?"

"God no. I use rat poison, or maybe a .22 if I see one in the barn. It's just that you two were getting kind of loud, so we thought it might be a good idea to drop by."

"I didn't like him sneaking in here like that," Kate said.

"Do you have 911?" Sarah asked.

"Yes, but it might take a while for the police to get here." Sam looked at her worriedly. "We can keep an eye out, but you'd better be careful 'til he stops coming around."

Considering how upset they seemed to be over Claude's visit, Sarah decided not to mention her near-death experience with the red pickup truck. Instead, she told them about Kincaid's letter, hoping to move to a happier topic. If anything, the elderly couple looked even more upset.

"Kincaid handled all her legal affairs," Sam said, a sour look on his face.

"Like suing the town?" Sarah asked. "Why did Myra raise such a stink over the Oak Hill development?"

"She grew up in one of the earliest houses in town, beside the Baptist church," Sam replied. "The place used to be right next to where the development's access road goes in, and Myra claimed they were desecrating the old Burndt homestead."

"That was one of her crazy lawsuits," Kate said. "Myra claimed the homestead was an historic landmark, and the town had no right to let the road go through."

"No matter that the house burned down sixty years ago," Sam added. "There's just a plaque where it used to be."

"There was another lawsuit too?" Sarah said.

"Myra claimed there was an old Indian burial ground on top of the hill," Sam replied, "in the middle of the development. She wanted to stop construction and do an archaeological dig. It took months to sort that one out."

"Was there an old burial ground up there?"

Sam snorted. "In Myra's imagination, maybe."

"Is Myra buried in the cemetery?" Sarah asked.

Sam looked at her for a moment and said, "Way in back, up the slope by the stone wall where the new graves are."

"There's no stone," Kate said disapprovingly. "Just one of those little markers the funeral home put in."

"Speaking of churches," Sam said, "we were talking about you making some friends around here, maybe visit a church."

"I don't know if the Baptist church would be much like the Catholic," Kate said, "but there's an Episcopal church out on the Goose—," Kate caught herself and turned to Sam. "What's that road called now?"

"Turner Plains road," he replied. "Take the Cross Point road and turn right. It's a big, shingled turn-of-the-century building. Can't miss it."

Kate and Sam sat wordlessly at the kitchen table for a while after Sarah had left.

"I feel like a pimp," Kate said at last.

"The church is a good idea, though."

"I don't trust him." Kate ran her finger over the tabletop where a patch of sunlight had warmed the surface.

"She's old enough to take care of herself."

"That's not what I mean, and you know it. Do you think she saw

Brian leaving?"

"He was long-gone by the time she got back," Sam said.

"He was asking a lot of questions about her. He looked nervous. Maybe she does know something."

"She's never given any sign of it, except maybe yesterday."

"I don't mean about then," Kate said, irritated. "I mean now. She hasn't even seen the will yet. Who knows what trouble may come out of that."

"The will is probably just about *Owl*," Sam said.

"I don't suppose you had any luck?"

"I didn't get a chance, and I probably won't get one at this rate," Sam replied.

"I'll bet Brian thinks Myra told Sarah something that would make trouble with the planning board, maybe block final approval of Oak Hill."

"I can't imagine what Myra would know that she hasn't tried already," Sam replied.

Kate sighed. "I hate driving by the old camp and seeing those monstrosities. I hate seeing that Oak Hill sign in the middle of town. We shouldn't have invited her up here."

"We've been through all that."

"Well it's not working out the way the way we'd planned."

The morning had turned sunny and warm, hinting at summer, but a light southerly breeze was stirring, and fog would likely bring disillusionment by afternoon.

The fine May weather was wasted on Oliver and Pearly as they stood on Pearly's float and stared like a pair of mourners at a newly-built boat, glistening in the sunshine and redolent of fresh paint.

"A fine mess you've got us into this time, Ollie," Pearly said in his finest Laurel and Hardy imitation. Oliver hated the nickname, and Pearly knew it.

The object of their attention was an eighteen-foot open motor-boat whose tan and white paint complemented the varnished mahogany trim. The hull was made of fiberglass, an anathema to Pearly Gaites, who normally built in the traditional way with wood. The boat's existence was a concession to Eldon, who had built the wooden interior to Oliver's design. The fiberglass hull was a stock design molded in quantity by a local firm.

A teak-planked deck covered the forward four feet, while a control console stood amidships. A big Honda outboard sat on the transom.

Eldon had finished off the hull with particular care, since it was to be Cathy Leduc's boat.

Oliver kneeled down at the edge of the float and looked at the boat's bow again. No matter how many times he checked, the damn thing was still bow-heavy by a good inch. Having designed the interior of the boat, the error was his responsibility.

"The fuel tank is full?" Oliver asked.

"Yeah."

"I hate motorboats."

"They don't seem to like you much either," Pearly replied. "I saw it when she hit the water, so I climbed in and sat on the transom to level her up. Eldon didn't notice a thing."

"At least an inch," Oliver said.

"How about I repaint the waterline?" Pearly suggested brightly. "Make it come out right."

Oliver rolled his eyes.

"The forward bulkhead?" Pearly said, referring to the watertight panel that sealed off the rear end of the forward deck. "Eldon might have used thicker plywood than you said."

Oliver stuck his head under the deck. "Can't tell with it all fiber-glassed over and painted. He's not sure?"

"I can't get a straight answer out of him on anything," Pearly said, glancing towards the boat shed. "It's like having a rabid elephant in there every time the cops come and question him."

"The plywood wouldn't be enough to explain it anyhow. Get in for a minute."

"In the old days," Pearly said nostalgically, "some builders would launch a boat, let her sit in the water for a while, haul her out, and paint to the scum line. Worked every time."

"Are you going to get in the goddamn boat, or not?"

A boat is like a seesaw, with the weight of everything in it balanced on an imaginary pivot called the "Center of Buoyancy." It's the designer's job to add up the weight and location of everything, including the hull itself, and make sure it all balances so the boat will float level. Somehow, Oliver had let something upset the seesaw.

Pearly clambered aboard.

"Start moving aft," Oliver instructed as he watched the bow. "Okay, stop there."

Oliver straightened up, and studied where Pearly was standing. "How much do you weigh?" he asked.

"Enough," Pearly said. "I'll just put some lead pigs in the stern locker to level her up. Not that it matters to anyone except Eldon, with Cathy gone."

"I still want to know where I screwed up." They both knew that errors like this happened more often than some would like to admit. Still, Pearly was bound to wonder if Oliver could make a mistake like this, why not a bigger one?

"I thought you used a computer," Pearly said, as though reading Oliver's mind.

"I could have entered one of the weights wrong."

"Garbage in, garbage out," Pearly intoned.

Oliver vowed to hunt down the error. "I've got to get back home before that woman you dumped on me comes over," he said.

"Woman?"

"The one with the Herreshoff."

"Oh, yeah," Pearly said vaguely. He was poking around the stern storage compartment, apparently looking for a place to hide the lead blocks. "Boat looked like a sinker to me."

"It's not too bad."

Pearly straightened up from his investigation. "You going to sister in some new frames, like a Christian, or use that sticky shit of yours?"

"Sticky shit. It's better than starting to take the boat apart and not being able to find a place to stop."

"She did a good job with that shear plank," Pearly mused. "Must have been a hell of a thing to fit, with so much edge-set."

"She knew Myra. Went to Migawoc as a kid."

Pearly climbed out of the boat, groaning faintly as he stepped over the rail. "I wonder if she knew old Evan. There was a piece of work."

"I never did hear how he died," Oliver said.

"Damn fool got drunk one evening, took his lobsterboat out, and ran up on Brill's Ledge. Old Winn Tupper found his body and some wreckage the next day. Wasn't much left of him after pounding on the rocks all night.

"My old man managed to raise the boat and bring it in, but she was too far gone to fix up. Bow all stove in, back broken. Must've been going a ton when he hit the rocks."

Pearly shook his head. "I ever tell you about Evan and the wasp?"

"Evan and the wasp?"

Pearly settled himself on the boat's rail. "My old man used to go over to Evan's place and play poker with a couple of his pals—this was in the late forties—and sometimes the old man would take me along for luck. I think he did it to get my mother ugly. I was pretty young then.

"Anyhow, one fall during wasp season—you know, when they come inside to stay warm—one of the buggers started buzzing around the table in that sickly way they do in the fall. We batted at it, and the thing finally landed on the door frame going into the kitchen. Damn if Evan didn't grab his deer rifle and bet us two-bits he could shoot the wasp from across the room. He was boiled as an owl, as usual, so we hit the floor when he swung the gun up."

Pearly paused theatrically. "Drunk as he was, Evan nailed that wasp, left a neat little hole in the molding. Of course, his .30 '06 blew the back side of the door frame to hell, splinters all over the kitchen. Myra came boiling out of there and lit into him something wicked. We got out fast. Evan was some crazy when he hit the bottle."

Pearly stared out over the cove for a moment. "Things were different back then," he said.

They climbed the ramp from the float to the pier. It was high tide so the going was easy, but Pearly took his time. "Too bad you didn't put your old man on the computer, have him check the numbers. I wouldn't need those pigs."

"He doesn't use a computer."

"He doesn't need a computer." Pearly adjusted his Red Sox cap. "About twenty years ago, I built a nice little sloop he designed. You should get him up here for a visit, have him straighten you out."

Pearly stopped at the end of the pier as though reluctant to return to the boat shed. "How is John doing?"

"Not bad for eighty-seven. I went down over Christmas."

The whine of an overloaded Skil saw echoed from the boat shed like a dying banshee. Pearly grimaced.

"Eighty-seven? You should see him more often."

Chapter 7

The city of Belfast sits on a hillside, where its brick store-fronts slope down to Penobscot Bay, one of the largest inlets that slice into Maine's coastline.

Sarah stood on the sidewalk at what was probably the center of town, where five streets converged into a broad expanse of pavement, without benefit of a stop light. The intersection, and its orderly flow of traffic, had always fascinated her. In Massachusetts a place like this would be piled high with twisted metal, severed limbs, and dead bodies in a matter of minutes.

Perhaps the intersection said something about the enduring character of Belfast's residents. Founded on shipbuilding and fishing, it had fallen into decay with the demise of wooden ships, was reborn in the shoe and chicken processing booms, only to crash when the shoe industry fled the country and the chickens headed south for warmer climes. The city's latest savior was the credit card business, whose vast telephone service center had replaced the huge corrugated metal chicken barns. Sarah wondered about the chickens of old and the denizens of today's cubicles, and put the parallel firmly out of her mind. At any rate, Belfast was riding a wave of prosperity.

Sarah turned from her musings, and headed up Church Street in search of Jamison Kincaid's office.

"IRISH!" A shout echoed off the store fronts and froze pedestrians in mid-stride.

Her red hair was streaked with gray and her freckled face was older, but the approaching figure was unmistakably Sarah's child-hood friend.

"Marlee Sue?" Sarah said.

After an enthusiastic embrace, they stepped back.

"You haven't changed a bit," Marlee Sue said, examining Sarah. "What brings you to Maine?"

"I'm spending the summer with the Merlews, but right now I'm looking for Jamison Kincaid's office. How about you?"

"I live here. Moved up seven years ago. God, what a coincidence bumping into you like this. I can hardly believe it."

Marlee Sue pointed out Kincaid's office and they arranged to meet for lunch after Sarah's appointment.

"Thanks for fitting me in this morning," Sarah said.

Kincaid looked to be in his forties, tall, with a luxuriant head of wavy brown hair done in a style that reminded her of JFK. "It was a pleasant surprise to discover that you were right here in Maine," he said. "We had your Sudbury address, but that's where we hit a dead end. Cathy Leduc might have known you were going to be up this way, but she's disappeared, and I never thought to check with the Merlews."

"I'm afraid your letter got delayed in the forwarding."

"Well, it all worked out in the end," he said with a dismissive wave of the hand. His expression turned formal. "You understand the original will was prepared years ago, not long after Evan Huggard died. Myra didn't rewrite it until last November when her health began to fail. As I said when you called, your inheritance is minimal. I gather that Myra never mentioned any of this to you?"

"No. It was a complete surprise to me."

He nodded. "She didn't want anyone to know the terms of her will. Some people are like that. I did some pro bono work for Myra, actions against the town, and found her to be a very secretive old lady. Didn't trust anybody." He paused. "At any rate, the bulk of the estate, the house and land, was left to her sister."

"She had a sister?"

"Cara Turbot. I'm told she moved away after graduating from high school. She lives in a nursing home outside Cincinnati. Pleasant, but a little vague." Looking as though he regretted the indiscretion, Kincaid shuffled some papers.

"I wonder what she'll do with Myra's place," Sarah said.

"No secret there. She's planning to sell it once the will is settled and she gets the title. Brian Curtis will have the listing. He's a Realtor in Burnt Cove."

Kincaid handed Sarah a copy of Myra's will. "As you can see, Cathy Leduc inherits Myra's Ford, which Myra gave her in advance, and the contents of the house, which were lost in the fire. Unfortunately for Cathy, the old woman didn't believe in banks, so any cash and other valuables must have burned. I tried to persuade Myra to get a safe deposit box, but she wouldn't hear of it. Fortunately, she let us hold the will for her, or that would have been lost too." He shook his head sadly.

"Anyway, as for your share of the inheritance—" Kincaid smiled apologetically and referred to his copy of the will. "Cutting through the legal jargon, you inherit her Studebaker and the contents of the outbuildings: a lawnmower, assorted hand tools, hoe, shovels, rake, and so forth. I stopped by the place after she died, but I haven't done an inventory. Perhaps a lawn sale would be in order." He read some more.

"She also left you any boats she might own," he went on. "Again, the original will was prepared right after her husband died, and that part wasn't changed when Myra made the revisions last fall. I gather she had several boats back then, including Evan's lobsterboat."

Sarah gave Kincaid a confused look. "I thought the lobsterboat sank when he drowned."

"Apparently it was raised after the accident, and later abandoned. I expect it rotted away long ago. I'm told there was a dory as well, but nobody knows where it went to."

Kincaid handed her an official looking document.

"Myra left you this as well. It's an old deed to her property, from when Evan Huggard's grandfather bought the place back in the 1800's. It's worthless, really."

Sarah looked over the handwritten pages and imagined a secretary painstakingly inking in the legalese. Why would Myra want her to have an old deed? "It's worthless?" she said.

He smiled indulgently. "Pretty much, except as a souvenir. It simply shows that Evan Huggard's grandfather owned the property, and the deed is on file with the registry of deeds. I gather she never mentioned it to you and it doesn't ring any bells?"

"It's all news to me," Sarah replied.

Surrendering to another fit of candor, he said, "Myra Huggard was a very opinionated and eccentric old woman, as I learned in my dealings with her. People that age sometimes get fixated on an idea that only makes sense to them, and often it's best just to go along with their whims."

Sarah and Marlee Sue had a leisurely lunch at Darby's Restaurant in downtown Belfast. Marlee Sue had recommended the place as they walked down High Street, describing it as "kind of like an Irish pub." Sarah's straight-laced upbringing hadn't exposed her to many such establishments, but the food was good, and the old-fashioned bar, embossed metal ceiling, and intimate tables provided a comfortable atmosphere for them to catch up on the past. Marlee Sue had moved to Maine after her parents died, and now she worked as an investment advisor at NGTS Bank and Trust, which employed many of Belfast's residents. In turn, Sarah told of her career as a nurse before marrying Claude, and their recent divorce.

"I'm going to spend the summer living in the Merlew's granny flat and sailing around Burnt Cove," Sarah concluded.

"Sailing? In what?"

"Remember *Owl?*"

"The old camp boat the Merlews had?"

"*Owl* was Myra's boat," Sarah said. "She gave it to me."

Marlee Sue's jaw sagged. "Myra's boat?"

"It turns out Myra bought it for the camp to use."

"I thought she hated the camp. I thought she hated the kids, too." Marlee Sue shook her head in amazement. "And she bought a boat for them to sail? There was more to the old bat than I thought. But isn't *Owl* a wreck by now?"

"I'm still working on it, but it's almost ready to go."

"You're doing the work yourself?"

"Mostly. I've got some help." Sarah told about Oliver.

"You sure are a glutton for punishment. I've got a boat of my own. A real boat. A power boat."

"You never did like sailing, as I remember."

"Darn right. Why sit around all day waiting for the wind to blow when you can go wherever you want in no time?" Marlee Sue leaned her elbows on the table and regarded Sarah. "So you're going to be a middled-aged beach bum for the summer, but then what? Any plans for after that?"

"You always were disgustingly practical," Sarah groused.

"Somebody has to be. Are you going to look for a job? I've got some pull at NGTS, and it's a great place to work, good benefits, health insurance, nice atmosphere, even travel. I got to spend three months at their branch in San Francisco last fall."

"But I trained as a nurse," Sarah protested.

"That's okay. They support a bunch of community projects too. Come to think of it, they're helping to fund a place for troubled teens called The Spruce Cone Center. You know, problem kids, drug abuse, and all that. It's just starting up, and you'd be a natural with your experience as a counselor at Migawoc."

"I'll probably go back to Massachusetts in the fall."

"What for? Why not make a fresh start here?"

"Don't rush me. I'll think about all that later," Sarah said, remembering how pushy Marlee Sue could be. Myra's letter was in her purse, and she pulled out the photographs.

"Remember this?" Sarah said, handing her the first photo.

Sarah's companion squinted at the picture. "I'd forgotten about Myra and her damn camera," she said. "She always seemed to have it in her pocket. Too bad she was such a lousy photographer."

The photo showed Sarah wrapped vampishly around an upright granite stone. Her companion lay on the ground nearby, sticking out her tongue and grimacing. Marlee Sue laughed. "It's the 'Heathen Brats' picture."

Sarah laughed with her. "I'd forgotten she called us that when she took it."

Sarah handed over another photo.

It was near the end of the summer, and they had come across a stray arrow in the underbrush, an escapee from the archery field. The snapshot showed Marlee Sue standing against a big oak tree at the edge of the field, holding the arrow against her stomach and grimacing. Beside her, Sarah was munching on an apple, desert from their lunch. Sarah didn't remember why Myra was there.

Marlee Sue dissolved in gales of laughter. "I remember that. It's the William Tell picture! God, the times we had."

The third picture had been taken in August of Sarah's last summer at Migawoc, and it showed Sarah kneeling in the vegetable garden. The Studebaker was visible behind her, with a small, chipped enamel saucepan full of baby potatoes sitting on its hood. Marlee Sue glanced at the picture and laughed again.

"We should call it the 'Missing Ring' picture," Marlee Sue said. "I remember her telling you that she'd lost her wedding ring in there. She conned you into digging up half her potatoes looking for it. I bet the ring was in her pocket the whole time."

"They were just baby potatoes," Sarah said, "and digging them was kind of like a treasure hunt. I think she wanted a handful for supper, and teach me where potatoes come from."

"We were stupid little twits, doing all that work while she stood around insulting us."

"It was her way of teaching us something about life."

"*Her* life, maybe. But who wants to live like that?"

Chapter 8

Route 1 ran through the town of Lincolnville, whose beach of fine grey sand was squeezed in between the Lobster Shack restaurant and the Islesboro ferry terminal. From there the road wended its way through Camden, where stately nineteenth-century mansions lined the streets, and the downtown was filled with upscale shops. Sarah scarcely noticed these sights as she thought about her morning.

It was exciting to find Marlee Sue right here in Maine, but her old friend's efforts to plan the rest of Sarah's life had been irritating. One of the reasons she had come to Maine was to do just that, but surely it wouldn't hurt to start off with a week or two of down time before thinking about her future. For all his faults, Claude was a successful tax attorney, and he'd agreed to a generous divorce settlement that would keep her from starvation, so there was no financial crisis. Sarah supposed it was just a part of her friend's nature to be a little-miss-fix-it.

Absorbed in all this, Sarah headed down Squirrel Point road towards Myra's place as though drawn there by a magnet.

This time she pulled into the driveway.

Sarah's shiny black Explorer looked like it had come from another planet compared to her newly acquired Studebaker. Beyond it and the decaying chicken coop was a small tool shed whose door was propped shut with a stick. The ramshackle structure was home to Myra's lawn mower as well as the gardening tools Sarah had come to know in her youth, and were now her inheritance.

She opened the shed door and peered at the assortment of worn-out tools. These odds-and-ends had probably been more important to Myra than *Owl*. Why on earth had the old woman left all this to her? Sarah knew that Myra had influenced her life, for better or for worse, but it hadn't occurred to her that she might have influenced Myra's life in return. The hard-faced woman had seemed like Maine granite: tough, independent, unchanging and unchangeable—certainly beyond being influenced by a teenage girl. Had she really been so important to Myra as to deserve all this? The idea was unsettling.

Sarah turned away from the tool shed, noticed that the outhouse was gone, and felt oddly comforted by the idea that Myra must have finally gotten indoor plumbing.

She walked slowly past the foundation, trying not to look at the spot where the front door had been, where Myra had died. The big, cast iron cookstove that started the fire lay on its side at the bottom of the cellar hole, rusty and half-buried by pieces of burned wood, but otherwise little the worse for wear.

She crossed the overgrown lawn, passing through the screen of trees, to the ledges along the water. A gull's cry echoed over the water, clashing with the whine of a saw from the vast mansion that was taking shape on the camp's former archery field. To her right as she reached the shore were the collapsed remains of Evan Huggard's lobster shack, where he had kept his traps and fishing gear. There was nothing left of the building now but a few rotting boards and part of the roof, gradually sinking into the brush.

It was half-tide and the granite, wet and slick, sloped towards the water. Sarah stared out over the sound, where she had learned to sail and later taught others as well. She could almost hear the youngsters' excited shrieks as *Owl* heeled to a gust of wind.

She shivered, not so much from the cool breeze as from the sudden feeling that the ghosts of her past were standing here, invisible, watching. Sarah looked around uneasily, and scolded herself for letting the place get to her.

Most of the frontage was deep water, but a cleft in the rocks held a small area of mud that exposed itself at low tide. Myra used to dig clams there when she wasn't too sore from arthritis and other vague ailments. She had persuaded the girls to dig clams for her one day when she was feeling "punk," and Marlee Sue had wallowed barefoot up to her knees in the mud, to Myra's disgust. Sarah had worn her sneakers, without the socks, and never could get them completely clean afterwards.

The air suddenly felt thick with malice as she stood alone, and her heart raced with the sense of being watched.

This was ridiculous. Next thing, she'd start imagining Myra crawling out of the cellar hole, her nightgown still smoldering. Sarah spun around again, saw a flash of movement through the trees as if someone had darted behind the Explorer as she turned. Cut it out for heaven's sake, she scolded herself, it was just a squirrel. The place is called Squirrel Point, after all.

She turned back to face the water. She was spending far too much time thinking about Myra and the past, and it was beginning to get to her. It was high time to start occupying her mind with other—

"Good Lord, it's Sarah Johnson!"

The voice at her elbow nearly catapulted Sarah off the rocks. She turned to see a vaguely familiar face. Who was it? Oh yes, Debbie Vincent. The Vincents, Debbie and George, had lived near them in Sudbury for a while before moving away. Sarah remembered him being in banking of some kind, and retired.

Sarah glanced back towards the Ford, but saw nothing. She struggled to catch her breath, willing her heart to slow.

"Debbie," she said, "what a surprise. I didn't know you were around here."

"Our house is next door, beyond the Borofsky's new place. The driveway with the iron gates." Debbie looked at Sarah worriedly. "You look pale. I'm sorry if I gave you a start. What brings you up to Maine?"

"I'm spending the summer here," Sarah replied.

"That's wonderful. There's a regular little colony of 'Squirrel Pointers' here—at least that's what we call ourselves. We'll have to get together for cocktails. You and Claude will fit right in. It will be just like old times to have the Johnsons back in the neighborhood."

"It's Cassidy now. Claude and I are divorced."

"Oh, well," Debbie said, "that's too bad, though I always thought you two had a lot of differences to overcome. And Claude? Is he still in Sudbury?"

"An apartment in Boston."

"Well, it is nice to catch a glimpse of you anyway," Debbie said briskly. "I saw the car pull in and thought you might be a Realtor, or someone looking to buy the place."

"I used to know Myra," Sarah said, suddenly wanting to needle Debbie.

"You did?" Debbie stepped back a pace. "How?"

"I went to camp here and met Myra then."

"What a coincidence," Debbie said distractedly. "I hardly laid eyes on her myself, though George dropped in to visit her once." She shuddered discretely. "It's terrible to think she died right here. The house had almost completely burned down before somebody drove by and saw it. There isn't much traffic here at night during the winter."

Debbie's eyes flicked towards the charred stones. "I can't imagine what people were thinking of, to let a crazy old woman live alone like that. I'm surprised the police didn't take her away. And the Ocean View nursing home is nearby too." She shook her head sadly. "Maine is still awfully backward. The welfare people in Massachusetts would have moved her out of there years ago."

Sarah pulled into Oliver's driveway early the next morning and parked beside *Owl*. A collection of timbers were braced against the boat's damaged side, held in place by a web of ropes that enveloped both *Owl* and the trailer she sat on. Pushing the hull back into shape, Sarah supposed. She was greeted by Wes, who barked and wagged at the Explorer's door. She could hear the whine of a saw from inside the shop.

Sarah got out and patted Wes tentatively on the head. "Good doggie," she said, much to his delight. Emboldened, she patted him some more and was rewarded with a look of joyful adoration and a busily wagging tail. The creature didn't seem to be fussy about who patted him, so long as he got attention.

An elderly riding mower, its seat replaced by a box-like frame filled with motors and electronics, sat inside the shop's door.

"What's that," she asked, indicating the contraption as Oliver shut off the saw.

"Lawnzilla. It's a robotic lawnmower."

"You built it?"

"It's a work in progress," he said vaguely. "I hate mowing lawns."

"And it works all by itself?"

"It will when I get the bugs out," he replied defensively.

"Anyhow, you're just in time," he added, giving her a handful of strips. They were the length of her forearm, the width of the old frames, and about the thickness of cardboard. "Your new frames."

"They are? They don't look long enough."

"You only need to replace a couple of feet around the breaks."

" And how do I do that?"

"You glue and screw them in. But first we'll have to taper down the broken ends of the old frames." Oliver picked up what appeared to be a big electric grinder.

"I'm going to use that thing?" She had never seen her father wield anything quite so big.

"It's a heavy-duty disk sander," he explained. "Better let me do this. It takes a light touch. One slip with this thing and you could go right through the side of the boat."

She bristled at the macho attitude. "And you won't?"

Oliver put on a dust mask. "Trust me. This is how I make the big bucks," he said.

"Do you make big bucks?"

The corners of his eyes crinkled above the mask. "No, but I can starve to death slowly."

"You didn't get anything done on your boat," Sarah observed.

"I got tied up on something else."

"Like Lawnzilla?"

"Partly. Come on, and bring the extension cord."

Sarah followed, feeling put out.

Soon, Oliver had sanded away a couple of feet of the broken frames so they gradually tapered down to a feather edge where the breaks had been.

"Now we can start gluing in the new pieces to fill in what I sanded away," he said, brushing off his arms.

"Do I get to do any of that?" she said, feeling still more put out. A cloud of dust lingered in the air. Oliver nodded absentmindedly.

She followed him back into the shop, along with Wes, only less enthusiastic. Oliver donned a pair of latex gloves and had her do the same. He worked the lever on a machine that dispensed two syrupy liquids into a plastic bowl, and handed her the bowl and a mixing stick.

"Epoxy," Oliver explained. "Stir it for a couple of minutes." He busied himself with a staple gun and other odds and ends.

Sarah did as she was told, feeling like an apprentice witch preparing some kind of gooey, noxious potion.

"Why did Pearly Gaites send me to you?" she asked. "Aren't you competitors?"

"Not exactly. For one thing, we make different kinds of boats, and for another, boatbuilders often end up working for each other. Sometimes I go down and help Pearly out, and sometimes he or Eldon comes up here."

Oliver dumped some white powder into her poisonous soup. "Keep stirring," he said. "I've got a sawmill out back, and I saw boat lumber for Pearly once in a while too."

"So he was just too busy to work on *Owl?*"

"He builds one, maybe two boats a year, but he also stores a bunch of boats for the winter, and has to get them ready in the spring. It's a hectic time of year."

"He didn't mention epoxy."

"God no. He would have steamed in new frames."

"Would that have been better?"

"That's a matter of opinion. It boils down to how important you feel it is to uphold tradition."

He eyed the sticky mess Sarah was mixing, and added a dash more powder. "Pearly uses epoxy once in a while for certain things, but plank-on-frame construction, like *Owl*, is the kind of building he grew up with, and knows how to do. And he's very good at it."

"How do you build boats differently, besides using this goo?"

"The Whitehall you've been helping sand is strip-planked. Instead of using wide boards to plank with, like *Owl*, you use narrow strips so you can nail and glue the edges together, which means you don't have to put caulking between them. It may take a little longer to build, but you end up with a hull that's all one piece, so it's stronger, doesn't need as many frames, and doesn't leak. No leaks means less chance for rot. At least that's the theory."

Sarah had wondered why *Owl* had so many more frames than Oliver's Whitehall. "Why do people call them frames? They look a lot more like ribs to me."

Oliver shrugged. "Some people do call them ribs, and that's what they're for, holding the shape."

They went outside, climbed into *Owl*, and crouched together in the cockpit.

"We'll just glue in a couple of the strips today and finish the rest tomorrow," he said, handing her a foam brush. "Spread some epoxy on the strips, and where I sanded the frames. Then we'll staple the strips in to hold them while the epoxy cures." He watched for a moment, making her uncomfortable. "Don't be dainty, slather it on," he advised.

"Am I keeping you from anything?" she inquired.

"This won't take long. It can't or the epoxy will set up."

"Don't you like this type of boat? Plank-on-frame was it?" She waved the foam brush around *Owl*'s cockpit.

"I think any kind of boat is great, and Maine is one of the best places in the world to find traditional construction, and men with skills like Pearly are hard to come by today. Too many of the old ways are dying out, like your pal Myra."

"And your point is?" She paused, her foam brush poised over the bowl of epoxy.

Oliver stared pointedly at the brush.

"You were here in the sixties," he said. "Look at the changes. Fishermen like Evan Huggard used to live on the shore, with their boats moored right in front of the house. Today, a lot of them have to commute fifteen or twenty miles to the harbor, because waterfront land is so expensive and property taxes are so high. It's not surprising that some of the old timers get resentful about all the incomers."

"But, that sort of thing is happening everywhere," she protested.

"Tell me about it. I grew up on Cape Cod in the sixties, and it was the same thing then. Myra, with her vegetables and chickens, was one of the last of her kind. Did you know she was the last native Mainer to own deep-water frontage on Squirrel Point? All the rest belongs to people from out of state, and most are just summer people, or land speculators. It's amazing Myra was able to hang on so long."

Sarah remembered Kate's comment about Myra extorting money from people. How did she do that? Was that how she managed to hang on? "You make her sound like some kind of heroine. Believe me, she was no saint."

"She gave you a boat," he said, as though that forgave all Myra's sins.

Sarah wandered around her apartment, tidying up while she thought idly about lunch. She had called her brother in Chicago and gotten his answering machine, and tried her son and daughter, with the same result. These brief, one-sided communications left her depressed. Maybe Muffy was right and she should she be putting her life back together among her friends in Sudbury.

It was even possible that her coming to Maine had shaken Claude out of his mid-life crisis, and he was serious about turning over a new leaf. His visit had almost convinced her—for a moment. And he was right, they had shared a lot, including two kids. Perhaps more counseling . . .

No, she scolded herself, that would be wimping out. Kate and Sam were right. What she really needed was to make some friends around here before she went crazy.

A pounding rattled the door in its frame. "Coming!" she yelled.

Normally, daylight flooded into the room when she opened the door, but not now, for the space was totally blocked.

A giant stared down at her. "They're wrong. You don't look anything like Cathy," he rumbled. "You're much too old, for one thing."

"You must be Eldon," she said.

"You don't sound anything like Cath, either."

Sarah's eyes were on a level with the words "Boston University" on the young man's sweatshirt. She guessed six-foot-six and a good

300 pounds. She held out her hand, which disappeared into his calloused paw. "I'm Sarah Cassidy," she said.

"Eldon Tupper." His smile revealed a surprisingly even set of teeth considering the broken nose that adorned his face. "I heard you were in town, and I was here anyhow, so I came to see if you'd heard anything from Cathy."

"Just a note right after Myra died."

"A note? What did it say?" he asked eagerly.

Seeing his desperate hope, Sarah dug out Cathy's note.

His eyes devoured the words. "That's all?"

"Yes. Sorry I can't help more."

"She's gotta turn up soon." He sounded forlorn.

Sarah had no response, mainly because she had a feeling that Cathy would most likely turn up dead, if at all. "How did you find out I was here at the Merlews?"

"Oliver told me. Said you had a big, ugly black SUV." He stood for a moment shyly. "You knew Myra from way back?"

"Back in the sixties when I went to Migawoc."

Eldon stood for a moment, as though contemplating her vast antiquity. "Cathy and I used to go over to visit Myra a lot, clean up the place. You know, the house and the grass.

"She was kinda gruff sometimes, but she was real generous, too," Eldon added, "even gave Cathy a car for Christmas. It worked out good because Cath's car had died a couple of weeks before that."

"That was generous," Sarah conceded.

"It was just an old beater Myra used to drive. Took me a week to get it running again."

"Myra was still driving?"

"Up 'til they pulled her license a year ago. She was a demon on the road."

Eldon's brows furrowed. "She kept having these little strokes, going downhill each time. Would have had to go into a nursing home before long, and the idea of it made her crazy, probably would have killed her. Cath wanted to help her stay at home, so she and I went over to help out, and Ziggy stopped by when he was around."

Sarah figured another five minutes of staring up at Eldon's face and she'd need a chiropractor. "Would you like to come in and have some coffee?"

"Can't stay. Mostly, I came to see if you'd heard from Cathy, 'cause she wanted to talk to you." He looked wistful. "Let me know if she calls. I'm at the yard most days."

"I will. Do you know what she wants to talk about?"

Eldon shook his head. "No idea. She and Myra had something bugging them, but I don't—"

"There you are," Sam's voice was muffled by Eldon's back. "I saw your truck and figured you must be around here somewhere."

Eldon looked defensive. "I was meeting missus Cassidy."

"You don't need to bother her with Myra's schemes," Sam replied with unusual gruffness. "Come on, I'll show you what needs fixing on the barn."

Eldon scowled, opened his mouth to say something, thought better of it, and turned to follow Sam. Her view of the outside world restored, Sarah's breath caught in her throat as saw the all-too-familiar front end of Eldon's battered red pickup truck.

Sarah treated herself to an afternoon drive and a little shopping in Camden. She took the Turner Plains road on the way back. A sign at the intersection of Route 1 assured her that "The Episcopal Church Welcomes You."

She was on the opposite side of the Squirrel Point peninsula from Burnt Cove and the inlet was narrower here, about a hundred yards of tidal creek, compared to the broad expanse of Kwiguigum Sound. The houses were more modest as well, in contrast to the mansions sprouting up on the Burnt Cove side. The road wound through stands of softwood, assorted houses, and hayfields. Occasionally, a glimmer of water showed itself down a driveway or a break in the trees.

After a couple of miles, the woods opened up to reveal a large church, clad in weathered grey shingles, whose high-pitched roofs, wooden buttresses, and narrow diamond-pane windows gave it Gothic pretensions. In the late 1800's, Sarah knew, the church had served a wealthy colony of rusticators who built a string of Victorian mansions, nestled on spacious estates, that lined much of the lower end of Squirrel Point. They lasted until the 1947 drought brought a forest fire that leveled them all except for the Hotel.

Sarah pulled up to the front door, where a glass-faced sign board announced that Sunday services were held at ten o'clock.

She got out of the car. A shaggy lawn, populated by a group of ancient pine trees, lay between the church and the still, greenish-blue water. An idyllic spot for a picnic.

She wandered down to the water's edge and found a dilapidated picnic table sitting in the shade of a big pine.

The inlet narrowed to the right as it withered away to a nondescript stream running through a culvert under Route 1. A tiny island populated by half a dozen spruce trees split the channel to the left. The still air held the aroma of pine, spruce, and salt water. A seagull gave a mournful call as it circled over the mirrored, blue-green surface.

Sarah brushed a few stray pine needles off the picnic table and sat down. She hadn't been inside a church since her mother died four years ago, and she had no real attachment to the Catholic church, or any other for that matter, though her parents had taken her regularly to Saint Brigid's in South Boston when she was growing up. It probably didn't matter which church she went to anyway, so long as she met some interesting people. She sat a little longer, until the black flies chased her back to the car.

The First Baptist church, a picture-postcard New England structure, sat beside the road just south of Burnt Cove village. Oak Hill rose up behind the church, and the cemetery rested on the hill's flank, starting just above the church's dirt parking lot. A stone wall enclosed the cemetery's back and sides.

A new road, freshly paved, ran just outside the cemetery wall and up the hill on the side farthest from the church. A large sign stood at the end of the road, proclaiming, "Oak Hill Estates, Ocean View Lots, Will Build to Suit." In smaller print at the bottom were the words "BCD Properties, LLC." Some wag had spray painted a dripping black arrow on the sign, pointing to the cemetery.

Sarah pulled into the church's parking lot, where a notice board informed her that the Baptists worshiped at nine-thirty, under the guidance of Pastor John Wilson.

She walked slowly up a path that bisected the cemetery. As Sam had told her, the newer graves were at the top of the slope, which gave them a nice view over the harbor—or would have if fog wasn't obscuring it. The sky was turning heavy and grey, the air cool and damp as the sun dimmed.

A thin line of trees stood between the back wall of the cemetery and Oak Hill Estates, from which came the sound of a bulldozer and a chainsaw, along with the smell of raw dirt and freshly cut timber.

The flimsy metal marker on Myra's grave stood in stark contrast to the granite-hard woman Sarah remembered.

She wondered about Eldon's description of Myra's generosity. That wasn't the person she had known. Perhaps Myra behaved differently with locals. Perhaps she just didn't like the wealthy kids from away.

As a matter of fact, Sarah's family hadn't been wealthy, and her parents scrimped and saved to send her to Migawoc, but of course Myra wouldn't know that. By its very nature, wealth is relative, and even the least well-to-do of Migawoc's campers were vastly richer than the camp's crusty neighbor.

"Why did you give me the boat, the deed, and the rest of it?" Sarah asked the marker. "Why me? What in the world were you thinking?"

She didn't expect an answer, but the lack of response irritated her nonetheless. That, plus the fact she couldn't help suspecting that Myra's legacy hadn't been given out of generosity, but some darker motive.

"Judgement is mine, saith the Lord," Sarah added, "but I still don't think you were a generous old woman."

As if in answer, Sarah turned to see a wall of fog creeping up the slope towards her.

Dense fog and a cold drizzle swallowed up the afternoon light, leaving Sarah with her nose up against the windshield as she groped her way down the road. The blurred glare of oncoming headlights slowed her to a crawl. She waved to Ziggy Breener, who was peddling soggily towards her, his eyes focused on the ditch. He gave no sign of seeing her.

She turned the church question over in her mind. As far as she knew, the Merlews didn't go to church. She wondered if Oliver Wendell went to church, and decided not. How had he made friends when he moved here? It almost seemed as though he didn't feel the need of friends, but that was unfair since she barely knew the man. All she knew for sure was there were none of the tell-tale signs of a woman's touch at the Hound Hill Boatworks. The place had a scruffy look of vague neglect that suggested a man living alone.

Sarah adjusted her rear view mirror to deflect the glare of headlights as she strained to see the road. A sharp turn suddenly loomed out of the fog and she hit the brakes. The lights behind her grew alarmingly before falling back. "Sorry," she said to the head-lights. At least there was less traffic on this stretch of road.

Maybe the look Kate and Sam had traded when she first mentioned Oliver's name had to do with his bachelorhood.

Sarah vowed to think of something else. She didn't need men cluttering up her life right now, and certainly not some oddball like Oliver Wendell.

Just then, the headlights behind her grew again, filled the car with a dazzling glare. A sudden thud rocked the Explorer. Sarah yanked at the wheel, struggling for control as a truck swept by inches away and cut in front. She swerved, the road fell away, and her car shot into the woods.

Chapter 10

The Merlews clucked, fussed, and worried over Sarah's mishap as though they were her parents. She described it as an accident to avoid upsetting them, but even so, she was pampered all evening and most of the next morning, so it was a relief when they finally dropped her off at Lulu's Lunch in Burnt Cove the next day.

Lulu's place was just beyond Tabler's Market, and it occupied the same swaybacked building that had been Al's Diner in Sarah's youth. Being situated on a low hill, one could catch a glimpse of Burnt Cove harbor through Lulu's front windows.

In spite of the Merlew's fussing, Sarah managed to arrive a few minutes ahead of the luncheon rush, such as it was, and she snagged a window table. The cafe-style seating made the place look a good deal brighter than Al's old booths, and Lulu was more diligent about keeping the windows clean than Al had ever dreamed of. Sarah sat and gazed down Water street, a hundred-yard strip of pavement that led from the intersection of Squirrel Point road and Cross Point road to the waterfront. A misty sun struggled to suck the last reluctant wisps of fog from the air.

She looked up as Oliver appeared and pulled out one of the arch-back chairs.

"Thanks for rescuing me," she said. "I really appreciate you coming to pick me up."

He eased his long legs under the table. "I never say no to a free lunch."

They were allowed just under a minute to read the menu before the waitress arrived. At six feet and 180 pounds, Lulu Pelligrini didn't look like a woman to be trifled with, and she loomed over the table intimidatingly, the stub of a pencil poised. "Whaddya want?" she demanded.

"I'll have the number three," Sarah replied.

Lulu turned to Oliver. "What about you, stringbean?"

"I'll try the number five," Oliver said.

"Try all you want, you'll get the number eight." Lulu snatched up the menus. "Who's paying?"

"I am," Sarah said.

"Then I'll get you something better than the number three, dearie." Lulu turned on her heel and marched off.

"Why does she bother to ask what you want if she isn't going to give it to you?" Sarah asked, more loudly than was strictly necessary.

"Lulu comes from New York."

Sarah wondered what that meant. "At least you know what your getting. What's a number eight?"

"Not what it says on the menu," Oliver replied fatalistically.

"And you eat here often?"

"It's cheap, and good. You have to trust Lulu." He looked at Sarah. "Are you okay?"

"Just some bumps and bruises on top of the ones I already had," she said.

"You were lucky. How about the car?"

"You mean 'the big, ugly black SUV?' It's not too bad. The air bags didn't even go off, and I was able to drive home, once the tow truck got me out of the woods. There's a broken headlight, a few dents, and a lot of scraped paint from all those saplings. It's over at Dinger's, getting the headlight fixed. They said it would be ready this afternoon, except for the bodywork. I'll worry about that later."

Lulu arrived and placed a huge chef's salad in front of Sarah. Oliver got a large bowl of what looked and smelled like beef stew. The aroma made Sarah's mouth water.

"Do I look like a chef's salad type?" she asked when Lulu was safely out of earshot.

"To Lulu? Who knows?"

"You want to trade?"

"No way. Lulu would kill us."

"Someone is already trying to kill me," Sarah pointed out.

"Have you talked to the police?"

"Not yet, but I'll have to report being run off the road."

Oliver looked at her thoughtfully, and Sarah noticed that his eyes were a bright blue in the morning light. "So you think it was intentional?" he said.

"What else could it be? It was someone in a red pickup truck, both times."

Oliver busied himself with the stew. "Maine is full of red pickups. Was it the same one each time?"

"How would I know? I was kind of busy both times trying not to get killed," she snapped.

Oliver's spoon hovered over the bowl, his eyebrows lifting slightly. "I'm only asking the kinds of questions the police will probably ask."

Sarah would have preferred sympathy, but his question gave her pause. It could have been two trucks, in which case the accident theory made more sense. Perhaps she was overreacting. The thought irritated her even more. "The truck that sideswiped me sure as hell looked like Eldon's."

"You've met him," Oliver said. "Does he seem like the type to do that kind of thing?"

"You tell me," she retorted.

"He's been going around town, playing detective, pestering everyone about when they last saw Cathy, and he beat up three guys doing it, but nobody filed charges," Oliver said. "And he did have some minor scrapes with the law as a kid."

"What kind of scrapes?"

"Kid stuff. He got drunk one night when he was in high school, stole a dozen lobsters for a party some of his pals were planning, and dumped them loose on the seat next to him in his truck. It would have been okay except the bands came off some of their claws, and they started crawling onto his lap while he was driving. A cop saw him 'operating a vehicle erratically' and pulled him over."

"Sounds more like a prank."

"Yes, though stealing lobsters is taken pretty seriously around here. Did Ziggy say anything about the first truck?"

"He just babbled on about me being 'incompatible with the space-time continuum,' whatever that means."

Oliver nodded. "It means he thinks it was somebody with a grudge against out-of-staters."

"I didn't know you could speak nutcase."

"Ziggy is a lot shrewder than he seems. And he spends most of the day traveling around town, so he knows what's going on."

Oliver paused. "Do you have any enemies that might have followed you up from Massachusetts?"

Sarah thought about Claude's jealous fits, that struck like lightning out of a blue sky. Like the time Sarah was having lunch with her brother at Panera's, and Claude had run up behind her unsuspecting sibling and started hitting him over the head with a tray. But that was a case of mistaken identity. It was Claude's bad luck that a pair of cops happened to be there—not to mention the blood and stitches.

No, he might be upset about her coming to Maine, but running someone down with a truck wasn't his style. Getting her in trouble with the IRS would be his way.

Besides, he seemed to be looking for reconciliation, not revenge.

"No, I don't. Maybe it was just mistaken identity," she said reluctantly.

"Cathy Leduc? I suppose it's possible. That lets Eldon off the hook, though. He's met you."

"I don't see why someone would try to run me down just for visiting Myra's grave or prowling around her place."

"Why were you visiting her grave and prowling around her place?"

"Why shouldn't I? I used to know her. Why shouldn't I pay my respects? I'd have walked around the campgrounds too if everything wasn't covered with MacMansions."

"Yes, but if someone killed Myra, assuming she was killed, then he might be nervous about having a stranger poking around. Especially a stranger who knew her."

"We'll see what the cops say."

"They'll probably say that it looks a couple of accidents. Or maybe some guys with one too many beers who don't like SUV's with Mass plates."

Sarah ate in stony silence.

It had clouded over by afternoon and a stiff southeast wind blew up Kwiguigam Sound, lashing the water to a surly, whitecap-speckled gray under steely clouds that threatened rain. The cove containing Pearly's boatyard also sheltered his dock from the southeast, so the water here was calm, except for a few ruffles that rushed across the surface. A handful of boats lay serenely at their moorings in the cove as though savoring the peace and quiet.

Pearly lay in the bottom of Cathy's boat as it sat tied up to the float. As a result, he couldn't see the whitecaps rolling up the sound, but he could hear the wind whistling through the trees that shaded two cottages nearby.

Even on a Saturday afternoon, the boatyard was a quiet spot this early in the season, at least when Eldon wasn't blasting the air with his country music. And with only four other cottages sharing the cove, it was off the beaten track as well.

Even so, a visitor was often wandering around, like the first robin of spring, though a few were more like the first black fly. Pearly looked forward to the robins—some being close friends—and he tolerated the black flies. In any case, he tried to be patient with all of them, in hopes of gaining a customer.

Cathy's boat floated level now, thanks to some judiciously placed lead bars. Pearly lay on his back in the bilge with his head jammed under the boat's center console, trying to assemble the throttle controls. Eldon had built the boat and by rights he should be under here, Pearly figured. On the other hand, working on Cathy's boat reminded Eldon of his missing girlfriend and turned him morbid and irritable.

The situation was made worse by the fact that Cathy's parents were still frantic over the girl's disappearance and were constantly prodding the police, who responded by questioning poor Eldon some more.

Pearly didn't blame the cops. After all, Eldon was Cathy's boyfriend and therefore their most likely suspect. Hell, he was their only suspect. Nor did he blame Eldon for playing Sam Spade, trying to find Cathy on his own, though his bull-in-a-china-shop approach didn't ingratiate him with the law, or the people he interrogated.

There's nothing like a brand-new boat sitting in the water to attract sightseers. The present rubbernecker came from New Jersey, was in "Marketing," talked too much, and had been here for the past twenty minutes by Pearly's reckoning.

"Was it hard to build this?" Rubberneck asked.

Pearly squirmed further under the control console, trying to worm his hand up through the collection of cables and wire. "Depends on what you mean by hard," he said.

"I'm thinking about getting out of the rat-race. Retire up here, and built boats. How hard can it be to learn?"

The small nut Pearly had been trying to fit onto its almost inaccessible bolt in the upper corner of the console slipped from his fingertips and rattled into the bilge.

"I'm thinking of getting into marketing," Pearly muttered under his breath. "How hard can *that* be?" He rolled onto his side in the cramped space and groped around the bilge.

Pearly's visitor was on a roll. "All I'd need is a piece of waterfront land and a shed," he mused. "Do you know of any cheap waterfront around here?"

Pearly retrieved the nut and wriggled around for another try. It was like working with his head in a bucket.

"There's no such thing as cheap waterfront any more," he said. Who could afford to start a new boatyard on the water, Pearly thought, considering the cost of land? It was hard enough just paying the taxes on this place.

"That's what the Realtors tell you," Rubberneck said, "but I'll bet if you knew the right locals you could get a good buy."

"Let me know if you find any of the right locals."

Rubberneck leaned on the rail, rocking the boat just as Pearly was about to fit the nut in place. "This doesn't look all that hard to make. I've done some woodworking—you know, bookcases and lawn furniture."

Pearly's fingers scrabbled with the nut. If he dropped the damn thing now, it would probably end up in his left eye. "That's a start," he said, mentally placing his visitor in the black fly category.

"You just screw the deck on, right? That's easy."

Rubberneck leaned further into the boat. "What's this?" he said, tapping on the panel that sealed off the bow.

"Flotation tank. Keeps the boat from sinking if it fills with water."

"You mean a watertight bulkhead, like on a ship or a submarine to seal off part of the hull," Rubberneck explained, already playing the role of an expert. Tap, tap, tap. He rapped on the bulkhead like a starving woodpecker. "What's it made of, plywood?"

"Yeah. Covered with fiberglass." Pearly's uninvited guest was sprawled over the rail now, half in and half out of the boat, and his efforts to keep from falling made it feel like they were off Monhegan in a full gale.

Tap, tap went the woodpecker. "How did you get it so smooth?" Tap, tap, thud.

Parlin Gaites, overwhelmed by an awful realization, didn't reply. Instead, he lay paralyzed by the ghastly image that filled his mind and raised bile in his throat. How could he have missed it? Christ almighty, it was hard to believe how quickly a nice spring afternoon could turn to shit. He owed Oliver Wendell an apology.

And that was the least of his problems.

Chapter 11

The sky cleared and the wind dropped by dark, leaving a cool stillness in the air when Oliver parked his ancient Honda in Pearly's lot. The moon hadn't risen yet, and the sky was bright with a blizzard of stars, like tiny snowflakes frozen in space. Around him, the sharp salt air was almost palpable as it caressed his skin and filled his lungs. He stood in the darkness, breathing deeply and listening to the water lap softly against the pier's pilings. Oliver lingered a while longer, reluctant to leave, soaking up the tranquility of the place. He had an uncomfortable feeling that tranquility was about to become scarce.

The boat shed's big front doors were closed, but light spilling from the windows guided Oliver to the side entrance. Inside, Cathy's boat sat on its trailer beside a nearly completed Alden sloop.

"You're late," Pearly said, looking tense.

"May I ask why you dragged me down here in the middle of the night?" Oliver inquired, less disgruntled than he was trying to sound. He had never been here after dark. The overhead fluorescents bathed Cathy's boat in an antiseptic pool of light, as though it was a surgical patient on the operating table.

Pearly locked the door. "It's only nine o'clock, and you're here because I'm going to make a modification to Cathy's boat, and I want your advice."

"This couldn't wait until tomorrow?"

"No."

"What kind of modification?" Oliver asked suspiciously.

"I'm putting an access port in the forward flotation tank."

"May I ask why?"

"To drain it if water gets in there, why else?"

"The damn thing is sealed up with fiberglass and epoxy. How the hell would water get in there?"

"Who knows what might get in there and need to be cleaned out. I'll use one of these four-inch deck plates." Pearly held up the circular device. "See? Clear plastic cover so you can see if everything is okay, and the cover unscrews so you can reach inside."

"I know what it is, for god's sake. What I don't know is where you got this crazy idea. Don't do it. You put an opening in there and someone will fill it up with anchor chain, beer bottles, and who knows what else. It'll turn into a storage locker instead of a flotation tank."

"I think I'll put it right here." Pearly announced, as though he hadn't heard Oliver's objections. He pointed to a mark near the bottom of the panel. "Pass the hole saw."

"Get it yourself."

Pearly sighed, picked the big drill off a bench, and climbed into the boat.

"I'm going home," Oliver announced.

"Don't go yet; I may need more advice."

"The only way you'd take advice is at gun-point," Oliver muttered, but he stayed put.

Pearly kneeled in the bilge and went to work. It only took a moment to do the job, and he soon put the drill down, making faint sniffing noises as his nose passed by the freshly drilled hole.

Oliver looked on in disgust.

"See? That wasn't so bad after all," Pearly said cheerfully.

Oliver shook his head in despair.

"Let's see what Eldon used for plywood." Pearly reached into the hole.

"Jesus!" He snatched his hand back, his face green.

"Now what?"

"There's something feels like a plastic bag in there," Pearly croaked. He held out a hand. "Pass the work light."

Oliver handed him the light, shaking the cord impatiently where it caught on a sawhorse. Pearly looked into the hole as though a rattlesnake was lurking inside.

"What the hell?" He gingerly poked at what looked like a black plastic trash bag. "It feels like a big rock."

"You're a piece of work, Gaites," Oliver growled. "You dragged me down here because you thought someone had managed to stuff Cathy Leduc in there—"

"Well, a chunk of her, anyhow."

"—and you wanted a witness when you opened it up."

"Better you than Eldon. Shit, now I'll have to cut the damn thing out of there."

"It's part of a headstone," Oliver said as they pulled the black trash bag away from the object on Pearly's workbench.

"Why would anybody hide a headstone in Cathy's boat?" Pearly stopped short. "Jesus, you don't suppose Eldon found old Gerhard Burndt's grave?"

"His grave disappeared more than a hundred years ago. And even if it is Gerhard's, why would Eldon hide it in there, and how would he have found it in the first place?"

"Myra might have known where to look," Pearly suggested.

Oliver examined the weathered surface, moving the work light around as he tried to read the inscription. "It's just the top half, and the way it's broken off, most of the dates are missing. Besides, it's too worn to read the letters anyway," he said at last.

Pearly absentmindedly scrubbed the stubble on his chin with one hand. "Eldon put the bulkhead in last winter before Myra died. We've got to get that stone out of here."

"You've got to give it to the cops. It probably has something to do with what happened to Myra or Cathy."

"Hell with that. They'll just run Eldon through the wringer

again. Or throw him in jail on some trumped up charge." Pearly began working the headstone back in its bag.

Oliver watched in silence while his comfortable assumptions about Myra's accidental death crumbled. Gerhard Burndt was Burnt Cove's founding father, and it would be just like the old woman to stir up trouble with it, involve Eldon and Cathy, and get herself killed in the process. He thought about Sarah and the red pickup truck. Had she come across something that might incriminate the killer? Oliver had known Eldon for years. Could he have misjudged him? The young man did have a temper.

"Maybe Eldon *should* be in jail," Oliver said quietly.

"He's just an overgrown kid. Would he be going around asking everybody what they know about Cathy if he was mixed up in something?"

"Who knows? You have no idea what he may have been up to, or what Myra may have got him mixed up in."

Pearly glared at his companion. "You don't know shit about Eldon, and you don't know shit about Burnt Cove. I've known that kid all his life. There've been Tuppers around here forever."

Strictly speaking, Pearly and Eldon didn't live in Burnt Cove, but the next town over. Even so, the message was clear, and a wave of desolation swept over Oliver. A door had shut in his face. He thought of Pearly as a friend, and perhaps he was, but they were strangers when it came to this. Oliver hadn't been born here, hadn't grown up with Eldon's parents and grandparents, hadn't seen Eldon as a baby, or watched him go to school and become an adult. He hadn't witnessed Eldon's triumphs and defeats, could never know the young man as Pearly did.

He would always be from away. The gulf could never be closed. His roots simply didn't reach deep enough into the rocky Maine soil, and nothing could change that. Could he ever know Pearly or Burnt Cove when it came to the important things?

"I'm just saying this is evidence." Oliver spoke into the awkward silence. "It could mean that Myra was murdered. The cops should have it. There are probably fingerprints on the bag that'll tell who put it there."

"I'll hang onto it for a few days," Pearly said in a softer voice, aware of the chasm between them and pulling back from the brink, "'til I figure out what's going on. What harm can a few more days do?"

"For one thing, Eldon is going to know what happened when he comes in and sees that hole."

"The boat won't be here when he comes in."

Oliver looked at his companion with a dawning horror. "Oh, no. I'm not taking—"

Pearly finished pushing the stone back into its bag. "You designed the flotation tank, didn't you?"

"What does that have to do with anything?"

"Makes it your job to figure out how to fix it." Pearly smiled faintly at this perverse logic, and clambered back into Cathy's boat, grunting as he maneuvered the bag through the jagged hole to its former resting place. "I'll back my truck in, while you clean up around the trailer."

"Dammit, Pearly!"

"You got a tarp up at your place?"

Chapter 12

Sarah arrived at St. Agnes just as the Sunday service was about to begin, and she sat near the back in order to be as inconspicuous as possible. Even so, there was a discrete turning of heads in her direction as she took her place. The nave was big enough to seat two hundred, though there were only about fifty worshipers clustered near the front.

She admired the Carpenter Gothic architecture. Whoever designed the place must have had big ambitions. Age-darkened beams arched up into a twilight maze of timbers, high overhead. Wagon-wheel-sized chandeliers, hanging on chains, cast a yellow glow onto the pews. Sarah could imagine a vast colony of bats living among the rafters, unseen in the perpetual gloom, ignoring the humans that crept about down below.

By way of contrast, sunlight slanted through the stained glass window and bathed the altar in a multicolored light.

An asthmatic pipe organ, played with more enthusiasm than skill, rattled the air and ushered in the procession. Father Millay, a round, gray-haired man with a florid face brought up the rear. The service was enough like a Catholic mass to be comfortably familiar, yet disconcertingly different in places. Sarah concluded that Episcopalians gave the Blessed Virgin short shrift, but otherwise the service was satisfactory, and even some of the hymns were familiar.

When it was over, Father Millay invited everyone—his eyes seemed to single her out—to the parish hall for coffee and a chance to meet each other. Finally, the organ set to work stirring up the bats with a recessional hymn, and the congregation began to file out. Sarah made herself get up. Meeting people was what she came here for, after all. How bad could it be?

"That's Sarah Cassidy over there," Brian told his companions. "I told you she'd come. There goes Mabel, the one-woman-welcome-wagon, homing in on her."

Harry Caldwell and Roy Tupper studied the stranger from their vantage point a little apart from the rest of the coffee hour attendees.

Roy Tupper was in his early thirties, medium height, sturdily built, and with a prematurely weathered face. "She does look like Cathy," he said. "An older version."

"She might be related to Cathy, trying to find out what happened to her," Brian suggested.

"Eldon talked to her and he doesn't think so," Roy said.

Harry Caldwell, tall, slender, bald and distinguished in a three-piece suit, turned to Roy. "Maybe Eldon doesn't want to think so. Just how real is that Sam Spade act of his anyway?"

Roy's eyes narrowed. "Are you saying my brother—"

"She is his girlfriend."

"She's your receptionist. Maybe she found something in your files."

The parish hall, like the nave, had a high, vaulted ceiling that extended up into the gloom, and Brian rolled his eyes heavenward, though not in prayer, or in search of bats. "Keep it down," he said, moving between the two.

"I've got plenty of other work without putting up with this stuff," Roy muttered.

Caldwell turned on Brian. "You were supposed to find out what she's up to. The planning board meets in two weeks. Have you even talked to her yet?"

"I got her here, didn't I?" Brian retorted. "Why don't you talk to her yourself if you're in such a fuss?"

Caldwell leaned into Brian's face. "Because I'm paying *you* to take care of that stuff," he hissed.

Roy was staring at Sarah again. "I think I saw her up at Myra's grave Friday," he said. "Black Explorer?"

Brian nodded.

"This keeps getting worse and worse," Caldwell said. "What else was she looking at up there?"

"I'm paid build houses, not spy on people," Roy said, glowering at Brian.

"Get off my back," Brian growled. "Come on, Tupper, you can meet her too."

"Hello, I'm Mabel Hardwick." The speaker was a tall, stork-like woman with a halo of gray hair. She looked to be in her eighties. "Are you visiting for the summer?"

"Yes," Sarah replied, "I'm staying at the Merlew's."

Mabel was staring at Sarah in a way that had long-since become irritatingly familiar. "Are you related to Cathy Leduc?"

"No. You're the organist, aren't you?"

"Organist isn't quite the right word," Mabel said. "I play the piano really, but I'm all we've got. That organ has so many pedals and things."

Mabel spotted Roy and Brian approaching, and stepped in to make the introductions.

"Royal Tupper, this is Sarah Cassidy. She's staying with the Merlews. Doesn't she look just like Cathy Leduc?"

"Call me Roy," he said, extending a calloused hand. "You do look like you could be related to her."

"Well, I'm not," Sarah said, more curtly than she intended. "Are you Eldon's brother? You two don't look much alike."

"Half-brother. He kept coming back for more when they handed out big, that's for sure. Going to be here long?"

"I'll be here for the summer, and I wanted to get out and meet some people," Sarah explained.

"This is a good place for it," Roy commented.

Mabel had been tugging at Brian's arm. "This is Brian Curtis," she said.

"We've met," Brian said. "I was hoping the Merlews might persuade you to come." He gave her an embarrassed smile. "Seriously, I know practically everyone around here—part of my job." His eyes flicked to Sarah's ring finger, "so if you and your husband want to look around, just give me a call."

Sarah flushed. She had removed her engagement ring, but for reasons that weren't clear to her, had kept the wedding band. "Former husband," she said.

"Been there, done that," Brian said cheerfully. "Not to be nosey, but do you know many people in town?"

"Just the Merlews and the Vincents."

"George and Debbie Vincent? I sold them that house lot, and Roy built the house. In fact he's building the new house next door to them for a couple named Borofsky. Going to be quite a place. Biggest house on the point, so far. Have you seen it?"

"Just from driving by."

"The Hotel is bigger," Roy pointed out.

"Stop in and take a look," Brian said. "I'm sure Roy would be glad to show you around."

"I've got a crew there, and I'm not always around," Roy said in a off-putting way. "I'm up at Oak Hill a lot of the time."

Roy saw Harry Caldwell approaching and began to sidle away. "Catch you later," he said.

Mabel's eyes lit up as she prepared for another round of introductions.

Chapter 13

Sarah pulled into Oliver's front yard Sunday afternoon and found a second boat and trailer parked next to _Owl_. A blue plastic tarp covered the boat's deck.

Sarah was feeling more cheerful than she had in days, probably the aftereffects of coffee hour at St. Agnes. Mabel Hardwick had been pleasant, though a bit earnest, and Sarah had met Edna Grimstone, a friend of Mabel's. Brian's attentiveness had been good for her morale, and he had asked her out on a "luncheon date," as he gallantly called it. In her present rosy mood, even Oliver was all right, though quirky.

She found that Oliver didn't share her good spirits.

"Where did that boat come from?" she asked, indicating the tarp-covered mound. A light westerly breeze flapped the blue material.

"It's Cathy Leduc's," Oliver growled in a tone that made it clear the subject was off limits.

They had finished epoxying the broken frames yesterday, and Oliver had screwed the planking to them and sanded the repairs while she was at church. Sarah went to work putting primer on the bare wood inside the boat while Oliver worked underneath, pounding what looked like strands of yarn into some of the seams.

"You're spending a lot of time working on _Owl_," Sarah said. "Aren't I keeping you away from your boat?"

"You can help me put another coat of paint on it later. Payment in kind."

"You must be building it for someone?"

"A guy named George Vincent out on Squirrel Point, your old stamping ground."

"I know the Vincents from when they lived near us in Sudbury. I bumped into Debbie at Myra's the other day."

"Small world." Oliver's voice drifted up, cool and slightly muffled, from underneath *Owl.*

"See?" She said mischievously. "The incomers aren't all bad. They're buying your boats and bringing money into the area." Sarah knew she was throwing gasoline on his smoldering ill-humor, but couldn't resist the temptation.

"Maybe that's not such a good thing."

"And poverty is a good thing?"

"Define poverty."

Sarah slopped on more primer than she intended. "I hope you're not going to give me a lot of idealistic baloney about Myra Huggard."

"Myra? Heck no. She could have sold her place and gotten a condo in Rockland, a nice cottage in Appleton with a vegetable garden, or an assisted living facility, and had money to spare." Oliver straightened up and watched Sarah busily wielding the brush. "She *chose* to live in a drafty old house that was falling down around her ears because she wanted to. Does that make her poor? Or crazy? What gives us the right to judge her lifestyle? Who was she hurting?

"I wonder how much grieving the newcomers down there did when Myra and her house burned up," he concluded.

Sarah put down the brush, feeling defensive because she had wondered the same thing. "Are you suggesting one of the Squirrel Pointers had something to do with her death?"

"'Squirrel Pointers?' It sounds like a breed of dog," he commented. "I'm saying she was standing in the way of progress, and people who do that can get into trouble, especially with so much money involved. Look at the surveyor's flags along Squirrel Point. All that waterfront, from Myra to the Hotel, will be house lots in a few years, and her place was an eyesore."

"But there was no need to kill her. Everyone knew she was dying. A few months and she would have been in a nursing home and her place would have been sold."

"Do you really think the fire was an accident?"

"Maybe." She wondered what was going on. Just the other day, he had dismissed Myra's death as a mishap.

"Do you agree with the police that Eldon killed Cathy?"

"He doesn't seem like the killer type to me," she said, remembering Eldon's bashful smile.

"No, but she's his girlfriend, and that makes him the most likely candidate. Besides, what about you and Eldon's truck?"

Sarah was getting more and more confused by Oliver's change of heart. Hadn't he been defending Eldon at Lulu's yesterday? "I met his brother at St. Agnes this morning," she said.

"That shingled monster out on the Goosespit Flats road?"

"The Turner Plains road," Sarah corrected, clinging to her cheerfulness.

"I suppose they had to change the name for 911."

"You should go to church sometime." She said, goading him again. "It's not good to live alone out here."

"Who's alone? You think I live in a cave like a hermit? I've got Wes, and there's always somebody coming around to make a pest of themselves."

As if on cue, Eldon's truck rumbled up the driveway and lurched to a stop in front of the barn door. Sarah thought she saw a fresh dent on the truck's right side, hidden among the older dings and scrapes.

"Dang it all to hell," Oliver muttered as he moved to put himself between the truck and Cathy's boat.

Pearly emerged and sauntered over. "Thought I'd see how you were coming along," he said. He looked at Sarah's battered Explorer. "Lord, what happened to that?"

Oliver scowled at his latest visitor. "She got run off the road by Eldon's truck."

"You've been reading Stephen King again and it's gone to your head," Pearly said. "Trucks don't run people off the road; people *in* trucks run people off the road."

"Look at that fresh dent." Oliver demanded, pointing to Eldon's truck. "I'll bet it matches the red smudge on Sarah's front bumper."

"Heck there are dents all over it. You know perfectly well Eldon drives by feel. Besides, everyone borrows his truck."

"Everyone borrows his truck?" Sarah said.

"He keeps the keys in it all the time, right over the visor," Pearly explained.

"Don't be surprised if the cops ask him about it," Oliver said darkly. "Did you drive up here in that thing just to give me a heart attack?"

"I borrowed it to keep Eldon from driving up here."

"You told him the boat's here?" Oliver looked nervous.

"Had to tell him something. I said you took it to get some measurements, take some pictures for your files."

"And he believed that?"

"He knows I wouldn't lie to him."

Oliver shook his head in disgust and pointed to Cathy's boat. "I want it out of here."

"Did you build it?" Sarah asked Pearly as she looked again at the shapeless mound under the tarp.

"Eldon built it," Pearly said. He turned to Oliver. "Have you fixed the hole yet?"

"*Fixed it?*"

"I can't take the boat back to Eldon the way it is now," Pearly replied, as though talking to an unreasonable child.

"It's your hole," Oliver pointed out.

"It's your flotation tank. Besides, I can't fix it down there with Eldon around."

Oliver's uninvited guest ambled over to the far side of *Owl.* "Gee," he said, "who taught you how to caulk a boat? Where's the hammer and iron?"

"Do you want the bag inside the tank when I seal it up?" Oliver spoke with elaborate sarcasm. Pearly ignored him and began pounding at *Owl's* seams.

"What bag?" Sarah said, visualizing a packet filled with illicit powders.

"I don't want it anywhere near the boat," Pearly said. What with the ringing of Pearly's hammer and his position under *Owl*, Sarah had trouble hearing him.

"Don't pound so hard," Oliver said. "You aren't caulking a four-masted schooner, forgoshsake."

Pearly muttered something unintelligible.

"What bag?" Sarah repeated. The tarp flapped at her.

"Just remember, she hasn't been in the water since the camp closed," Oliver warned.

Pearly muttered again.

Oliver left Sarah's side, marched around *Owl*, and stood over Pearly's back.

"It's not staying here, dang it," Oliver said.

"What's not staying here?" Sarah demanded.

"I won't be the only one who ends up in jail if the cops come around," Oliver growled.

The tarp had been fastened to the trailer with bungee cords, and Sarah snatched it off before the two men could react.

A black trash bag lay in the bilge. It had shifted in its journey, revealing what appeared to be a weathered slab of marble. The worn stone and rough-cut hole made a jarring contrast to the boat's pristine newness.

"What's that?" she said.

"You don't want to get mixed up in this," Oliver replied. He tried to pull the tarp back in place, but she wouldn't let go. With a resigned sigh, Oliver gave up the tug-of-war.

"It's a headstone," he said, stating the obvious.

Pearly lurched over, painfully straightening his back, which seemed reluctant to unbend after its labors beneath *Owl*. "All we know is that somebody hid it in the flotation tank."

"Eldon," Oliver said.

"Maybe not," Pearly replied. "I've been thinking, and as I remember, Eldon put the plywood in on a Friday afternoon."

"When was that?" Sarah asked him.

"I figure the beginning of December. We didn't fiberglass it until Monday, so someone could have gone in over the weekend when we weren't around and opened the thing up. It was just screwed together at that point."

"You think Cathy might have done it?" Sarah said.

"Sure. She used to hang around, visiting Eldon and helping him work on her boat. Besides, Eldon could have found lots of other places around the yard to hide something."

"But how could she get into the shop by herself?"

"Easy," Pearly said. "There's a trick shingle next to the side door. Slide it out and the key is right there. Eldon made it because he's always losing his keys. He can't keep track of the things for love or money. That's why he keeps his truck keys over the visor."

"Okay, maybe it was Cathy," Oliver said reluctantly. He turned to Sarah. "Pearly is going to give the stone to the police."

"Pearly is going to look it over first, because he's not sure it's any of the police's business," Pearly said.

Sarah pushed back the trash bag some more. "It's just the top half of the headstone."

"We know that much," Oliver replied.

"Whose is it?"

Pearly looked over the rail. "We're not sure. The writing is too worn to read."

"Do you have some tracing paper?" she asked Oliver.

"Sure he does," Pearly said, obviously delighted to have an accomplice. "Let's go inside where we can work on it and see what we find." He lifted the stone and headed for the kitchen door.

Oliver's house stood at right angles to the barn, and a few paces away. Sarah followed Pearly with Wes bumping companionably against her leg. Oliver brought up the rear, somewhat less companionably.

Chapter 14

The door opened into a large kitchen, with a big wood-burning cookstove sitting on a hearth at one side of the room. The modern appliances were arrayed defiantly along the opposite wall. A stack of dirty dishes covered the counter beside the sink, while the kitchen table hid under piles of magazines and newspapers. Wes trotted to a water bowl beside the refrigerator and drank noisily.

They went into what had once been the dining room, where a drafting table covered with papers occupied one wall, a computer hutch next to it. The walls were lined with book shelves and Sarah's quick glance caught a collection of what looked like engineering texts, boating books, and hundreds of mystery stories.

A fireplace on the far side had been fitted with a wood stove, and beside the hearth was a dog bed with an assortment of stuffed dog toys. On the mantle, a framed photograph showed a younger Oliver and a woman with two children, a boy and a girl.

Pearly lowered his burden onto what would be the dining room table in the event the room was ever used for such a purpose, pushing aside a collection of papers, letters, and assorted boat fittings in the process.

Pearly looked around the room warily. "You don't have any of those dang machines running around, do you?" he asked.

Oliver shook his head.

"Machines?" Sarah said.

"He makes vacuum widgets and mechanical spiders," Pearly said ominously.

"You mean like a Roomba?" Sarah said.

"You know what a Roomba is?" Oliver said admiringly.

"Roomba? You should be so lucky," Pearly replied. "This thing will suck your shoes off. Just kick it out of the way if you see something coming."

Oliver scowled.

"You build robots?" Sarah said, intrigued.

"Force of habit," Oliver replied. "I was an electrical engineer before I moved to Maine."

"How about you two clean the rest of that junk off the table, so we can get a look at the stone." Pearly said, heading for the kitchen. "I'll make us some coffee."

Oliver and Sarah cleared the table in silence and placed the headstone on it. Oliver's grouchiness seemed to have lifted by the time Pearly returned with coffee mugs, and they soon produced a rubbing of the stone with tracing paper and a soft pencil.

"The Gothic printing makes it hard to read, even where it isn't weathered away," Oliver observed.

"It looks like the right number of letters to spell Gerhard Burndt," Pearly said.

"The way the stone is broken off catty-corner, you don't have the birth date," Oliver said. "The death date looks like it might be 1828."

"It could be a 23," Sarah said. "Or even a 26."

"That's still about right for when he died. We could look it up and see," Oliver said.

"The last name looks like it starts with a 'B'," Sarah added, squinting at the paper. "Do you think this really is Gerhard Burndt's headstone? I don't know much about him except that he was one of the founders of Burnt Cove, and nobody knows for sure where he's buried."

"A lot of Germans settled this area in the 1700's," Pearly said. "Here, Waldoboro, and along the St. George River.

"The town was originally named Burndt Cove after Gerhard, but there were hard feelings when the Germans torpedoed the *Lusitania* during World War One, and a bunch of people led by Cyrus Huggard called a special town meeting to have the name changed. Half the town belonged to the Burndt family, and they weren't too happy with the idea, but the Huggard tribe had bought up most of Squirrel Point below the village by that time, a big chunk of town, and they threatened to secede. The place nearly had a war of its own before they finally voted to drop the 'd' and become Burnt Cove. There were hard feelings between the two families for years after that. Those people in Burnt Cove just love to fight with each other."

"Nobody really knows where Gerhard was buried," Oliver added. "Most people think his grave is in the Oak Hill cemetery and the stone sank into the ground, or got lost over the years. Some people figure one of the Huggards may have desecrated it after the *Lusitania* business, but nobody can say for sure."

Sarah ran her fingers over the stone. "Wasn't Myra the last of the Burndts?"

"She and her sister," Pearly said. "The family girled out. Evan was the last of the Huggards."

"It's ironic they should marry. The end of the feud."

"Not hardly," Pearly said. "They fought like cats and dogs."

"Do you think Cathy or Eldon found Gerhard's grave and hid the stone to protect it?" Sarah asked.

"Protect it from who?" Pearly said.

"Cathy is a bug on town history," Oliver said. "Maybe she was keeping it until she could be sure it was Gerhard's."

"It's kind of romantic to think that Cathy might have found his final resting place," Sarah said.

"We don't know this is his stone, for sure" Pearly pointed out, "and even if it is, we don't know where the actual grave is. People just assume he's buried somewhere in the Oak Hill cemetery. He lived next door."

"It was the oldest house in town, until it burned back in the 1940's," Oliver said. "The Oak Hill development's driveway runs right through where the back yard used to be."

"I think we'd better keep this quiet for a while," Pearly said.

"Until we call the cops," Oliver said.

"Don't be such a fuss-budget."

"Why would Cathy hide it in the boat?" Sarah said.

"She had to hide it somewhere," Oliver replied, "since it was illegal for her to take it in the first place. Nobody would have ever found it either, if Eagle-eye here hadn't noticed the boat was down at the bow and cut the stone out."

"Wish I hadn't, now," Pearly grumbled.

"But it's not exactly convenient to get at," Sarah said.

"Getting at it isn't hard," Oliver replied. "Fixing the hole afterwards is a pain." He shot Pearly a dark look.

"Maybe she didn't need to get at it easily," Sarah said. "Maybe it was in the way of some construction project, and she and Myra were blackmailing the contractor."

"Blackmail?" Oliver looked at her thoughtfully.

"All they'd need is a photograph to prove they had it," Sarah went on, "and they wouldn't dare to leave it at the construction site where it could be taken away."

"It would be nice to find out where the stone came from," Oliver said, "but I don't see how, without knowing who hid it in the boat."

"I thought you said Oak Hill was the most likely place," Sarah said.

"Sure, but there's construction going on all over town," Pearly replied.

"We keep talking about Cathy, but why couldn't it be Eldon and Myra? Or just Eldon?" Oliver said.

Pearly strode over to the mantlepiece, picked up what looked like a gallon wine jug on a stand, and brought it back. An exquisitely detailed model of a three-masted schooner sailed across a tiny sea inside the bottle.

He handed the bottle to Sarah. "That's Eldon's work." He eyed Oliver, adding, "Hard to think someone who could do that kind of thing would be involved in a murder."

"It's hard to imagine anybody with hands like his could make something so tiny," Sarah said, marveling at it delicate rigging and ant-sized figure at the ship's wheel.

"It isn't the size, it's the steadiness," Pearly said.

Oliver frowned. "Making ships in bottles doesn't mean—"

"You know how Eldon is with secrets," Pearly retorted. "If he knew anything about this, everybody in the world would know too. The trouble with Eldon is when he starts nosing around, he's like a rhinoceros sniffing at your hip pocket—you can't miss it. He means well, but you still get nervous."

"Nervous? You mean like the three guys he beat up?"

"They shouldn't have accused Cathy of killing Myra when he asked where they'd last seen the girl."

Sarah and Oliver stood at the rail of Cathy's boat and stared at the rough-cut hole in the flotation tank.

"It's too bad," Sarah commented.

Oliver glanced around, but Pearly had wandered off towards Eldon's truck with the trash bag. "It won't be that hard to fix," he said quietly.

"No, I mean about Gerhard Burndt. First, people forget where he was buried, and when his grave is found, someone takes the stone away in a trash bag."

"Must be hell for him," Oliver observed solemnly.

Sarah glanced at Oliver, but his eyes, blue-gray this morning, looked serious. She let it go.

"Cathy's boat doesn't have a name either," she added.

"She'll think of one when she turns up."

"If she turns up."

Wes sat and leaned comfortably against Sarah's leg. She patted the dog's head and he looked up, panting happily. "What kind of a dog is Wes?"

"Springer Spaniel. Always had them."

"He's so friendly. Why do you call him Wes?"

"He's named for Weston Farmer."

"And who is Weston Farmer?"

"A yacht designer. It's a family tradition, naming pets after yacht designers. When I was a kid, we had a cat named Nathaniel Herreshoff, the man who designed your boat. We called him Nat-the-cat."

Sarah digested this for a moment. "But you haven't always been a yacht designer like your father? You were an engineer?"

"Yes." Oliver let the single word hang in the air, and Sarah was beginning to think that was all he was going to say on the subject. Finally, he added, "I took some yacht design courses, and I had worked in a boatyard as a kid. My father always said there was no money in yacht design, and I should do something else for a living. There are only a few hundred full-time yacht designers in the whole world. Mostly, I just build them."

"The stone looks like it was half-buried for a long time. The back has dirt stains on it," Sarah said.

Oliver didn't seem fazed by her sudden changes of subject. "The bottom half would be harder to get at if it sank completely underground. I wonder where it is."

"I bet Myra told Cathy or Eldon where to look. Who else would be likely to know?"

"Myra was the most tight-lipped, paranoid old woman I've ever known," Oliver said. "I expect she kept the place a secret to protect Gerhard. Protect him from what, only she would know, and her mind was a little strange. She'd need a good reason to tell anyone."

"Maybe Pearly is right, and it isn't about blackmail, or Myra being murdered," she said. "Myra knew she was dying. Maybe she wanted to pass on the location of his grave for the future."

"But why dig the thing up if it wasn't blackmail?" Oliver paused. "That might be what Myra and Cathy were arguing about last fall."

Pearly wandered back empty-handed. "Don't forget to fix that flotation tank. I'll bring some paint over tomorrow so you can touch it up. And don't forget the lead. You won't need it now."

"Make Eldon fix it, if your so sure his girlfriend put the stone in there."

"Have you forgotten about the rhinoceros already? Just keep quiet 'til I sort things out." With that, he headed for the truck.

"You won't believe what I'm going to charge to fix your hole," Oliver called after him.

Pearly didn't seem to hear as he clambered aboard and swung the door shut with a rusty creak. The gears ground as he fumbled for reverse. He backed around and leaned out the window. "I put the stone behind your trash barrels. Don't throw it out by mistake."

Sarah watched Pearly drive off and said, "What's with him and the headstone? Is he just protecting Eldon?"

"Pearly's son drowned years ago when his lobsterboat sank, so Eldon is the closest thing Pearly has to a son, but there's more to it than that. Everything is tied together in a small community like this. It's like a spider web, and we don't know all the connections. There's Cathy, helping Myra stay in her house as long a possible. Lot's of people were unhappy about that, including Cathy's boss, Doc Caldwell, who thought Myra should be in a nursing home."

Oliver leaned back against the side of Cathy's boat so he was facing *Owl*, propping his foot on the trailer's fender. "Then there are Myra's lawsuits against the town and the planning board. That gets Sam Merlew involved.

"And speaking of the Merlews, Myra made trouble when they began selling the camp for house lots. Sam was frantic because they were desperate for cash to pay Kate's medical bills, and Myra held up the sales for months. Heck, she was still making trouble for the Borofskys right up 'til she died."

He leaned forward and poked at a spot of dirt on *Owl*'s varnish. "It goes on and on. Pearly grew up around here, and he's worried about stirring up grief for a lot of people he cares about."

Oliver glanced at his watch. "Let's make a phone call, see what we can learn about graveyards."

Back inside, Oliver turned on the speaker attachment for his telephone and dialed a number.

It picked up on the second ring. "Rosen."

Oliver had designed and built a small daysailer for Lev Rosen, a retired lawyer, three years ago. After identifying himself, Oliver said, "I have a legal question for you."

"Do I get paid for answering it?"

"Are you crazy? Where would I get that kind of money? I'm looking for a freebee. Suppose you were putting up a house and came across an old graveyard—you know, where the headstones had sunk into the ground over the years. What would that mean?"

"That's easy. There are state laws governing what they call 'ancient graveyards.' If you buy a piece of property and you find an old cemetery, even if it isn't shown on the deed, you have a legal obligation not to disturb it."

"What does that mean, exactly?" Oliver said.

"You found an old cemetery up there in the woods?"

"I'm just asking for a friend."

"Hah! They all say that. If you leave the cemetery alone, no problem. If you want to do any construction work, you have to notify the town code enforcement officer, he has to verify that it's a grave-yard and what you're doing is legal. For instance, you can't build anything within 25 feet, that sort of thing. Or, you can petition to have the graves moved."

"Petition?" Sarah murmured.

"Whatsay?" Lev demanded.

"What do you mean by petition?" Oliver said.

"That's getting into more than a phone call, but for instance, if there are any descendants, you could try to get permission from them to move the graves. Or you could ask the court for permission. What are you up to?"

"It's just a hypothetical question."

"Hah! They all say that too. Next thing you know, I end up visiting them in jail."

"Does that sort of thing happen often? I mean finding old graves on your land?"

"It happens, and it usually isn't a big problem to deal with, but

I expect there are a lot that never get found. Little family plots were pretty common around here in the old days. Mom and Pop buried out back, and the graves get lost over the years."

"I suppose some people might just toss an old headstone aside," Oliver said.

"And they'd probably get away with it, so long as some guy with a backhoe didn't dig up the coffin."

Chapter 15

B rian asked Sarah about her Explorer the minute she got into his Volvo. She told him about her "accident" without incriminating Eldon, or his truck.

"There are still some rough people in Burnt Cove," Brian said as he backed out of the Merlew's driveway. "Not as many as there used to be when I was growing up, thank god. Even so, there are always a few bad apples in any small town."

The Monday morning traffic was a lot lighter than it had been over the weekend. He gave her a tentative smile.

"What are you doing to keep busy?" he asked.

"Working on *Owl*," Sarah said. "I'm hoping to get her in the water next weekend."

"You working over at Pearly's yard?"

"Oliver Wendell's place."

"Ah." Brian was silent for a while. "I sold him that property when he moved here ten years ago. Nice view land."

"It seems isolated."

Brian nodded. "It's about a mile to his nearest neighbor, but I guess he likes it that way after what happened."

"Oh?"

"He won't talk much about his past, but I do know his wife and daughter were killed in an automobile accident down in Massachusetts about twelve years ago."

They came to a decorative concrete wall. "The Duvals," Brian said. "He made a fortune in real estate."

"A competitor?"

Brian's laugh was as infectious as his smile. "No, he builds shopping centers down in New York." They passed a driveway paved with cobblestones. "That's the Copellos. A big-shot corporate lawyer. They come up for a month or two in the summer."

He drove at a crawl, ignoring the cars that impatiently swung out to pass. "Most of these are summer houses, except the Vincents and a few others."

"It seems like a waste to build these big places for just a few weeks in the summer," Sarah said.

"Pays my bills, so it can't be all bad," Brian said. "I sold most of the land and Roy built some of the houses."

"Do any local people own waterfront along here?"

He gave her a perplexed look. "Depends on what you mean by local—a lot of people from away have lived here for years. If you mean people who were born here, then no, not along this stretch, except for Myra, and she's gone. Plenty of locals own land away from the water, and some of the tidal frontage."

He gave her another high-wattage smile. "The way I see it, none of us are local if you go back far enough."

They paused at the huge new house going in between the Vincent's and Myra's place. "The Borofskys," Brian told her. "He's a chemist. Figured a way to take the smell out of overripe fish, or something like that. Made a fortune."

Brian looked at Sarah as though trying to gauge her reaction. "Doesn't look much like the old camp, does it?"

"No," she said wistfully.

"Too bad, but times change, and we have to make the best of it."

A good, pragmatic Maine attitude, Sarah thought. She suspected that Brian was one to make the best of anything that came along.

"I worked at the camp back in the days when you were there," Brian said. "Sam hired a bunch of us kids every spring to help open the cabins and tidy up the grounds. Then we'd come back in the fall and put everything away. Of course you wouldn't remember me because we'd be done by the time you all arrived."

"In the sixties?"

Brian nodded. "Started when I was about fourteen and kept on right through high school. Sam paid well and he didn't work us too hard. Money was scarce in those days, but I saved up and got a boat and some traps, like most of the kids around here."

They came to Myra's scruffy driveway. "That was one of the oldest houses in town," Brian said. "Built by one of the Burndts in the early 1800's, back when they owned most of Squirrel Point, before the Huggards began settling here."

"And you'll be selling the place?"

"Yes." Brian smiled. It was certainly one of his better features. Sarah suspected that grin sold a lot of real estate. "It'll sell for well into six figures, especially with houses like the Vincents and Borofskys next door. I'm hoping we can sub-divide the property. We'll get a lot more if we sell it in two lots."

"I suppose there are restrictions," Sarah said.

"We don't have zoning laws here, like you do in Massachusetts, but we do have restrictions on lot size and so on. For instance, Burnt Cove requires a minimum of 200 feet of water frontage for a new subdivision, and Myra has just a little short of 400. I think we can get a waiver from the planning board for two lots, though. I'll file an application once the estate is settled."

"Did Myra know how much it was worth?"

"She didn't care. She was just determined to stay there. I talked to her a few times, trying to get her to sell. She could have gotten rid of the place and lived like a queen somewhere else, but a million bucks didn't mean any more to her than a thousand." He seemed baffled by Myra's attitude towards money.

"She must have been very attached to the place."

"I don't think Myra had the get-up-and-go to move. At her age, she was too scared of any kind of change to try something new, even if it would be better. Besides, she didn't need the money all that much anyway."

"She didn't?"

"Myra lived pretty cheap. She got Social Security—Evan used to make good money lobstering, even if he did go on a bender every weekend. On top of that, the Merlews paid top dollar when they bought the three lots from Evan in the fifties and early sixties. Myra kept the purse strings, and she never spent a dime without wringing its neck first, so I'll bet she still had some of that money stashed under her mattress."

Sarah suspected that Brian was being overly optimistic about Myra's finances. "I suppose her place will sell pretty quickly," she said.

Brian gave a far more predatory grin than his usual smile. "Oh, yeah. People are already stopping in to ask about it."

"Didn't Myra drag down land values?"

"Probably, but what with her health, everybody knew she wouldn't be there much longer."

It occurred to Sarah that someone might not have wanted to wait that long for Myra to die.

"As a matter of fact, Myra owned a parcel right across the road from her house," Brian added, pointing to the strips of orange flagging. "It's on the market now. They're selling it to raise cash to settle the estate, taxes and so on."

"It's not on the water. Is it worth much?"

"Oh, nothing like waterfront, of course. Still, this is a good neighborhood and it's a nice piece of land, good house site. We've had a nibble or two."

They drove on past Myra's driveway. "Speaking of investment, see the flagging?" Brian said, pointing to the tape. "The lot beyond Myra was surveyed last fall. Prime frontage."

"Will you be selling that too?"

"Hope so. It belongs to a guy in Boston, Jim Grinshnell. He bought it about seven years ago as an investment. A lot of people do that, of course. I talked to him when he was up last month."

Brian sped up. "I thought we'd have lunch at the Squirrel Point Hotel. Then we can take a drive if you like and I'll give you my Realtor's Special guided tour."

"Do you think I'm dressed up enough for the Hotel?"

"You're fine," he assured her. "It's a lot more casual than it used to be. What did you make of St. Agnes?"

"It looks awfully big."

"It fills up in the summer. Those rich summer people with the big estates down by the Hotel had big ideas back then. The mansions may have burnt down, but St. Agnes lives on. You picked a good Sunday to visit. Much nicer than a Low Sunday."

"Low Sunday? Is that a different kind of service?"

He laughed again. "You could say that. It's the tide. Those millionaires got cheap when it came to land for their church and they bought tidal frontage. For some reason those mud flats really stink at low tide, hydrogen sulphide gas or something. It gets pretty rugged if the wind is wrong. Attendance can be thin on a Low Sunday."

He grinned at Sarah. "A little bit of St. Agnes tradition: check the tide before you go to church."

"I suppose the town has been laughing at those idiots who built a church next to Goosespit Flats ever since."

The grin faded. "I imagine some people have," he said.

Henry Wilson, president of the Burnt Cove historical society, was in his eighties, bald, and with the look of a retired college professor, which in fact he was.

"Nobody knows where Gerhard Burndt is buried." Henry spoke with a mid-western accent. "The fact is, he was more famous in death than he was in life. The town wasn't even named Burndt Cove until 1857, long after he passed on. We may think of him as the founding father, but in his day, he was just a farmer who happened to build the first house in the area, raised a big family, and died. Beyond that, he was an enigma."

"So nobody paid much attention to where he was buried?" Oliver inquired, putting the delicate, bone-china teacup in the saucer beside his chair.

"Nobody paid much attention to him at all. It wasn't until the area began to be settled that the Burndt family decided to put their mark on the place by naming the town after him."

The wood stove in Henry Wilson's study was cranking out an impressive amount of heat. Between that and the scalding tea, Oliver was starting to sweat. "But surely there must be some town records," he said.

"There were, until the town hall burned down in 1871. We know he built the first house in town, but we can't be sure he died in it." Henry, in a cashmere sweater and wool jacket, seemed unaware that the room was hot enough to roast an ox. "Most people assume he's in an unmarked grave is in the Oak Hill cemetery, but for all we know, he may not even be buried in town."

"Could Myra Huggard have known where he was buried?"

"It's possible." Henry sighed. "I would have loved to interview the old woman. That sort of oral history is priceless. Unfortunately, she saw me as an outsider and wouldn't share her memories."

"What about Cathy Leduc?"

Henry brightened. "She's a member of the historical society, you know. Unusual for someone her age to be interested in the past. She gives me hope for the younger generation. Anyway, Myra did share some of her memories with Cathy, and she's planning to write them down. I urged her to start as soon as possible, because memories do fade, even with the young. Want me to hot up your tea?"

"Oh, no thanks," Oliver replied, fearing heat prostration. "Did she ever talk to you about her conversations with Myra?"

"Not as much as I would have liked. Myra talked to Cathy about Gerhard's house in town. Having grown up there, Myra had some interesting anecdotes. Originally, all the land from behind the cemetery to the top of Oak Hill went with the house."

"Where the development is?"

"Yes. Myra could remember when it was still farmland. As a child, it used to be her job to herd the cows up to the pasture on top of Oak Hill every morning and round them up every afternoon. Myra must have had quite a life."

• • •

It was mid-afternoon when Brian pulled into the Merlew's driveway and lurched to a stop well short of Sarah's door.

The front end of Eldon's truck was visible beside the barn.

"I'll let you out here," he said hastily. Barely waiting for a response, Brian left her standing in the dust as he retreated.

Apparently, he and Eldon didn't get along.

It had been a delightful afternoon. The Squirrel Point Hotel served a sumptuous meal in an atmosphere that recaptured the glory days of the Grand Hotel. Brian seemed to know everybody, stopping at several tables to greet people as they went into the restaurant.

Sarah wandered over to where Sam and Eldon were working on a corner of the barn. A large timber jutted from the back of Eldon's truck, another stuck out from under the barn itself.

"Give it another tunk, Eldon," Sam said.

Eldon, in worn jeans and a sweat-stained Grateful Dead tee-shirt, picked up a heavy sledge as though it was a tack hammer and swung it one-handed at the timber. The entire barn shook, rattling the windows. The timber slid further beneath the building.

"I saw you come in."

Sarah turned to find Kate beside her. "You startled me," she said.

"Why did you lie to us?" Kate demanded.

"Lie? About what?"

"About being run off the road. You said it was an accident. Pearly told us it wasn't."

"I didn't say anything because I'm not sure it was intentional, and I didn't want you to worry over nothing."

"It *was* intentional," Kate replied with surprising intensity. She was shivering. "I'm sorry we got you involved in this. If only—"

"Now, mother." Sam interrupted. He had left Eldon to rattle the barn with his sledge. "Let's all go inside and have some tea."

Chapter 16

Sarah returned to her apartment after tea and traded her turtle-neck and slacks for a sweatshirt and jeans. What had Kate meant about being sorry for getting her involved? Involved in what? Why had Sam hurried over to interrupt their conversation? In any event, Kate had recovered her composure by the time they got inside, and the couple were evasive on the subject in spite of Sarah's prodding. What were they keeping from her?

The phone interrupted Sarah's train of thought.

"Hi, mom." Her son Jeffery's voice sounded disconcertingly like Claude.

"Hi, Jeff," she said. "I hope you got my message. I just wanted to say hello, and see how you were doing."

"I'm doing fine, but you had me worried when I couldn't get through on your cell," he said.

"There are dead spots up here," she replied evasively. In fact, Sarah had turned the phone off when she arrived, partly to keep Claude at bay, and partly as a self-imposed exile from her old life.

"You're settling in all right then?" Jeff said.

"Everything's great. The weather's been good, the Merlews are wonderful, I'm meeting lots of people, going to church, doing some shopping, and *Owl* is almost ready to go in the water—" Sarah caught herself babbling and stopped.

"Wow, sounds like you've been busy. Sorry I wasn't around when you called. Dad and I have been worried about you up there all alone."

"I'm not all alone, and it's a nice break after everything. I really need some time away."

"I can understand that, and I'm glad you're having fun. You deserve it."

Jeff went on, tentatively now. "You know, I haven't taken sides in the divorce. It's been hard enough for both of you as it is, but I hate to see either of you hurting—"

"I'm healing, not hurting," she said, knowing the words sounded trite.

"I was thinking about dad. He's been so upset and angry and depressed since you went to Maine. I'm scared he'll do something foolish."

Dang it all , Sarah thought furiously. Aloud, she said, "I can't do anything about Claude. He needs a good therapist to work through his problems."

"Hard to make him see that. Getting rid of Lurlene would be a start. Then maybe you guys could—"

"Dang it, I had to go to the doctor and get tested because of your father's girlfriends!" she exploded. "Do you know how humiliating that was?"

There was a long pause.

"I'm sorry, mom. You're right. I can't know what you've been through, and I shouldn't have stuck my nose into your business."

"I'm sorry too, sweetheart. I know it's been hard on you kids, but Claude will be all right. Really. He's a lot stronger than he seems." She hoped it was true.

Sarah switched on a few lights against the evening after Jeff hung up. They had moved on to safer topics, but she was still feeling shaky from her outburst, and she nearly went through the roof when a pounding shook the room. Eldon must have finished "tunking" the barn and was shifting his attention to her door. She ushered the young man inside, hoping he was as harmless as he seemed, and seated him on one of the dinette chairs.

Her guest drained the glass of lemonade she handed him, and sighed comfortably. "That sure hits the spot," he said. The chair creaked in agony.

Sarah refilled his glass. "I hear you've been looking into what Cathy was doing before she disappeared."

"Me and the cops. Figure I'd better do my own looking before they frame me with some crazy charge."

"What have you found out?"

"Not much. Cath talked to the Merlews the morning after the fire, and they said she was upset, but she didn't really tell them anything. People saw her driving around some after that, and she got gas up at the Irving station around the middle of the day. Nobody saw her after that, but her car ended up at Pearly's shop, which didn't look good since my prints were on the steering wheel. I told them I'd pushed it out of the way 'cause it was parked in front of the door, but they don't believe me."

"That isn't much to go on," Sarah replied, wondering why Cathy would leave her car at Pearly's yard. If she had left town, wouldn't she have taken her car? Had she been killed there? No wonder the police suspected Eldon.

"I'm still asking around at stores and places," he said, looking discouraged.

Sarah decided to try for a happier subject. "You two must have seen a lot of Myra."

"We used to go over once or twice a week. Cath would tidy up the house, and I'd fix up stuff, or work outside. Myra had a little patch of vegetables, and I'd work on that."

"What did Cathy and Myra talk about?"

Eldon fidgeted. "The usual stuff. Growing vegetables, cooking. And Cath loved to hear about the old days."

Eldon fidgeted some more. "They were death on all the development going on around here. Myra would give me heck 'cause Roy is a builder—like I could tell him what to do. He has to make a living, doesn't he? Myra went nuts when they started the Oak Hill development. Said somebody had to fight to keep the town from being ruined, teach those rich people a lesson."

Eldon gave her a forlorn look. "Myra made so much trouble, I wonder if some of it rubbed off on Cathy. I keep asking, but nobody's talking."

"She'll turn up," Sarah said, trying to sound as though she believed it. "Do you know what Myra meant by teaching the rich people a lesson?"

Eldon emptied the pitcher into his glass.

"I'll mix up more," she said.

"No sweat. I'll get some water. The Merlews have a good well," he said, heading for the sink . "I don't think Myra knew what she meant. She was a little batty about things towards the end."

He filled his glass.

"You remember that old movie *The Russians are Coming?*" he said. "We rented it last fall, took the DVD player over, give Myra a treat. Big mistake. After that, she started seeing Russians everywhere. Cath worried about her imagining things, and all." He shook his head sadly. "Maybe we should have paid more attention to the Russians. We figured she saw one of the surveyors running a line."

"Didn't she go to check on any of them?"

"She could barely make it out to the mailbox by then."

"I heard that Cathy and Myra had been arguing," she said before she could catch herself.

Eldon scowled at her, and Sarah wondered if she had gone too far. After a moment he said, "They got going over something around Thanksgiving time last year, but they wouldn't say what. Said it was better if I didn't know. Myra could be real tight-mouthed, but I got the idea she wanted to do something and Cath didn't like it. I told Cath if Myra was trying to make her do something wrong, she should talk to somebody about it, you know, like the Merlews."

Eldon sat down again. "Did you know Myra well, back when you were in camp?"

"Not all that well, I suppose. A friend of mine and I went over a few times each summer."

Often when they appeared, Myra would chase them off with curses and threats. It was partly the thrill and uncertainty that kept luring them back.

"I bet she was a terror in the old days," Eldon said.

He was right in more ways than one. Sarah remembered one afternoon when she and Marlee Sue had traveled the brushy path through the woods to Myra's back yard. It was their fourth year at Migawoc, and as it turned out, Marlee Sue's last visit with Myra. As usual, they paused at the tree-line to see how they might be greeted.

Myra had her back to them that day, an ax in one hand, a wildly flopping chicken in the other. A dull thunk on the wood-splitting block and the body fell to the ground, where it staggered in desperate circles while blood spurted. Marlee Sue screamed.

Myra spun around. "Dern you brats! Don't you know better than to go sneaking up on someone like that?"

She advanced on them, the bloody ax still raised. "What's the matter with you two? Ain't you ever seen a chicken with its head cut off? Where do you think the saying came from?"

Sarah watched the dead bird collapse near one of its defunct companions. Choking and gagging, Marlee Sue bolted for the woods. She never darkened Myra's yard again.

Myra lowered the ax, and a thin smile curled her lip as Marlee Sue vanished among the spruce. "That little gal won't ever make it." She turned to Sarah. "But you're a survivor."

Eldon had been watching as Sarah sat, lost in the past. Now he interrupted her reverie. "What happened to your car?"

Sarah told him about her encounters with the red pickup.

Eldon's face purpled. He stood up and grabbed her arm, snatching her out of the chair. "We'll straighten this out right now."

"Where are we going?" Sarah demanded.

Eldon had practically tossed her into his truck, and now they were hurtling down the road.

Sarah's companion glared through the windshield in a way that made her nervous. "If someone came to me looking for someone to run a car off the road," he said, "I'd send them to this guy I know. He's got a reputation from here clear to Rockland, and he's been hanging around the yard while I worked on his boat. He might even know something about Cath, but he ain't talking."

Eldon sighed. "Besides, he borrowed my truck about when you got run off the road. He's a little dim."

Meadow road ran through a stretch of low, wet ground, verging on swampland, as it meandered inland for a few miles before joining Merrifield road.

They rattled over the narrow, pot-holed pavement, past decaying single-wides and lopsided houses. Almost every weedy, rutted yard sported a derelict car or a lobsterboat in some state of disrepair. They passed a tiny pond, little more than an overgrown mud puddle, its banks littered with old tires and a rotting Lazy Boy. A Fisher Price tugboat floated in the murky water.

A rusty mailbox with the inscription "Z. F. Breener" attracted her attention. Behind it, a swaybacked shack leaned drunkenly. The muddy front yard was filled with a staggering array of junk from rotting rowboats to rusting freezers. A derelict car, with one door missing, served as a chicken coop. Three piglets rooted in the mud beside the shack, while a goat, tethered to a sapling behind the building, grazed on the rough grass. The Breener estate was run down, even by Meadow Road's relaxed standards.

"Ziggy's Zoo," Eldon commented as they thundered by.

In typical Maine fashion, there were contrasts even here. On the right, across from a battered trailer with a rotting couch on the lawn, stood a neat cottage with a small paddock in front, where a pair of handsome, well-groomed horses were grazing.

Eldon noticed Sarah's reaction. "There's more money around here than it looks," he said.

"Even Ziggy?"

"Can't tell about Ziggy. He's different."

They lurched off the pavement into a small field containing five lobsterboats and an assortment of junk. Three men dressed in jeans and grimy tee shirts were peering under the hood of an aged pickup truck. The truck was red.

A fourth, older man with gray crew-cut hair, was scraping the paint on a lobsterboat nearby.

"Oh   , not again," one of the trio said fervently as Eldon and Sarah alighted.

Eldon ambled over. "This ain't about Cathy, Hoot," he said. "Want you to meet a friend of mine." Eldon rested a paw on Sarah's shoulder, almost knocking her over in the process. "She's staying with the Merlews, and somebody's been giving her grief ever since she got here."

The men studied Sarah for a while. "So, why are you telling us?" one of them demanded.

"Because I'm passing the word that I'll straighten out anyone who bothers her," Eldon said.

The man called Hoot bristled. "Well, I don't like your altitude, coming down here threatening people. People shouldn't be poking around other people's places anyway."

Sarah noticed that Hoot had a large wrench in his hand, the second man was now holding a length of pipe, and the third was sidling over to a hammer on the truck's fender.

If Eldon was concerned by this turn of events, he gave no sign. He stepped forward menacingly, putting himself between Sarah and the men. "I don't like people trying to run down a harmless old woman, or taking my truck to run her off the road."

A harmless old woman? Sarah darted in front of Eldon. "I wasn't 'poking around' Myra's place," she said. "I knew her when I was a kid, and I was just paying my respects."

Crew-cut came over. "For gosh sake give it a rest, Hoot," he said. "I don't want my dooryard all stove up like last time, and I'm sure as heck not going to haul the three of you into Pen Bay to get patched up again."

Crew-cut turned to Eldon. "I'm not saying I know what happened, but my guess is that someone was driving by and saw your friend at Myra's place and figured maybe it was somebody—"

"—looking to steal something," Hoot interrupted.

"—looking to buy the place and put up no trespassing signs, cut people off from that nice little clam flat of Myra's," crew-cut said. "Hell, there's hardly any flats left around here where you can go clamming. Maybe this person was pretty drunk and figured he'd give your friend a little scare, only maybe he nudged her by mistake."

Crew-cut turned to glare at Hoot and his friends. "It might be that somebody came around later and offered a chunk of money to have a car followed and run it off the road, give the driver a scare. But that's just an idea I heard going around."

"Who was the guy with the money?" Eldon demanded.

"Never saw him before," Hoot said, looking mulish.

Why would Hoot borrow your truck?" Sarah asked as they drove back in the gathering dusk.

"His is busted half the time. Can't take care of machinery worth a dern. I'm not even sure he has a license since they got him for DUI." Eldon sighed. "Guess I'll have to find someplace else for the key."

"I wonder if it was your truck the first time."

The vehicle in question lurched as Eldon shifted in the seat. "Doubt it. The first time sounds like a spur of the moment thing."

"The red truck back there is Hoot's?"

"Yeah. He, or somebody, probably saw you at Myra's and decided to do something about it."

Sarah was willing to concede that the first time was a "spur of the moment thing," but the second time wasn't.

"Would Hoot know Sam or Brian?" she asked.

"Sure. Brian may think he's too good for this place now, but he grew up here, poor as dirt, and Hoot knows him real well."

Eldon turned on the headlights. "But maybe Hoot's lying, or whoever's behind it hired someone to set things up, cover his tracks. Easy for Brian to pay a stranger to talk to Hoot."

Sarah started to disagree, but thought better of it. She didn't know Brian, and though she liked his fun-loving way, she had sensed a hint of ruthlessness as well. The kind of ruthlessness that sometimes comes to those who have fought their way out of poverty.

"You don't seem to like Brian much," she said.

"He and Doc Caldwell both wanted Myra out of her house, but at least Doc was thinking about her health. Brian just wanted to make a pile of money, and he's got more than he needs already."

Eldon nodded at the window. "Brian doesn't come back here now. He's not too popular in these parts any more."

Chapter 17

Sarah stepped outside Tuesday morning into air that was cool and damp. It took her a moment to notice what had happened to the Explorer. Scrawled across the driver side in blaze orange spray paint was the word "slut."

She circled the vehicle warily and gingerly touched the lettering. The paint was dry. How long would that take, two hours? She worked at it with a fingernail, to no avail.

Kate and Sam were sitting at the kitchen table when she entered. "Do you have a can of spray paint I can borrow?" Sarah asked. They looked up in surprise.

"Any particular color you'd like?" Sam said.

"Dark."

"There's a can of forest green in woodshed," Kate said.

Sam returned with the can. "What's the project?"

"My car. Somebody vandalized it."

Kate's face looked as though it had turned to stone.

Sam headed for the door. "I'd better take a look."

The luminous orange looked even brighter from a distance.

Sam approached the Ford slowly. "You're going to paint over that? How about trying some paint thinner on it?"

Sarah was shivering. "It's dry and won't scrape off."

"We could tape some cardboard over it until you go to Dingers. They can touch that up for you in no time."

"Spray it! The rest of the car's already trashed, dar it!" She fought back angry tears. "Just look at the poor thing."

Sam turned to her, his face grave. "I can see this happening on the street in town, but in our driveway? I hate to say it, but I don't think you're safe here."

"Somebody painted *what* on your car?" Marlee Sue asked incredulously. She struggled to suppress a grin.

"Slut," Sarah repeated, "and it's not funny."

They were seated in the Quarterdeck restaurant at a table overlooking Camden harbor. At least they got the lunch they had ordered, unlike Lulu's idiosyncratic eating place.

"No, it's not funny," Marlee Sue replied soberly, "and Sam's right. I don't think it's safe for you to be staying at the Merlews, either. First of all, anybody who would drive out there to paint your car isn't just doing it on a whim. They've got to be serious. And second, for all you know it could be the Merlews themselves who are after you."

"That's crazy. They invited me to come up here."

"How do you know they didn't lure you here for some nefarious purpose?"

"'Nefarious purpose?'" Sarah smiled in spite of herself. "Isn't that kind of melodramatic?"

Marlee Sue ignored her. "Think about it. They haven't seen you for years, and suddenly, out of a clear blue sky, they invite you up to spend the summer. Why would they do that? Out of all the hundreds of kids who went to Migawoc, why would they think of you?"

Sarah stared at the windjammers as they lay tied up to the dock. With Memorial Day only weeks away, people were swarming over the big schooners' decks, getting them ready for summer.

"I don't see why the Merlews would ask me up here just to harass me," Sarah said stubbornly.

"You were almost killed twice, your car is a wreck, and you call it harassment? You may be stubborn, but this is ridiculous. Somebody is out to get you in a big way, and I think it could be the

Merlews. You still haven't told me why they invited you to Maine."

"They knew Myra had given me *Owl*, so they wrote when she died to let me know she was gone and invite me to spend the summer. The divorce was going full steam then, so the invitation seemed like a godsend."

In a way, Sarah regretted having told Marlee Sue about her various adventures. On the other hand, her friend did have a fresh perspective, unlike Oliver and Pearly, who were much too close to the people involved. She remembered Kate's comment yesterday about being sorry they had "gotten her involved." In what? Crazy as it seemed, perhaps Marlee Sue was right about them.

"All I did was walk around Myra's place, and her grave," Sarah said plaintively. "I don't see why that should cause so much trouble."

"Dang it woman, that's not the point. Someone is stalking you. Doesn't that make you nervous?"

"It does, when you put it that way," Sarah admitted, though mostly she was feeling just plain anger at the unreasonableness of it all.

"Good. There's hope for you yet," Marlee Sue said, sounding relieved. She leaned over the table. "Look, someone may *think* you know something dangerous or incriminating, even if you don't. Or maybe you do know something without realizing it—a trivial little thing about Myra that could make trouble."

"I've wracked my brain and I can't think of anything. I barely knew the woman. Just our visits over there. You probably knew her as well as I did."

"Yes, but she liked you and hated me," Marlee Sue said in a matter-of-fact way. "Face it, Myra was a troublemaker. A lot of people didn't like her, including me, and now you've got yourself stuck in the middle of something she probably cooked up."

"Myra had some friends."

"Like who? Myra's special pal, Cathy Leduc, you were talking about? Nobody knows what happened to her, except that she may have killed Myra and run off. And what about this Eldon character, who beats people up? He drags you down to see his disreputable pals, and just happens to know who has been playing bumper tag with you. That's a little too convenient for me."

A young man in a tee shirt and cut-off jeans that were a size too small was carrying a large cardboard box across a swaying gangplank onto the nearest schooner. Sarah admired the view, then turned away, disgusted. Is this what her life had come to, ogling men half her age through a restaurant window? Was she going to end up like Claude, chasing after underage sex-toys?

Marlee Sue flashed a sly grin. "I see your game, Cassidy." She waved her salad fork at Sarah. "You're playing Nancy Drew, hunting down Myra's killer. Don't do it. Leave it to the cops. Why stick your nose into this?"

"I wasn't 'sticking my nose' into anything   !" Sarah retorted, pent up rage bursting through. "But I'm *not* going to sit still while people go around attacking me! I'm going to put a stop to it."

"Putting a stop to it may get you killed. Did you think about that?"

Marlee Sue saw the anger on Sarah's face, and shook her head in frustration. "Dang Irish blood. At least let me help. Two heads are better than one, you know. It'll be like when we were kids at Migawoc. Remember when we used to play spy and they called us the Deadly Duo? We'll have a blast detecting stuff. Better yet, why don't you come and stay with me for a while? You and your car will be safer. God knows, somebody has to take care of you."

Touched by her companion's offer, Sarah stared out the window again, where Buns was returning to the parking lot for another box. She had kept Pearly's secret and not mentioned the headstone, even though she would like to have Marlee Sue's thoughts on the subject. She tried to think of some other way her friend could help.

Marlee Sue took Sarah's silence as a refusal, for she added, "What about your boyfriend, the one who's working on *Owl*? Could you stay with him for a while?"

"Oliver Wendell? He's definitely not my boyfriend."

"Okay, don't get huffy. I'm just trying to help."

"There is one thing," Sarah said slowly. "Could you use your banking connections to find out who's behind the Oak Hill development? The sign said 'BCD Properties LLC,' whatever that means."

Marlee Sue thought for a moment. "Sure. But why don't you just ask that Realtor, what's-his-name, in Burnt Cove?"

"Brian Curtis? I'd rather not ask him about that."

"You don't trust him?"

"I don't know who to trust, after talking with you. Besides, I thought you could find out about the developer's finances too."

Marlee Sue gave her a stare. "That might be a little harder." She thought a moment. "But doable. What are you looking for?"

"I wish I knew," Sarah replied.

Marlee Sue, ever practical, looked worried and mildly disapproving. The concern on her friend's face made Sarah realize how alone and isolated she had been the past week.

Suddenly, she missed Muffy, and her friends in Sudbury. She was even beginning, heaven help her, to miss Claude. Fighting back the tears, she decided, for better or worse, that she would call him tonight.

A well-manicured lawn sloped from the Vincent's terrace to granite ledges at the water's edge. The late afternoon sun left the terrace in shade while striking sparks on the wave-tops of the sound.

"Can I freshen up your drink?" George Vincent asked.

"Oh, no thanks," Sarah said.

George turned to his other guests. "Anton? Sasha?"

Sarah guessed that Anton Borofsky was in his late forties, with dark hair showing a touch of grey at the temples. His round face was deeply creased with smile lines. Sasha looked younger, a slight, blond woman with huge brown eyes.

The couple declined, and George turned back to Sarah.

"I suppose the area has changed a lot since you were here last," he said.

"Sarah went to the Migawoc Camp when she was young,"

Debbie explained.

Anton looked at her curiously. "You did? I've wondered about the idea of a children's camp on the ocean. Wouldn't a lake be more suitable?" He spoke with a slight accent.

"Lake water is warmer," Sarah conceded, "but we still did some swimming and a lot of sailing, nature hikes, tennis, archery, crafts, and other camp stuff."

Resenting the fact that his question made her feel defensive, Sarah changed the subject. "Are you here for the summer?" she asked.

"Not until the house is finished," Sasha said. "We're staying at the Samoset and driving back to New York tomorrow."

"Checking on the progress," Anton added. "You have to watch these contractors or they'll rob you blind."

"It will be wonderful to have you here with our little group of Squirrel Pointers," Debbie said enthusiastically.

"It's beautiful, and I love the sea air," Sasha replied.

"We have to make sure it doesn't get spoiled by inappropriate development," Anton said, "otherwise it will be ruined. We ought to have some kind of protective building covenant for Squirrel Point, especially now the Huggard place is gone, but I don't know how to go about it."

"Young Curtis might have some ideas," George said. "He's very capable."

"I'll talk to a lawyer friend of mine in the City," Anton decided, nodding his head.

"You ought to buy the Huggard place," Debbie said to Sarah. A note of artificial enthusiasm seemed to peek through the words.

"It may be a while before it comes on the market," George said. "They're hoping to sell Myra's woodlot first to raise some cash before they settle the estate. She didn't have any liquid assets."

Anton scowled at this, and Debbie turned to Sarah, saying hastily, "You could buy Myra's woodlot. It's a nice place for a house, even if it isn't on the water."

Sarah looked across the lawn to the water and thought about

living near the Vincents again, like Sudbury.

Sarah recalled the Maine of her youth: the long summer days spent sailing, playing, and exploring along the water's edge. They were gone now, as she could see by a glance around her. It proved the old saying that one can't go back—not to Maine, maybe not to Sudbury.

Thinking about the last few days, Sarah decided it was more than not being able to recapture the past, she couldn't entirely escape the past either.

The Vincents had cut the trees along the shoreline, opening up a spectacular view across Kwiguigam Sound. They had also built a new pier, to the disgust of local lobstermen who found their fishing grounds pre-empted by the structure.

"I don't have any plans beyond the summer," Sarah said.

"That's wise. Take your time," Anton advised.

"I tried to buy Huggard's place myself last fall," George said. "It was such an eyesore. I told her she could name her price."

"She threatened you with a shotgun," Debbie said, outraged.

"It may have been my Cossack hat, because she yelled something about Russians." George said, glancing at Anton.

"She was an awful woman." Anton burst out, his friendly expression vanishing as his face flushed red.

"Now, Anton," George replied, "I know she gave you a hard time over the boundary, but she was difficult with everyone."

"She was a crook! She and her accomplice, that girl—"

"Cathy Leduc," Debbie prompted.

"—Leduc," Anton spat out the word. Sasha put a restraining hand on his arm. He shook her off. "She was the one who ran around doing the old woman's dirty work. And as for that hovel—"

Anton caught himself and gave a rueful smile. "But there you are. I probably would have thought she was a fine old lady if she hadn't extorted money from me over the property line. It was quicker and easier to pay her off than fight over that dern foolishness with the tree."

"She probably needed money for the taxes," Debbie said.

"If she couldn't afford to live there, she should have sold the place to someone who could," Sasha replied.

Irritated, Sarah wondered how often that tired bromide had been trotted out to justify someone's greed.

Later, as Sarah was leaving the Vincent's, she saw a familiar bicycle enter Myra's driveway. Impulsively, she followed.

Ziggy had leaned his machine against Myra's chicken coop and was standing in front of what had once been her front door.

Someone had mowed the lawn since Sarah's last visit.

Ziggy turned with a start at Sarah's arrival. "You're the woman who lives in Myra's ditch," he said as she got out of the Explorer.

"Paying your respects?" Sarah inquired.

Ziggy peered into the blackened cellar hole, perhaps looking for an empty beer can for his collection. Or perhaps looking for something more.

"We had compatible neuroses," he said. "We talked about survival and rebirth, things we had in common. She survived by enduring, fighting the odds. When Myra is reborn, it will be as Myra. I admire that."

"How will you be reborn?"

"I already have been," he replied, his voice flat.

Turning away from the desolation in his eyes, she nodded at the cellar hole. "Do you think someone killed her?"

"Nobody asks my opinion. Why should I give it to you?"

"Because I live in Myra's ditch."

He looked at her intently, a shock of unruly hair showing beneath his watch cap. His nose and cheeks were sunburned where the skin wasn't covered by unkempt whiskers. Sarah decided that Oliver was right. The Can Man wasn't as flaky as he appeared.

"If she was killed," he said, "Mammon will possess her land, and darkness will have won, and she will be forgotten. And being forgotten is the worst fate of all."

Ziggy's beard bristled as his jaw muscles worked. "But your

question is meaningless, rooted in a culture of materialism and defeat. She was able to live at home until she died. That was her fondest dream, and it came to pass. Nothing else matters."

He turned away abruptly, to the blackness of the cellar hole.

After a moment, he said, "Time was Myra's enemy."

"You mean her strokes?"

"I mean Time with a big T."

"What if she was blackmailing someone? Could she have been poisoned with something to cause the strokes?"

Ziggy turned to look at her again, shrewd and appraising now. Oh yes, Sarah thought, there was definitely more to the Can Man than met the eye. Suddenly, she felt vulnerable.

"She wouldn't have called it blackmail," he said, evading her question.

"Did she mention a headstone? Or Gerhard Burndt?"

"If you mean the Oak Hill development, she hated it. If you mean his final resting place, he should be left in peace, wherever he is."

Back in character, Ziggy gave her a solemn look. "Be careful in your ditch, or risk darkness."

Marlee Sue called early that evening as Sarah was finishing supper. "You could be on the trail of something, Irish. It looks like Doctor Harold Caldwell is the one behind Oak Hill, and he's in deep. He underestimated how much it would cost to develop that property, and if they don't sell more lots soon, he's headed down the tubes. Does that help?"

"I'm not sure, except Cathy Leduc was Caldwell's receptionist, and she helped Myra fight the development."

Marlee Sue was silent for a moment. "Okay, but how are you going to prove that's why Myra was killed? Besides, Myra and Cathy weren't able to actually stop the development."

"But they were delaying it, and time is money." Sarah thought about the headstone and added, "And maybe they were cooking up some new trouble."

Another pause, and Marlee Sue said, "You're right. It all boils down to money, and Sam Merlew is the key in my book. He's chairman of the planning board, and he cast the deciding vote in favor of the first two lots on Oak Hill. The rest are coming up for a vote in a couple of weeks. If they aren't approved—and there's a lot of opposition in town—Caldwell goes belly up. Sam's vote is vital. Think payoff."

"Why do you keep picking on the Merlews?"

"I'm just trying to make sure you keep an open mind. There are lots of possibilities out there."

Chapter 18

S arah arrived at Oliver's place on Wednesday morning, and was greeted by Wes, who bounded out to say hello as he woofed and cavorted at her feet.

Oliver stood in the barn door and admired the Ford. "Dinged up grill, wrinkled fender, and now a green side. A little body rot, some mud, and you'll look just like a native."

"Very funny."

"What happened?"

Oliver listened, his face grave, as she talked.

"Why in the world would anybody do that to your car?"

Sarah felt her face flush. She was sure Oliver must be wondering if the word had any significance.

"It may have just been random vandalism," she said.

"Way out there? Did you call—" Anticipating her answer, Oliver groaned with irritation. "Doesn't anybody around here *ever* call the cops?"

"What could I tell them? What could they do?"

"You could tell them someone is stalking you. You could tell them someone may be trying to kill you. That would be a good start. At least they'd know."

"It's my problem. I'll deal with it."

" Good day you sound like that lunatic, Gaites." Oliver glared at her. "It is possible the cops could help, you know, maybe even keep you from getting killed."

He kicked at a pebble in the driveway, sent it spinning onto the lawn. He glared some more at her stubborn expression, then shook his head in frustration.

"We might as well get to work," he growled at last.

They started in on *Owl*. Sarah sanded the seat and frames for more coats of varnish and paint, while Oliver worked underneath, applying anti-fouling paint. Later, she would help him put more varnish on his boat.

While they worked, Sarah told him about her encounter with Eldon and her trip to Meadow road.

"You got more out of Eldon the rest of us," Oliver said.

"I'm probably a mother figure for him. According to Eldon, Myra had a thing about Russians."

"As in Borofsky?"

"Or George Vincent. He wears a Cossack-style hat."

"All that Russian stuff is probably just be Myra's prejudice showing through."

"Which gets us back to the headstone."

"It does?" Oliver looked over the rail at Sarah. His latex gloves were speckled with green anti-fouling paint.

"Protecting her ancestor from the alien outsiders. Myra got the Borofskys to pay her off over the boundary line. Maybe she tried to do the same thing with the headstone."

"Do you think the grave is on Borofsky's land?"

"It's possible. There might have been a family plot in the strip of woods they cut down for their driveway."

Oliver pulled off his gloves. "I can't imagine killing someone over a misplaced grave."

"I met Anton Borofsky, and he's got a temper."

"My guess is that Myra had Cathy dig up the headstone last fall, but the bottom half was frozen in too deep, and that's why we don't have it. Cathy probably decided Myra was going too far trying to blackmail someone with the stone, and that's what they argued about. We know Cathy told Eldon that Myra wanted her to do something wrong without telling him what. Suppose she followed his suggestion about getting advice. Who would she talk to, besides the Merlews? Brian? Doc Caldwell?"

"Cathy said she wanted to talk to me in the note she sent along with Myra's pictures," Sarah said. "But why would she want to talk to me about the headstone?"

Oliver shrugged. "No way of knowing. I still think Oak Hill is the most likely place for the stone to turn up, though. The access road runs along the edge of the cemetery grounds, about where Gerhard's house was."

"And I was run off the road right after I left there."

"True, but let's not be too quick on the trigger. There's the Vincent's new tennis court. They cleared a lot of woods and brush for that. Then there's the land on the other side of Myra that was surveyed last fall." He reached over the rail and scraped a stray blob of paint off the varnish.

"You're using a Boy Scout knife on my boat?"

"It's a Swiss Army pen knife," he informed her.

He held it out for her inspection. "You should get one yourself. It comes in handy for all kinds of things."

"How about self-defense?"

"Doubtful. Too small."

"Caldwell is behind the Oak Hill development," she said.

"How did you find that out? Brian? Sam?"

Sarah told him about Marlee Sue.

"He probably didn't want people to know he owns it to avoid stirring up hard feelings among his patients," he said.

"I think we should look into Caldwell."

"Say what?"

"He keeps turning up. If Cathy learned that Caldwell had disturbed Gerhard's grave, she might have confronted him. Do you go to Caldwell?"

"I'm not sick; I don't go to anybody."

"Then it's high time you got a checkup."

"And the purpose of this would be?"

"To pump him for information."

"Then why don't *you* get a checkup?" he demanded.

"Because I don't live here. Don't you care what happened to Myra and Cathy?"

"Dang right I care, and I pay a ton of taxes so the cops can find out what happened to Myra and Cathy. That's their job, and I'm going to let them do it." He stalked off.

Finished with her painting, Sarah found Oliver a half-hour later, poring over a pile of drawings jumbled on the workbench.

The top drawing showed a small sloop. "It's beautiful. Are you going to build it?"

"I'll start next week."

"Did you design it?"

"My father did."

"That must be nice for both of you."

"Mmm."

"Do you build boats for him often?"

"No."

Sarah figured the monosyllables meant that either he was still sulking or she was hitting close to home with Oliver's father.

"Why not?" she asked.

"Because he designs traditional, plank-on-frame boats, like *Owl*, like Pearly builds. I specialize in strip-plank and cold-molded boats."

"What's this, then?"

"Cold-molded. It's his first one," Oliver said.

"What does cold-molded mean?"

"You build a temporary form, what some people call a plug, of the hull and put on several layers of really thin planks, called veneers, over it cris-cross, glueing them together. When you're done, you take it off the plug and you have what's basically a boat-shaped piece of plywood, all in one piece. It makes a very light, strong hull."

"It's exciting that you're building it for him. It will be something new for both of you."

"He put in too much framing and made the planking thicker.

than he needed."

"Have you told him that?"

"Look at the number on the drawing."

"Design number 327?"

"That's a lot of boats," Oliver said. "Would you tell Moses that he had misspelled Jehovah?"

"But he isn't Moses, and I'm sure he'd want your opinion."

"Maybe."

"Will he be coming up to visit?"

"Maybe."

"It would be fun to meet him," she replied sweetly.

Oliver frowned at her. "If you really want to give Caldwell the third-degree, I can pick you up around five and we'll go down to the Rockland marina. He'll probably be there working on his boat, and he won't think twice about me turning up. Just don't expect to get anything out of him."

Chapter 19

P early's Mazda pickup was a good deal smaller than Eldon's oversized GMC, but then Pearly himself was a good deal smaller than Eldon, and he looked smaller still as he stepped out of the Mazda in front of Oliver's shop later that afternoon.

Oliver's heavily modified lawnmower crouched on the grass nearby. It appeared to have sprouted a collection of new bits and pieces. "Are you going to turn that thing loose again?" Pearly said suspiciously as Oliver came out to greet him.

"Lawnzilla? I'm about to."

"Should have brought my shotgun."

"I've told you it's harmless," Oliver said. "There are safety interlocks up the gazoo."

"_Right_," Pearly retorted.

"Anyway, I fixed that software glitch from last time," Oliver assured him.

"That was a glitch? I call it downright homicidal."

"If you hadn't tried to run away, it wouldn't have gotten confused."

"Confused? Not even your dog trusts the _dern_ thing."

"Did you just come here to bust my chops?"

"I need the trash bag," Pearly said. "They found Cathy's body."

"_Crap._ Where?"

"In Myra's well. Been there a long time."

"Myra's well?"

"She had a dug well at the edge of her lawn," Pearly said. "The Grabow kids were playing over there and pulled the cover off it—said they were trying to get a snake out of the stonework—and they saw something floating inside. Talk about poisoning the water."

"Symbolic," Oliver mused.

"Symbolic, heck.Probably just convenient, if you figure she was killed in January. They won't know for sure 'til the autopsy, but Charlie says it looks like she was shot in the head. Small caliber, most likely a .22. They had to use dental records to identify the body, and the cops going after Eldon again."

"You're giving them the headstone, right?"

"I'm going to take it back to the shop and let them find it themselves," Pearly said. "I figure we'll leave Cathy's boat here for a while. Keep Eldon from mooning over it."

The Rockland waterfront was a far cry from Pearly's quiet pace. Dozens of boats sat on the pavement, propped up on tripod-like metal stands. Oliver led Sarah through the maze, dodging around boats, stands, electrical cords, ladders, and hurrying people.

Suddenly, they were face-to-face with Caldwell. An oversized sponge in his hand and a bucket at his side, he was scrubbing a stain on the hull of a power cruiser whose deck stood well over Sarah's head.

Caldwell looked at her. "You're Sarah Cassidy, from Sunday," he said.

"I'm showing her around," Oliver said. "Did you hear they found Cathy's body?"

"The State Police called," Caldwell replied. "I hope they lock Tupper up and throw away the key."

"Why do you think Eldon killed her?" Sarah asked.

"He killed Myra too, as far as I'm concerned. He's the one who persuaded Cathy to help keep the poor old woman at home, when she was in no shape to be alone. And her tending a wood stove, for sake. Her mind was going, and she could hardly get up and down those stairs. No wonder the place burned down. Myra would still be alive if they had put her into a nursing home where she belonged. Eldon was a bad influence on Cathy from the start."

"I understand that Myra was against the Oak Hill development," Sarah said.

"She was against everything."

"Did Cathy ever say anything to you about the development? I know you're BCD Properties."

Caldwell dropped his sponge into the bucket, splashing Oliver's left sneaker. He stared at Sarah. "Who are you anyway?"

"Just a friend of Myra's," she replied.

"My being BCD Properties isn't a state secret," he said. "I knew Cathy didn't approve, but she never made a big thing out of it. A lot of people don't like developments."

"Did Cathy mention Gerhard Burndt's headstone?"

"What headstone? Everybody knows he's in an unmarked grave somewhere in the cemetery."

"His grave has been disturbed," Oliver murmured.

"Disturbed? What do you mean?"

"He might have been buried behind his house," Oliver said, "where Oak Hill's access road is."

"Not possible. The graves are inside the cemetery wall and the construction is outside."

"Unless the wall was built after he was buried," Sarah said.

"Why in the world would they leave him outside the wall?"

"Ground-penetrating radar," Oliver said thoughtfully.

"What?" Caldwell said.

"Ground-penetrating radar," Oliver repeated. "Utility companies use it to locate buried pipes, and archeologists use it to find old ruins and grave sites."

"Is this some kind of a joke?"

"It wouldn't take long to scan the area for graves."

Caldwell glared at them. "This is ridiculous. There are no graves on our right of way, and I'm not spending a fortune on some wild goose chase. Furthermore, if we had found an old grave we'd have gone to the town and dealt with it legally. Unmarked graves turn up all the time, and it's no big deal."

Unless you're dealing with Myra Huggard and are running out of money, Sarah thought.

Harry Caldwell returned home that evening and called Brian.

"That Sarah Cassidy woman was asking about Gerhard Burndt's grave, practically accused me of paving over his coffin. She knows there isn't room to move the access road."

"Did you pave over his grave?" Brian asked.

A brass lamp lit the mahogany surface of Caldwell's desk with a reddish glow, and left the rest of his den in shadow.

"How do I know? Where did she get the idea, anyway?"

"She went to Migawoc years ago and visited Myra back then. Maybe they kept in touch, or Cathy talked to her."

"The way we're burning up money, I can't afford to have her stir up the town, the planning board, the historical society, and god knows who else. It could take *years* for ‘gosh sake."

"Nobody knows where Gerhard Burndt was buried. It's all just guesses," Brian reassured him.

"She's got Oliver Wendell involved too. He's talking about using ground-penetrating radar, whatever that is, to go over our right of way," Caldwell said.

"Oliver is involved in this?" Brian paused. "They must know something. I'll see what I can get out of her."

Harry Caldwell sat at his desk and thought for a long time after hanging up the phone.

Chapter _20_

The Beetle Cat sailboat is about twelve feet long, six feet wide, and shaped like a melon-seed, with its mast well up in the bow. The shallow cockpit lacks seats, leaving its occupants to sit on the often wet floor.

Oliver and Arlene had picked a hot July morning for a sail to West Island. It was a perfect day for a pair of newlyweds to enjoy the brilliant sun and warm waters of Buzzard's Bay, and Arlene sat very close. Her hair, smelling of shampoo, brushed Oliver's ear as the light breeze stirred the golden strands. Her bare legs glistened with lotion and she wore one of Oliver's shirts over her bikini. They had a picnic lunch stowed under the fore deck for when they reached the island.

If they made it to the island. The closer they got, the more perverse the wind became. They could only get within a few hundred feet of the sandy beach before the wind veered and drove them back. Again and again, they tried, only to be defeated.

The skies were suddenly filled with black, writhing clouds, and the wind became a howling fury that drove them helplessly out to sea where towering waves crashed down on the boat, washing them into the sea. He made a grab for Arlene's arm, but it was just out of reach in the churning water. Her face, just below the surface, was open-mouthed in a silent, pleading scream—

Oliver awoke, covered with sweat. It was years since the dream had last haunted him.

It was partly based on fact. They had borrowed the senior Wendell's Beetle Cat and sailed to West Island a few weeks after their wedding. The wind hadn't thwarted them, though. In fact, they sailed right up to the beach, anchoring in the shallows.

They were alone, except for a couple with a toddler, splashing in the water a hundred yards further up the shore.

They swam, spread a towel on the hot sand, ate lunch, then lay in each others arms under the sun's warmth.

After a while Arlene murmured, "The hook's in front."

"What a brilliant idea."

"They made it that way with you menfolk in mind." She ran her hand down his lower back.

"Very thoughtful." He kissed her again.

"I don't want to be a spoil-sport," she said a little later, "but there are people over there."

"Shiver me timbers," Oliver replied, in his Captain Hook voice, "mayhap we should retreat to our pirate ship."

"Will all that timber shivering involve a lot of boat rocking?"

They had often joked that John Junior was born nine months later.

Wes growled, and Oliver realized that it wasn't the first time. A faint noise came from outside.

Oliver dressed hurriedly in the dark—an easy chore since he was in the habit of leaving his clothing in a heap beside the bed. He fumbled for the flashlight on the night stand. There was another, louder noise outside.

An old 12-gauge Remington pump-action shotgun stood behind the closet door. It was only loaded with birdshot, but that would have to do.

He worked his way downstairs in the darkness, hushing Wes as he went, and looked out the kitchen window.

Owl, with Cathy's boat beyond it, sat in front of the barn, indistinct blobs in the faint moonlight. A pickup truck was slowly backing up the driveway towards the barn. As he watched, the truck stopped, pulled forward a few yards, and then started to back up again. Somebody was trying to hitch onto the trailer of Cathy's boat and appeared to be having trouble lining up the truck in the dark.

Oliver started to ease out the kitchen door while keeping the struggling dog inside, but Wes was too quick. With a series of ferocious barks, he hurtled into the night.

The truck lurched to a stop, the sharp crack of a .22 rang out, and Wes yelped.

Without thinking, Oliver vaulted down the porch steps and fired. He was jacking another round into the chamber when the pickup roared off into the night.

Patches of ground-fog still clung to the low spots as Pearly and Oliver headed towards Route 1. A white BMW, doing close to ninety, leaped at them over the crest of a hill. Pearly jerked the pickup's wheel, his tires churning dirt from the shoulder. The BMW, still straddling the crown of the road, swept by with inches to spare.

" Dad-gum ," Pearly said as he pulled back onto the pavement.

"Summer is coming," Oliver observed.

"It doesn't have to come so dern fast."

"Can't live with them, can't eat without them."

"You're quite a philosopher, for someone who was up half the night shooting at people," Pearly said. "You want to saw the cedar for shares, like last time?"

"Sure, so long as I can borrow Eldon to help me run the sawmill."

"I don't need any oak, so that's on you."

"Yeah. It's only a couple of trees," Oliver said.

"I wouldn't drag you up there except you wanted logs with some sweep, so I figured you'd better make sure they're crooked enough for you. You met Fournier and his crew?"

"No."

They landed on Route 1 and hit the Thursday morning tourist traffic, early birds hurrying north to get ahead of the weekend rush.

"They're kind of rough-hewn."

"Like you?" Oliver said, meaning it as a joke.

Pearly didn't take it that way. "I went to college, Ollie. Four years at UMO. To Jack Fournier, if someone went to college it means they did a stretch at the Super Max in Warren. Don't get me wrong. He's honest as the day is long."

They turned onto the quiet of Route 46, heading inland.

"What did the police say?" Pearly asked, breaking the silence.

"Mostly they bawled me out for shooting at the truck."

"Not much sympathy."

Oliver's face was red. "The   dam bastard shot my dog."

"Winged him, anyhow. Could have shot you too," Pearly pointed out. "Just be glad the vet is letting you pick up Wes, alive, and not in a box."

Oliver nodded, still fuming. The bullet had grazed the top of Wes' neck. The vet told him an inch lower would have been fatal.

"I hope you didn't finger Doc Caldwell for it," Pearly said.

"I was tempted. We talked to him yesterday evening, Sarah asked about the headstone, and this happens."

"She asked him about the headstone?"

"Just in general. Nothing specific."

"She ever report being run off the road?"

"She had to, for the insurance, if nothing else." Oliver glanced at Pearly. "She didn't tell them it was Eldon's truck."

"She probably couldn't be sure."

"Yes she could. She just didn't know who was driving."

"It's a mess," Pearly said. "Leave it be."

"Are you kidding? Somebody waltzes in and shoots my dog, and you tell me to leave it be? I'm going to get the guy who did this."

Pearly sighed. "What about Cathy's boat, then? You want me to take it away and lock it up if someone was trying to steal it?"

"No, I'm going to use it for bait."

"What do you mean, bait?" Pearly said. "I've got money tied up in that boat. Cathy never made the final payment."

"Don't worry. I hid a Tracfone in it, so it'll call for help if the boat is moved."

"I thought you hated cell phones."

"They have their uses," Oliver said. "Maybe I'll rig it to set off a smoke flare if you call."

"No way that's legal," Pearly replied.

"I set it to call your cell, by the way."

"The heckyou did," Pearly grumbled.

An hour from the coast, they entered what is often called "The Other Maine," a place that gets somewhat less attention on post cards and travel brochures. Traffic was sparse here—mostly battered pickups with Maine plates. The scattered houses were tired and worn, surrounded by the remains of things too broken to use, too valuable to throw away, too expensive to replace.

"Sarah told me Myra had a sister." Oliver said as they swept by one of the hardscrabble farms.

"Cara was the ambitious one, moved to Boston right out of High School, never set foot in town again. She ended up running a bank in Chicago. The farthest Myra ever got from Burnt Cove is when Cathy drove her down to Portland for those tests last year."

Oliver wondered about Cara's ambition, and Myra's rootedness. What made some people cling stubbornly, in the face of all reason, to the place and ways of their youth, while others couldn't wait to rid themselves of the past? Was it fear of change, lack of ambition, or an inherent timidity, that motivated people like Myra? Was he naive in thinking that her choices were based on valuing community and tradition above ambition and wealth? Wherever it came from, Myra's rootedness was a Mainer's great strength—until those roots were torn up.

Oliver emerged from his musings to ask, "What happened with the headstone?"

"Told the cops I found it in the back of the shop. I put it in a new trash bag first, since our prints were all over the old one."

"You swapped trash bags?Dang," Oliver said, "have you ever

heard the term 'tampering with evidence?'"

"You ever heard the term 'jail cell,' Dick Tracy?"

"We could tell the cops the truth for a change—try something different. How are they going to find out where the stone came from without dusting the bag for prints?"

"No problem. I told them Cathy put it there last winter."

"But you don't *know* it was Cathy, Pearly."

"Sure I do. Besides, you want them to find your prints on it? Or Sarah's? Don't worry, I wore gloves."

"*Gloves?* What the hell are they going to think when there aren't *any* prints—" Oliver caught himself, took a deep breath, went on more calmly. "You can't protect Eldon forever, Pearly. If he did something wrong, it'll come out sooner or later."

"For Pete's sake Ollie, make up your mind. First you're Osama bin Laden, booby trapping boats and threatening the most respected doctor in town, and now you're Dudley Do-Right, fussing, over a dang trash bag."

They pulled off the pavement a little way beyond a scraggly farmhouse whose attached barn was missing an end wall and half of its roof. A muddy tote road cut into the woods, and a pile of tree-length logs were yarded up beside the road.

"Wet time of year to be cutting trees," Pearly said as they tramped through the woods, skirting water-filled skidder ruts. They followed the track until they came on three men seated in a clearing, eating lunch. An ancient Chevy Nova was parked beside them. The car was mostly tan, except for the driver's side fender and door, which were blue. A length of wire held the tailpipe off the ground. Oliver saw a skidder in the woods nearby, it's chain-encased tires thick with mud. Three trees were hitched to the skidder's cable.

"How'd they get the dang car in here, a helicopter?" Pearly muttered.

"Well, we thought you'd got lost." The speaker looked to be in his late fifties, unshaven, wearing a sweat-stained tee shirt and worn jeans with the knees blown out.

"Jack Fournier, this is Oliver Wendell, the guy I told you about," Pearly said.

Fournier sketched a salute and they traded introductions. "BB" Pearson, referred to as the best skidder driver around, was small and wiry with a greasy sweatshirt. Ralph, bald and looking to be in his seventies, was sharpening a chain saw.

"So you're the one who wants them crooked trees." BB flashed Oliver a nearly toothless grin. "We've got some good 'uns for you down the slope." Unlike the coastal drawl, he spoke with the short, clipped accent of inland Maine.

They haggled in a lackadaisical way over the price, amid glum comments about the plight of the small-time wood cutter.

"That's a lot of work for a half-load of cedar. We've got to go all over, jerk them out one at a time. It's not like we can make up a good twitch, haul a bunch at a whack," Jack said.

"What do you want them crooked trees for?" BB asked.

"It's just the oak he wants crooked," Jack said. "He wouldn't be here if he didn't have a use for them."

"They're for deck beams. Decks are curved," Oliver said, sketching an arc with his hands.

"Well, if you need crooked trees, we got 'em," BB said.

Jack seated himself on a dead log. "I went to Camden a while back to see the ocean." He nodded at the Chevy. "She don't look like much, but that old bird's a runner."

"Just like mother," BB added. "Heck to get goin' in the morning, but once she's rollin', watch out."

Ralph propped open the Nova's trunk with a stick and rooted out a jug of bar oil.

"Lot of fancy boats down there," Jack continued.

"I imagine they all had crooked beams," BB said happily.

"Drove right up to the yacht club," Jack went on. "They must have been having a party, men all dressed up in fancy straw hats, blue jackets, and everything."

"Was they glad to see you?" BB asked.

"I don't imagine."

"Them city people don't know nothin' about the woods," Ralph said, sloshing oil into his saw. "They sit around Augusta and make up rules, but they ain't cut down a tree in their lives."

"Most of them's from away," BB said, as though that explained it. "I visited my sister down in Massachusetts a while back. Lord, what a goshawfull place to live."

"That's why they move up here," Jack said.

BB frowned. "Trouble is, they come up here and make all those rules, and regulations, and crap—pardon my French—so it's just like where they left. If they come up here 'cause it's so good, why don't they leave it the way it is?"

Jack nodded, glancing sideways at Oliver. "Why don't they stay where they are and fix up their own country, and let us take care of ours?"

Ralph dropped the oil jug back into the Chevy. "I helped my old man cut over this territory when I was 'bout twelve. Had an old Ford jitterbug. Took all summer."

"When was that?" BB grinned at the old man.

"During the war, around '44. Jimmy Bright and I cut her off again in '75, and here I am doin' her one last time." Ralph let the trunk lid drop with a crash. "The woods'll be here long after them city people are gone."

Chapter 21

"You paid too much for that oak, considering it wasn't worth diddly 'til you came along," Pearly said as they tramped back to his truck.

"Maybe, but Fournier is right, Pearly," Oliver said. "The guys in the boaters and blazers can afford it. Look around, we're an hour's drive from all those million-dollar houses on the coast."

"You sound like a Massachusetts liberal," Pearly retorted. "You've got stock options and who knows what else from when you worked at that engineering company in Massachusetts. If I don't make enough money to eat, I starve. I can't afford to be so generous to people like Fournier that they get spoiled."

"I don't think we have any choice, in the long run."

Pearly shook his head. "I think you should take care of your own first, and worry about the next county later. Besides, these people don't like it when someone tries to help them, anyway. They're as ornery as a wet boot."

"These people? What about Myra Huggard?"

Pearly glanced at his companion, sensing a trap. "What do you mean by that?"

"Myra wasn't living very high on the hog, but at least she wasn't dependent on all the out-of-state money the way we are. Look at Fournier. He can tell us to screw off because we need him more than he needs us."

"You're too soft. And gullible too."

They walked on in silence, and soon a chain saw started up behind them. "Do you suppose Fournier really crashed the Camden yacht club, or was he just putting us on?" Oliver said.

A faint smile wrinkled the corners of Pearly's mouth. "Who knows, but I sure would have liked to be there if he did."

Oliver pulled into his driveway that afternoon with Wes sprawled on the seat beside him. The dog's neck was wrapped in a bandage, and he was still groggy from the anesthesia. The vet had given Oliver a paper bag full of bandages and antibiotics, and assured him that the wound wasn't as bad as it looked, but the dog would need rest.

A turkey meandered reluctantly out of the driveway and into the field as they approached. Wes looked, gave a half-hearted sniff, and lowered his head. Oliver fumed.

Owl sat in front of the barn, and Oliver felt an unexpected twinge of jealousy. Sarah had mentioned going out in Brian's boat this afternoon if the weather was good.

He helped Wes out of the car. "Come on, you mangey old reprobate, let's get something to eat."

There was half a pizza in the fridge, left over from some dimly remembered meal. He zapped it in the microwave.

For some reason, Sarah reminded him of Arlene. He wasn't quite sure why, since they were very different people. Even so, having the woman drop on him like this had rattled his cage.

The memory was seared into his brain: the day he had answered the page to Phil's office, the expression on the older man's face when Oliver entered. Phil Hendrix rated a corner office, and the afternoon sun that danced along the trees lining the parking lot shone through the windows to deepen the shadows lining Phil's face. Oliver saw Betty Malloy from Human Resources standing in a corner, and felt his heart stop.

A drunk in an SUV had run a stoplight. Oliver's wife and daughter had died in the intersection, their car flattened. At least his son was spared.

Oliver had adjusted, in a way, to being a single parent with a teenage son, but he never recovered from his loss and never expected to. His training as an engineer taught him to value logic only up to a point, beyond which lay chaos and uncertainty. Logic told him that life went on and change was inevitable, but in the end, trying to maintain the old life proved too hard to bear, and he had moved to Maine. Some of his friends accused him of running away from his emotions, walling them off, burying them along with half of his family. After ten years, he still wondered if they were right.

Oliver forced his mind onto his father's drawings, still lying on the work bench. He would start lofting the lines this afternoon, an enjoyably soothing process that involved recreating the boat's curves full-size on the white-painted plywood sheets spread out in the barn loft. Using the full-size lines, he would then the cut out the pieces to build a framework over which the hull could be formed.

Brian Curtis appreciated the Good Life and his taste in boats reflected that appreciation. *Good Times* was built on a lobsterboat style hull, but with a plush cockpit and a cabin that included cruising accommodations for two.

"I did some lobstering when I was a kid, like most everyone else around here," Brian said. "Had my own lobsterboat, so I decided to get the kind of boat I knew when I bought one to play with."

They rumbled out the mouth of Burnt Cove harbor and into the sound, *Good Times*' exhaust burbling throatily from the stern. The early afternoon sun dappled the water and highlighted the many-colored lobster pot buoys.

"It looks like more lobster pots than I remember," Sarah said.

Brian smiled at her. "They put video cameras in some traps once and found out that most of the lobsters crawl in there, eat the bait, and crawl right back out, no problem. Seems to be just the real dumb ones, or the unlucky ones, that get caught. Turns out, we're running a bunch of fast-food joints for lobsters down there."

He nodded at a boat pulling pots across the sound. A flock of gulls circled over it hopefully. "I'm glad not to be doing that any more. It's darn hard work. Not bad on a day like this, but wicked miserable in rough weather."

They watched as the boat moved on to the next buoy, a cloud of smoke belching from it s exhaust stack. A few seconds later the engine's roar reached their ears.

They ran along the rocky shore of Squirrel Point. "Your old stomping grounds," he said, pointing to the granite ledges that fronted the camp and Myra Huggard's property.

Sarah turned away. "I'm in Myra's will," she said.

"Yeah?"

"Her lawnmower, gardening tools, and the Studebaker."

"Well good for you," Brian said with a smile.

"She also left me a deed."

"A deed?"

"To her land."

Brian laughed. "Oh, *that* deed."

"What's so funny?"

"Nothing, but if it's the deed I'm thinking about, she drove the Borofskys crazy with it, claiming she owned a hunk of their land. "

"And you think this is the deed?"

"I'd have to look at it to be sure, but—"

Sarah pulled her purse out of the canvas tote bag she had brought along and extracted the deed.

Brian looked bemused, but took the paperwork from her fingers somewhat faster than Sarah expected. He cut the engine to an idle and studied the document.

"This is the one, transferring the land from William Burndt to Cyrus Huggard, back in 1883." He pointed to the handwritten text. "See where it says 'from the young oak tree by the shore marking the property line of Conrad Burndt?' The tree had been blazed, but the mark was pretty much grown over, and Myra claimed they had the wrong oak and she owned another forty feet of Borofsky's land."

Brian scanned the deed some more and said, "Myra called the cops when Roy started excavating the foundation, said he was on her land, and got the digging stopped 'til the dispute was settled. Borofsky came roaring up from New York that afternoon, mad as heck".

"Couldn't they prove she was wrong?"

"Sure, they could. The tree thing was a crock. That line was surveyed when Evan sold the land to the Merlews, and it was surveyed again when Sam subdivided the camp into house lots."

Brian refolded the deed. "Borofsky and I went and talked to Myra about the line. She started off by saying the surveyors were incompetent, and threatened court orders, law suits, and all that. Then, she offered to 'sell' him the forty feet of land. I thought Borofsky was going to have a heart attack, but he finally paid her something just to get her out of his hair, so he could get his house built."

"What if Myra had been right about the tree?"

Brian shrugged. "Without that forty feet, Borofsky wouldn't have had anywhere near enough frontage for the legal minimum to build. It probably would have ended up being a lawyer's free-for-all: the Borofskys suing the Merlews, everybody suing the surveyors, maybe even the town."

"So, why didn't the oak tree cause a problem when the Merlews bought the land?" Sarah asked.

Brian laughed. "Good question. Thing is, Evan was the one who sold the land. If it had been up to Myra, she'd still own every inch. Evan had inherited the land, and he probably didn't agree with Myra about which tree marked the line, but then he and Myra didn't agree about a lot of things."

"Why didn't Evan sell the woodlot?"

"It wasn't worth much back then. Besides, they needed it for the firewood. Eldon was still cutting wood off it for Myra." Brian replied.

"They had a fair chunk of land to start with," he want on, "mostly old hayfields. The Merlews bought two pieces from Evan when they started the camp, and they added the lot the Borofskys have now in the early sixties."

Brian returned the deed. "It's funny she would give you that deed. I wonder what she was thinking."

Sarah had wondered too. Was the troublesome old woman expecting her to carry on the Borofsky feud? What was the point, now that she had been paid off, and the house was almost finished?

"I have no idea," she said.

"She never mentioned it?"

"No."

"Funny, I figured you two must have kept in touch," he said.

"I haven't talked to her since I left camp. I tried calling her several times last fall when I learned she was giving *Owl* to me, but she never answered the phone. The Merlews suggested I just write her a note, so I did that."

"She didn't like talking on telephones." Brian shrugged. "Weird she should give you a worthless deed like that without saying anything, but she was getting pretty batty."

"That's what the lawyer said."

Brian opened up *Good Times'* throttle, saying, "A lot of farmers used to sell pieces of land back and forth all the time in the old days. The trouble is, most of them weren't very careful with the boundaries, so they'd write a deed with a lot description like, 'Go easterly from the dead spruce tree to the corner of my cow pasture.' A hundred years later, that kind of stuff can drive a surveyor crazy."

They reached the tip of Squirrel Point, where the rambling shingled hotel looked out to sea.

"Water looks pretty calm," Brian commented, "Let's go out to Brill Ledge and see if we can spot a whale."

It was late afternoon as *Good Times* made its way back up the estuary to Burnt Cove. The wind had died, the fog had stayed off shore, and Sarah hadn't even needed her windbreaker. Best of all, they had seen a whale, a little Minke that let them watch for nearly a minute before it dived. A most satisfactory afternoon.

Sunlight, low in the sky, lit the town with a reddish glow.

"The cove looks like it's on fire, like the name," Sarah said.

Brian cut the engine and *Good Times* rolled gently in the swell.

They watched the deepening glow for a while, and Sarah found Brian's arm around her shoulder. She moved away.

"Sorry," she said.

"Hey, I'm the one who should apologize. I know how you feel, being divorced myself."

Sarah doubted that he really knew how she felt. "I've had a great afternoon, though."

"Me too. Maybe we can take a picnic out to one of the islands sometime."

His enthusiasm gave her a pang of guilt. She had accepted Brian's invitation partly to see what he could tell her about Myra. She had learned some interesting things, though she didn't know what they meant. Still, Sarah felt guilty at using him in this way, even though he was fun, and she enjoyed his company.

Chapter 22

S arah pulled into Oliver's driveway on Friday morning, and Wes ran out to greet her as usual, front end barking and rear end wagging. From a distance it looked as thought he was wearing a bandanna around his neck. Then she realized it was a bandage. She got out and scratched his ears, careful of the bandage. He panted happily at her.

"What happened to Wes?" she said when Oliver appeared at the door.

Sarah listened with growing indignation as Oliver told her.

"Poor thing." She scratched his ears again. "You're one lucky dog."

"The scum bag who did it won't be so lucky, if I find out who it was," Oliver growled.

"Whoever was trying to steal Cathy's boat must have known the headstone was in it," she said.

"Caldwell is my first guess. We stirred him up with a stick Wednesday evening, and that night somebody tried to take Cathy's boat. It's a mighty big a coincidence."

Stirring up Caldwell had been Sarah's idea, and she felt guilty. "But how would he know the headstone was in there, and what's so important about it anyway? It's not a very obvious hiding place, and I can't see why Cathy would tell him, of all people."

"Maybe Caldwell was lying when he said she knew he was behind Oak Hill, and she asked him for advice about the stone."

"I wondered about that too. Of course, she might have talked to someone working at Oak Hill, like Roy Tupper, and he told Caldwell," Sarah said. "Would that ground-penetrating radar really work, or were you just trying to scare Caldwell?"

"It might. The trouble is, there's a lot of marine clay along the coast here, and the radar can't see very deep through that stuff."

Oliver shrugged. "Besides, it might not be the headstone at all. Caldwell was wrong, or lying, about one thing, though. Cathy was the one who wanted to help Myra stay in her house, not Eldon."

Sarah nodded. "Eldon went along with Cathy because he was smitten."

"We still can't rule out Myra's neighbors. We know she got money from the Borofskys, and she didn't make life easy for the Vincents either."

"And there's Grinshnell's land on the other side of Myra," Sarah said. "Maybe she was giving him a hard time too."

Having only questions and no answers, they turned to *Owl*, which sat on her trailer in the mid-day sun, ready at last. Oliver double-checked to make sure everything was firmly lashed down, then turned to Sarah. "Have you got life jackets, flares, pump, and all the stuff I put on the list?"

Suddenly fussy and officious, Oliver cross-examined Sarah about her preparations for *Owl*'s launching. The inquisition seemed unnecessary, if only because Pearly wasn't launching the boat until tomorrow morning. "Everything is in the car," she said brusquely.

Oliver abruptly turned to her. "Would you like some lunch? I've got sandwich stuff, cold-cuts, BLT makings, that kind of thing."

They assembled their meal in silence while Wes supervised the proceedings with a hungry eye. Oliver certainly lacked Brian's easy charm, light patter, and brilliant smile.

Sarah noticed the dishwasher was full of dirty dishes. It smelled as thought they had been there a while.

"You want me to run this?" she asked.

Oliver looked dubious. "Is it full already?"

She wrinkled her nose. "Where's the soap?"

They left the dishwasher to splash and gurgle, took the sandwiches outside, and placed two lawn chairs in a sunny corner where there was enough of a breeze to keep the black flies at bay.

"I think you need to be careful about getting involved in all this," Oliver said.

Sarah put down her sandwich. "You mean as in Brian?"

"I don't have anything against Brian. He probably has nothing to do with it, but think a minute. Myra is dead, and Brian is the broker for her land. That means a big commission for him."

Sarah felt her face turning hot. "Are you suggesting Brian killed Myra so he could sell her land?"

"I'm just saying there's a lot of money involved, between Myra's place and everything else. Even if you put the money aside, there are people with strong feelings about all the development going on. Look what's already happened to your car. Someone has it in for you for some reason."

Sarah was still focused on Brian. "It's crazy. How could Brian be sure Myra's sister would want to sell and make him the broker?"

"I just think you should be careful."

Fuss, fuss, fuss. But her irritation faded as she looked at the worry on Oliver's face. "I'll be careful," she said, "but you should be careful too. Look what happened to Wes."

Wes followed them into the house, looking hopeful, as they returned their plates to the kitchen. Oliver explained that he usually walked the dog after lunch, and Sarah surprised herself by asking to go along.

Sarah admired *Owl* once again as they passed by on their way around the barn. The ugly bulge was gone now, the bottom was freshly painted, and the boat glistened in the sun. Sarah realized with a thrill that if the weather was good, as the forecast promised, she could be out sailing by this time tomorrow.

They rambled through the woods on an old tote road, slathering on Uncle Ben's to discourage the black flies. Wes, impervious to such pests, bounded ahead.

"The camp was still going when I moved here," Oliver said as they skirted a trickle of water that crossed the trail. "It was on its last legs by then, though. The Merlews were getting kind of old to run it, and Kate began having health problems. That's when they started selling off the camp's land."

Wes nosed a red squirrel from the underbrush and it raced up the path ahead of them with Wes, panting and snorting like a furry locomotive, in hot pursuit. Being shot didn't seem to have slowed him down much. The squirrel darted up a beech tree, chattering insults from a safe height. "You're a disgrace to your bird-dog ancestry," Oliver scolded mildly.

"Do you think having the Merlews sell off the camp is what started Myra on her anti-development campaign?" Sarah said.

"Maybe, though they started selling lots, one at a time, years ago when the camp closed. It wasn't until the last couple of years, when the Vincents, Oak Hill, and the Borofskys all came one right after another that Myra really got going."

"Having the Borofskys build right next door must have been the last straw," Sarah said.

Oliver called Wes away from his squirrel and said, "Wouldn't you kids have noticed a grave if there was one in that strip of woods between the Borofskys and Myra?"

Sarah thought about the first time she and Marlee Sue had explored those woods, gotten lost in the jumble of brush, and ended up in Myra's back yard. "Not necessarily. It was so thick in there you could hardly see a thing."

They had been working their way steadily up hill, and now they passed through a tumbledown stone wall at the edge of an abandoned blueberry field.

Sarah stood transfixed by the view that stretched out below, a sweep of green that rolled down across the miles to the water. A handful of tiny white specks dotted the bay, and Sarah wondered if there were any Herreshoff 12's out there.

A huge boulder, its profile shaped like a dog's head, jutted from the hilltop. So this was the hound of Hound Hill.

"Let's climb onto the rock," she said. Wes, apparently under-standing her suggestion, bounded off to the boulder. Without thinking, she took Oliver's hand.

She felt him tense, and let go.

Why had she done that? The excitement of finally getting *Owl* into the water? These impulsive lapses always got her in trouble. "Reckless Irish blood" her mother had called it. Marrying Claude had been one of those lapses, she supposed.

They clambered up the back of the rock where it sloped into the ground. The front end loomed some fifteen feet over the field and offered a truly spectacular view. Sarah sat on the weathered surface of the hound's left eyebrow, and Oliver found a spot at a companion-able distance beside her.

Wes sniffed around the base of the rock and she noticed his bandage was wet and muddy. "Would you like me to change that? I was a nurse once."

"You were?"

"For a year, before I got married." She had met Claude when he had surgery for a ruptured appendix. He was smart, handsome, witty, and full of fun. He had graduated from Harvard law school, passed the bar exam that month, and made a joke of his new job as a tax lawyer for the IRS. She fell for him like a ton of bricks.

Oliver looked down to where Wes was nosing the brush at the base of the rock. "Sure. I've got all the stuff in the house."

"Do you come up here often?" she asked. "Wes seemed to know where we were going when I suggested it."

"He's got a pretty good vocabulary," Oliver said, gazing into the distance. "It's a good thinking spot."

For the most part, any signs of human habitation were lost in the trees from this distance, and Sarah could imagine that she was looking down on Burnt Cove and Squirrel Point as they had been forty years ago, or a hundred and forty.

Perhaps it was just another of her impulsive lapses, but whatever the reason, Sarah told him about the day that Evan Huggard died.

She had half-planned to tell Kate about it, now that Myra was gone, but something had held her back. For some reason, Oliver's "thinking spot" seemed to be the right place and he seemed to be the right person, perhaps just because he was here. In some strange, almost magical way, the quiet timelessness of the place managed to bring past and present together.

Sarah was eighteen that last summer, and the camp was due to close the next day. She and Marlee Sue had both been camp counselors for two summers by then, and since one of Sarah's duties was to teach sailing, she crossed the archery field to take a last look at *Owl*.

The afternoon was fading into twilight, and she found the boat sitting peacefully at her mooring in the stillness.

Several Buffleheads were paddling just offshore, and Sarah sat on the ledge above them, watching as they gradually worked their way into the shallows nearby, occasionally quacking softly to each other. Then, apparently sensing her presence, they swerved and swam quickly away.

It had been a bittersweet week as Sarah prepared to leave Migawoc for the last time. With college starting, she would need a better-paying job next summer, and Sarah had been saying farewell to her favorite haunts.

The air turned cooler, causing Sarah to welcome her sweatshirt and regret her shorts. She got up and wandered along the shoreline in front of Myra's house.

The ledges were wet below the high-tide line, and that was where Sarah walked, looking for little creatures among the seaweed and small tidal pools that filled hollows in the rock.

It was so sudden there was no time to react.

Sarah was pushed from behind and fell headlong onto the seaweed. She scrambled to get up, but Evan Huggard flipped her over like an oversized fish.

"So, it's Myra's little friend," he said, leering into her face. His breath reeked of alcohol.

She started to scream, but he was kneeling over her and holding her upper arms. He slammed her down against the ledge. The wet fronds of seaweed covering the rock were probably all that prevented him from shattering her skull. Dazed, she struggled and was slammed down again.

"Shut up, or I'll smash your head in," Evan said. He jerked her sweatshirt up and held it over her face like a sack.

Her head spun, and the world seemed to recede. With a strange detachment, she felt her shorts being yanked down, and heard Evan grunting as he struggled one-handed with his own clothing.

Chapter 23

It wasn't happening to her. The wet, cold weed-covered rock was soaking someone else's clothes.

Suddenly, there was a thud, Evan's body twitched and was still, his weight pinning her to the rock. She lay paralyzed with terror for what seemed an eternity, a time beyond time.

"Damn you!" Myra spat. Then the weight was gone.

The woman picked Sarah up as though she was a rag doll. "Don't look," Myra said urgently as she held the sweatshirt over Sarah's face.

Myra crooned comfortingly, almost desperately, as she carried Sarah up to the house, lay her on the sofa, covered her with a musty blanket.

Sarah had never been in Myra's house before. It smelled as though the windows were seldom opened to the fresh air. Myra dried Sarah's face with a stale-smelling towel and patted the blood on the back her head, talking softly all the while. The words didn't register in Sarah's mind, only that Myra had never spoken like this before.

After Sarah had stopped shivering, Myra went into the kitchen to make tea. Sarah heard her on the phone with somebody, probably Kate Merlew. From the snatches of conversation she could hear, Myra was saying that Sarah had fallen on the rocks.

She returned with a chipped mug. "Drink some tea. It'll make you feel better."

Sarah had never tasted tea so strong or so heavily sugared, but the hot liquid had a bracing effect. Myra sat on the edge of the sofa and tucked the blanket around Sarah's feet.

"Kate will be here in a few minutes," Myra said, "but we've got to talk first. What Evan tried to do was bad, but it could have been worse."

Myra paused, her words hanging in the air, filling the shadowy room with menace.

Sarah relived the attack. Her stomach heaved, and Myra took the mug, holding Sarah's hand until the moment passed.

"He had to be stopped before he did worse," Myra went on. "You know that, don't you?"

Sarah nodded her head and winced at the pain.

"It was drink made him do it. We mustn't judge him for that. It's best we put it behind us. Keep it a secret between you and me, and God. Remember, 'judgement is mine says the Lord,' so we should let Him hand out judgement. Do you understand?"

Sarah had never thought of Myra as a religious person and the hard-faced woman's references to God had always been pro-fane—until now. She nodded again, winced again.

Myra studied Sarah's face. "We need to make things right, but no good will come if you tell what he tried to do, just trouble for you. People will start looking at you funny, like you was some kind of slut, from no fault of your own. You're not like me. You've got a good life ahead of you. Don't ruin it by dragging this out."

Myra brushed a strand of hair from Sarah's face.

"Put it behind you, like it never happened," Myra said. "You're strong. You're a survivor. I saw that the first day you came over."

Headlights swept across the dimly lit room.

"There's your car," Myra said. "Remember, let God punish the evil doers."

Kate came in, a pale, frightened look on her face. She checked the blood-stained back of Sarah's head and held her face to the light, checking Sarah's eyes.

Kate never questioned her about what had happened. Perhaps she didn't dare, and perhaps it didn't matter, because Sarah left for home the next morning, started college a few weeks later, and never came back to Burnt Cove or Migawoc camp again.

The story took a while to tell, and they sat in silence when she finished, staring out over far-away Squirrel Point.

Wes had scrambled onto the rock, and he lay between them, his head on Sarah's leg. The bandage was grimier now, covered with twigs and bits of dead leaf. A dime-sized bloodstain had seeped through the gauze.

"And you never told anybody?" Oliver said after a while.

"No. I probably should have. At first it was like keeping a promise to Myra. Later on, there just never seemed to be a good time, or a good reason. After all, Evan drowned that night."

Sarah realized she had been absentmindedly scratching Wes' ear while she talked. He gazed up at her, and his soulful brown eyes seemed to be filled with the love, wisdom, and sorrow of the ages.

"I know it's silly, but I've always felt guilty, as though he wouldn't have attacked me if I hadn't been wandering around out there, and he might not have ended up so drunk that he drowned that night." She glanced at him, but Oliver was staring off towards the ledges of Burnt Cove.

"Myra even sent me a note," she said, "saying what happened to Evan wasn't my fault. 'It was drink that did him in,' was the way she put it."

He turned to her. "A note?"

"Myra asked Cathy to send it to me if she died."

"It sounds as though Myra thought you'd feel guilty about what happened."

"Well, she was right."

"There might be another reason for her to think that, too." Oliver said, looking at her pensively. "If Myra knocked Evan out with a rock, or whatever it was, he must have come to with a heck of a headache, on top of being drunk. Why would he take his boat out in that condition? Wouldn't he just sleep it off?"

He went on so gently, so quietly, that she strained to hear, "I hate to suggest this, but maybe Evan was already dead when she took you up to the house. If your face was covered, did you actually see anything?"

She felt exhausted and her stomach churned as it had that afternoon on Myra's couch. "No."

Oliver reached over and touched Sarah's hand where it rested on Wes' back. His fingers felt warm on her skin. "It would explain a lot if Myra had killed Evan and then sank his boat to get rid of the body."

Suddenly, she knew with an awful certainty that he was right, that she had refused to admit the truth to herself all these years.

The hideous, crunching thud of the blow echoed through her brain in all its gruesome clarity. Evan was dead when he collapsed onto her. Why had she refused to see it? Her vision tunneled. Then Oliver was there, his arm around her. She leaned into his shoulder and cried, great heaving sobs.

After a while, she became aware that Wes was licking her hand and whining worriedly. Oliver handed her a handkerchief that smelled faintly of cedar.

She dried her eyes, blew her nose, and returned the soggy piece of cloth. "Myra must have been wondering all along if I knew she had killed him, wondering if I'd turn her in."

"But you didn't."

"I didn't, or wouldn't see what was right in front of my face."

"Happens to all of us. It would help explain why she gave *Owl* to you," Oliver said.

"Yes. Set her house in order."

Oliver looked at her with worried eyes. "The trouble with this theory is, that if she really did kill him, then I don't think Myra was alone," he murmured.

She stared at him.

"Think about it. Myra would have needed to carry Evan's body over those rocks, load it into the dory, row out to Evan's boat, and hoist it in. That's heavy work for one person."

Oliver went on relentlessly. "It isn't easy to run a boat onto the rocks at night all by yourself and get away in one piece, either. Did they have an outboard motor for the dory?"

Sarah shook her head.

"Then she would have had to row a good three miles in the dark to get back home. Unless someone else had a power boat."

Sarah was shivering. There must have been someone else. The same person who decorated her car and ran her off the road. Sam had owned a motorboat. So had Brian Curtis.

"You understand this is all guesswork, and a little far-fetched at that," Oliver said reassuringly. "It's more likely that Myra only knocked him out, like you remembered."

"Don't try to coddle me," Sarah retorted. "She killed him. It made such a crunching noise."

He looked at her for what seemed like a very long time. "You have *got* to take this to the police."

"What will they think, having me come in and report a forty-year-old murder I can't even remember for sure. What can they do? Wouldn't it just stir up trouble without solving anything? I feel like Pearly with the headstone."

"This is *nothing* like Pearly and the headstone, dammit! This is a threat against *you*, probably by a killer."

Oliver and Wes stood in the driveway watching Sarah's piebald and dented Explorer tow *Owl* away. Her story about Evan's death answered some questions, but raised others. If Myra had an accomplice, who could it be? Was this why the Merlews invited Sarah to Maine? Had they known all along that Evan was murdered? Had Myra's accomplice panicked when Sarah turned up in town after all those years, and run her off the road? Was Evan's death tied in with the murders of Myra and Cathy?

Wes sat and leaned against Oliver's leg.

He had underestimated Sarah, Oliver thought ruefully. She hadn't come to Maine just to get away from a failed marriage, the way he had come here to run away from Arlene's death. Sarah had come to confront a trauma that must have scarred much of her life. He stood, feeling both humbled and worried, and stared down the driveway where dust from the Ford's passage hung in the air.

Chapter 24

Saturday morning was sunny and unseasonably warm when Oliver arrived at Pearly's boatyard, where he found *Owl* sitting on her trailer at the top of the launching ramp. Pearly had set up the boat's mast and spars, and Sarah was standing in the cockpit attaching the sail. Pearly looked up from sorting out a tangle of lines.

"Don't just stand there," he said to Oliver, "make yourself useful. Take care of this." He handed Oliver what looked like the jib sheet.

"Where's Eldon?"

"He'll be in this afternoon. I told him to take the morning off, because the cops were on his case again yesterday. They haven't got him in jail, but that's about the best you can say." He handed Oliver another coil of line.

A light breeze from the northwest was blowing puffy clouds across the sky and bringing warm, blossom-scented air from inland. A mixture of sailboats, outboards and lobsterboats were taking advantage of the weather.

At last they had the boat rigged and her sails bent on.

"You got a good pump?" Pearly asked Sarah. "A bucket?"

Sarah held up both from the equipment still littering the cockpit. They had been on Oliver's list as well.

"She'll probably leak like a sieve for a couple of days where she's been stored so long," Pearly warned. "Back her into the water. We'll tie up to the float and see how bad it is."

Sarah climbed over the rail onto the fender, and dropped to the ground.

"You can use one of the moorings out front 'til I get one set up in Burnt Cove." Pearly looked around. "Where's your dinghy?"

Sarah looked flustered, and Oliver noticed a red welt on her neck, a black fly bite, probably from yesterday.

We don't have launch service," Pearly added patiently.

So much for lists, Oliver thought to himself. "I've got an old Puffin she can use," he said hastily.

"I'll pick it up this afternoon," she said, shooting him a grateful look.

Sarah fumbled for the Explorer's keys in her jeans pocket and started towards the Explorer, then stopped.

"What ever happened to Evan Huggard's boat?" she asked.

Pearly, startled by the question, stared for a second. "Evan Huggard's lobsterboat?"

"Myra left me her boats."

Pearly shook his head as though conceding there was no limit to the astonishments of life. "My old man managed to raise her after the accident, but she was too stove up do anything with. Evan must have been going a ton when he hit the ledge. Stem was gone, back broken. It sat in the back of the yard for years. I finally salvaged what I could and burned the rest."

He glanced at Sarah, looking a bit defensive. "It wasn't as though Myra was paying storage or anything, and it used to be legal to burn stuff like that back then."

"What about the dory?" Sarah asked.

"Never found it. We figured Evan was towing it when he went onto the ledge, and it sank or drifted off."

Sarah and Oliver traded glances. If Myra had been alone and rowed the dory back after sinking Evan, then where was it? Surely Myra would have brought it back to the mooring.

"How did they find Evan?" Sarah asked.

"Winn Tupper was out pulling pots, saw his body and some wreckage floating out by Brill ledge."

• • •

Pearly and Oliver stood on the float and watched *Owl* glide out of Pearly's little cove and into the sound, where a gust of wind caught the Herreshoff and heeled it as the boat built up speed. Another cat's paw sent a flurry of ripples racing off across the water, searching for another sail to fill.

"I don't like her being out there all alone," Oliver said.

"Looks like she can sail pretty well," Pearly replied. He looked at Oliver's face. "Heck, the worst that could happen would be to spring a leak, or have a plank-end pop loose, and you checked the fastenings. Beside, there's plenty of boats out there to pick her up."

"Mmm," Oliver said distractedly. Something about Pearly's conversation with Sarah teased the back of his mind, just out of reach. But what? He continued to watch *Owl* gradually shrink into the distance, and his uneasiness grew. Was Myra's gift to Sarah really driven by guilt, or a dying old woman's thank-you for Sarah's years of silence?

Or was Myra manipulating people from beyond the grave? The more Oliver thought the more he worried.

Sarah set out across the sound towards Myra's place. The stretch of water was only a couple of miles wide here, not far, even in her little sailboat.

The wind blowing off the land was erratic and required constant adjustments as *Owl* heeled to a gust one minute and sat almost becalmed the next. Sarah hadn't sailed in many years, so she was rusty, but the old skills quickly returned, and the wind steadied as she got further from shore.

She had almost invited Oliver to come—he looked so hopeful, but the picnic lunch she packed was barely enough for herself. Besides, she wanted to savor her first sail alone.

This was what she had come to Maine for—the feeling of

freedom and peace. That, and the chance to rethink her life. Unfortunately, much of her thinking centered around Myra Huggard. And now Evan.

She still didn't know whether it had been the place or the person that had caused her to confide in Oliver about Evan. Kate, or almost anyone else, would have been a more logical choice. Except that Oliver hadn't been around when Evan died and couldn't have been involved. Someone she could trust.

Sarah realized now that it had been wishful thinking, some kind of psychological block her youthful mind had erected, that made her believe Evan was only unconscious, and had died later in a drunken accident. Oliver had demolished her comfortable illusion as easily as shattering a mirror. Now, the only question was whether Myra had an accomplice, as Oliver suggested, to help dispose of the body on Brill Ledge.

Reality was so awfully slippery. Just when you thought you had a firm hold on it, something happened to knock everything askew. Seeing the reality of Evan's death after all that time had shaken Sarah's self confidence to the core. If she had misread something as obvious as that, what other illusions was she harboring? What about her assumptions around Myra? What about her own marriage? Did she share more of the blame for its failure than she had thought? Was she dismissing Claude's talk about reconciliation unfairly? There were no answers, only a churning fog of uncertainty.

Her mind returned to Evan's death. Oliver could be underestimating Myra's strength. Sarah had been no lightweight, even in her youth, but Myra had picked her up and carried her back to the house effortlessly. Couldn't she have done the rest of it too?

On the other hand, the missing dory, not to mention the incident with the truck, suggested a second person. Someone who had been wondering for years how much Sarah knew, or had actually seen, that afternoon. But who? Sam was a strong possibility. The phone call Myra made that afternoon might have been to ask Sam's help with the body, as well as ask Kate to pick up Sarah. But why would the Merlews invite her to Maine if they thought she could implicate Sam in Evan's death?

What about Brian? He might have been there, helping Sam get an early start on the fall cleanup. Was Brian's attentiveness just an attempt to find out what she knew, and see if she was planning to stir up trouble over Evan's death?

Sarah had always suspected Evan beat his wife, or at least that they fought. The unexplained aches and pains, the occasional bruises, suggested as much. She wasn't an expert on abusive relationships, but Sarah thought if she were in Myra's shoes she would have been glad to see the last of Evan, no matter who did the killing.

A seal popped its head up among the lobster buoys and watched *Owl* glide by. The big, soulful eyes and bristling whiskers reminded her of Wes, and she felt a surge of anger. Sarah had never cared for dogs before, but somehow Wes had won her over. What kind of person would shoot a dog like that?

Sarah resolutely tacked *Owl* away from Squirrel Point. She would go down the other side of the sound and pass through the gut between the mainland and Long Island.

Since Oliver didn't carry a cell phone and didn't approve of them or the ugly towers they spawned, he was forced to stop at the big Irving gas station on Route 1, where he tried Brian from one of the few remaining pay phones. There was no answer, and Oliver guessed that the Realtor was probably out with a client.

He continued south on Route 1, turning onto Merrifield road towards Burnt Cove.

Ten minutes later, he pulled into the Merlew's driveway. Their van was gone, but Kate was cleaning up the flower bed beside the house. A forest of daffodils filled part of the garden with yellows and whites, while green sprouts dotted the rest. Freshly planted violets ran along the front. Kate rose stiffly to her feet as he stopped.

"Oliver, what a pleasant surprise," she said. "Sam is away running some errands, if you're looking for him, and I'm just about to go inside and make some tea if you'd like to join me. Half an hour of kneeling is my limit nowadays."

He sat at the kitchen table while the old woman fussed with tea. She finally joined him at the table.

"What have you been up to this morning?" she asked.

"I was down at Pearly's watching *Owl* go into the water."

"Sarah told us this was the big day. She's been very excited. It was awfully nice of you to help her fix up the boat."

"It was nice of Myra to buy a boat for the camp," Oliver said.

"She got a kick out of the kids, I suppose."

"It was generous of Myra to give the boat to Sarah," he said. "I wonder why Myra asked you to send it down to her last fall."

Kate busily stirred her tea. "Myra knew she didn't have much time."

"Of all the campers who visited Myra over the years, Sarah must have been quite a favorite," Oliver said.

Kate took a careful sip from the steaming cup.

"We knew a few of the girls went over there occasionally," she said. "Looking back, we shouldn't have let them wander around so much, but the world was a safer place in those days, and Myra enjoyed having them—the ones she liked, anyway. She ran the others off."

"And she obviously liked Sarah."

"Sarah was a nice, level-headed little girl as a camper, and a good counselor later on. And she was one of the few girls who visited Myra with any regularity. The rest were put off by her ways."

"It must seem funny to have *Owl* fixed up after all those years. I suppose it brings back a lot of memories."

Kate looked at him warily. "It had been sitting in our barn for years, just taking up space. And Sarah loved *Owl*."

One of those long, rectangular pill boxes with a hinged cover for each day of the week sat on the table. He could see through the translucent plastic that most of the compartments were empty. Kate fiddled with the box, her thumb twitching at Saturday's lid.

"You must have wondered why Myra hung onto the boat, when she could have sold it and gotten some money."

"We put it away in the barn when the camp closed, and forgot about it. She never mentioned *Owl*, so we assumed she'd forgotten about it too, or decided to let us have it."

"She never came over to look at it?"

"Look at *Owl*? G*osh*, no. Why would she?" Kate replied.

"When did you learn something was hidden in the boat?"

Kate put the cup down carefully, holding it in both hands, as though afraid it might escape. "How did you find out?" she said.

"It's the only answer that makes sense."

Chapter 25

"We thought it was all over when Myra died," Kate said. "We figured it was finished and we could forget about her blackmail schemes. And we could forget about what happened to Evan."

She paused. Oliver waited.

"It all happened so quickly," she went on. "Sam was walking along the edge of the archery field, picking things up. You know, the stuff that kids always leave lying around at the end of the season, and Myra came over to check on him, see what he was up to. Myra was like that, especially when she thought somebody might be walking on her property. She was very possessive that way."

Kate's gaze moved from the teacup to the sunlit window.

"They were talking and thought they heard noises, like a struggle, down on the rocks. So they went over to see—"

She looked into Oliver's eyes, searching for understanding.

"Those girls were like our own children, it was like his own daughter was being attacked. If he'd been thinking . . ." Tears ran down Kate's wrinkled cheek. "Anyway, Myra carried Sarah up to the house . . ."

Kate stopped, like a wind-up toy running down.

"And then?" Oliver prompted after a while, afraid of breaking the spell that was leading Kate on.

"Evan kept his dory on a haul-line out front, and Sam loaded Evan into it while Myra was waiting for me to come and pick up

Sarah—it was fairly dark by then. Later, Sam and Myra took the body and rowed out to Evan's boat. Then Myra took the boat out to run it onto the ledge, and Sam followed in our Whaler."

"And the dory?"

"There were some blood stains, and Myra was worried about them, so they weighed it down with an anchor and sank it out beyond the ledge."

Rage colored Kate's face. "Myra's dammed camera. It was while they were rowing Evan out to his boat. It was so dark Sam didn't even realize she had it until the flash went off."

"She took a picture?" Oliver's jaw dropped.

"Four of them, before she was done." The indignation was fresh in spite of the years. "There would have been more, but she only had one flashcube. Sam tried to take the camera away at first, but he was rowing, the dory was tippy, and Myra was pretty strong. Besides, he was in a state of shock. I don't think he knew what he was doing."

"Myra used the pictures to blackmail you? But she was as guilty as Sam."

Kate looked exasperated. "Don't you see what would have happened if it came out that one of our campers was attacked, and there had been a murder? Parents would have pulled their kids out in droves. We'd have been ruined. We were on pins and needles for years, worrying that Sarah would say something."

She took another sip of tea. "On the other hand, when we thought about it, we weren't absolutely sure it was an attack. Sarah wasn't screaming or struggling all that much."

Oliver stared at Kate, appalled. The girl had been slammed onto the rocks, stunned, terrified, the breath knocked out of her, her sweatshirt pulled over her head. How much screaming did Kate expect? He bit back a retort.

Kate was too absorbed in her memories to notice Oliver's expression. "Myra wasn't all that greedy, really. She was just trying to survive. We all have to survive. For years she'd ask for money to help pay the property taxes and we gave it to her, at least until the camp closed. I think the tax assessors tried to go easy on her, but even so, waterfront land like hers isn't cheap."

She looked at Oliver defiantly. "It cost us a lot of money over the years, but we didn't kill her. Why should we? We weren't even giving her anything the last few years."

Oliver nodded, hoping she was telling the truth, hoping she spoke for Sam as well. "When did Myra ask you to send *Owl* down to Sarah?"

"Cathy brought Myra over for a visit last fall, around the middle of October. That's when we learned Sarah was going to get the boat. Myra said she wanted Sarah to have it right away, before she died. I suppose we should have been suspicious, but it never occurred to us that she might have hidden copies of the pictures in *Owl*, of all places."

Kate sighed. "She must have snuck out some night while the boat was still in the water and hid them aboard it, probably the fall Evan died. I suppose it appealed to her twisted sense of humor to hide copies in *Owl*."

"How did you find out they were there?"

"Cathy came over the morning after Myra died. She was in a state, crying and blubbering. She told us Myra had hidden what she called 'blackmail stuff' in the boat. I don't think she knew what the blackmail stuff was. She just felt badly about Myra extorting money from us."

"And that's why you invited Sarah to spend the summer up here?"

"We thought it would be fun to have someone in the apartment, too," she said defensively. "We figured it would be easy to find the pictures once we had the boat in the back yard. It's not as though they're really important any more, with the camp closed and Myra dead. We just wanted to get rid of them and be done with it once and for all."

"Tying up loose ends."

Kate nodded. "The trouble was that Cathy never told us where to look before she disappeared, and then Sarah took *Owl* right up to your place, so we never had time to go over it."

"There are a lot of places to hide a few pictures, even in a small boat," Oliver said, thinking he knew where to look.

"I don't see what Myra expected Sarah to do with the pictures," Oliver added. "Why not just let you have them?"

"She was getting kind of batty, so we assumed that she must have forgotten about them, and gave *Owl* to Sarah as payback for keeping her mouth shut about Evan. Then things started happening to Sarah."

"You think Cathy told somebody else about the pictures?" Oliver said, a knot tightening in his stomach.

"What else could it be? As I said, I don't think Cathy knew what they were, just 'blackmail stuff,' Myra had used against us."

Kate leaned forward earnestly, putting her hand on Oliver's arm. "We should have seen it coming. First, she blackmailed us for money, then she tried to influence Sam's vote on the planning board. That's when we shut her down.

"Knowing Myra, we should have realized right away that there was something fishy about her giving *Owl* to Sarah, and done something about it. It's our fault all these things are happening to the poor girl."

He had been a fool, Oliver thought. The burglar in his yard had been trying to steal *Owl*, not Cathy's boat.

"But why did Myra dump all this on Sarah?"

"I suppose she didn't trust us, because of the planning board. And Cathy was just a kid."

"Still, why Sarah?"

"Partly because Myra knew she could keep a secret, because she had with Evan, but it was more than that."

Kate leaned back in her chair with a sigh. "You have to understand how it is. Gosh, we've lived her fifty-two years, and I still struggle with it."

She looked at him sadly. "I suppose prejudice is part of human nature, the need to have someone else, someone different, to look down on. The Migawoc kids were good children, but most of them were from well-to-do families. They thought of Myra as a backwoods hick, who didn't even have running water, and kept her chickens in the living room during the winter. They made fun of Myra and her ways, and naturally she resented that."

"And Sarah respected Myra." Oliver said.

Kate nodded. "She was the only girl who tried to understand Myra and not make fun of her."

"And so Myra respected Sarah."

"It works both ways, doesn't it? To Myra, Sarah was someone she could trust who knew the bigger world that Myra didn't."

"Someone who would know how to carry on Myra's crusade, whatever it was," Oliver said.

Kate nodded, and her voice turned brisk. "When we learned about Sarah being run off the road, we began to worry that someone was out to get her because of the pictures. By then, we just wanted her out of here, out of harm's way, regardless of the pictures. Two people had been killed already, and someone was obviously after her."

The Honda's engine had noisy tappets, and they ticked like a chorus of impatient clocks as Oliver sat at the end of Kate's driveway and tried to make sense out of what he'd heard. Oliver figured it was a safe bet that *Owl*'s flotation tank held photographs implicating Sam in Evan's murder. That was probably what Cathy had wanted to talk to Sarah about.

But how incriminating could the photographs be? Shots of Sam rowing, with Evan draped over the rail? "Smile for Mother Huggard while I get a nice picture of you and dear old Evan?" No, her accomplice wouldn't have posed while Myra flashed away. He would have tried to hide his face, and Evan's body, from the lens.

And what did the pictures, assuming they hadn't rotted away, have to do with anything now? Oliver could see Kate and Sam paying Myra to keep the whiff of scandal from destroying Migawoc, regardless of what the photos actually showed. But as Kate said, the camp was closed now and Myra was dead, so the pictures weren't a threat any more. They couldn't force Sam to do anything, like alter his vote on the planning board, so why did someone still want them?

On the other hand, in the world of secrets that Myra had created, it wasn't what you knew, but what you thought you knew, that was dangerous. And somebody could easily think the "blackmail stuff" in *Owl* had enough leverage to influence Sam's vote, and therefore was important enough to try stealing the boat, and take a gun along in the process.

It was also possible that Myra had hidden something more dangerous than photos of Sam and Evan in *Owl*, something that involved Sarah and put her life in danger. There was no telling what else might be stashed away in *Owl*'s flotation tank.

If there was something else, and the Merlews weren't involved, then who was? Who else knew that something incriminating was hidden in *Owl*? Who else might Cathy confide in besides the Merlews? He couldn't think of anyone except Eldon, who was notoriously bad at keeping secrets, or Ziggy, who had been away for the winter.

There was still the question of why anyone who wanted to get their hands on something hidden in *Owl* would arrange to run Sarah off the road and possibly kill her.

Unless she and *Owl* were both threats. If that was true, the killer might be trying to eliminate whatever was hidden in the boat's flotation tank, and in the recesses of Sarah's mind.

What about the headstone? If it fit into the puzzle somewhere, Oliver suspected that Sarah had some ideas that she hadn't shared. He headed north to Route 1, and Pearly's establishment, trying not to think about the fact that somewhere out there, Sarah and *Owl* were alone. Two targets together at last.

Chapter 26

G entle, sandy beaches are scarce along this part of the Maine coast, where a grain of sand can be the size of a dump truck, and sailors live in dread of the crispy-crunch of granite against their tender keels.

But Maine is a place of contrasts in many things, and the northern end of Long Island offered a small beach tucked in among the ledges. Sarah admired the yellow sand as *Owl* glided by just offshore. She remembered when the Migawoc girls had picnicked here. Sarah would take a bunch of campers in *Owl*, while Sam ferried the rest in the Boston Whaler, a scow-like craft that was said to be unsinkable.

The Whaler, with its big Evinrude engine, was fast even when loaded down with screaming kids. As a result, Sam would wait until *Owl* was at least half way across Kwiguigam Sound before he started out with his group, soon passing Sarah's crew amid traded catcalls and insults.

A young couple had pulled their outboard onto the beach and were unloading picnic supplies. They waved as she glided by.

Sarah had brought a picnic lunch and she toyed with the idea of anchoring off the beach and swimming ashore. A hand in the icy water quickly put an end to that plan. Oliver had mentioned loaning her a Puffin to use. She had no idea what a Puffin was, other than an odd-looking bird that nested on some of the offshore islands. She hoped that Oliver's version would be small enough to tow behind *Owl*.

She looked across the sound to where the Vincent's house and the Borofsky's nearly completed mansion covered Migawoc's old playing fields. A new pier jutted out from the shore in front of the Borofsky's house. An unbroken procession of houses ran from Burnt Cove all the way to Myra's land.

Sarah had read that the Maine coastline was some 3500 miles long, counting its myriad coves and inlets. Forty years ago, she wouldn't have thought it possible for all that shoreline to be cut up into house lots, but that seemed to just what was happening.

The thought reminded her of high school biology class experiments with Petri dishes. One placed a minute speck of bacteria onto the pristine medium and watched it grow, spreading faster and faster, an avalanche of grayish-green that didn't stop until the dish was covered.

The northwest wind that had brought Sarah this far turned fickle as it faded away, and soon *Owl* was completely becalmed, rolling listlessly in the swell.

Sarah unzipped her soft-sided picnic cooler and extracted lunch, a container of yogurt, carton of iced tea, a small bag of potato chips, and a bunch of grapes.

The yogurt was a concession to the bathroom scales. It hadn't occurred to her that she might have two eligible men squiring her around, though she suspected that Oliver was more interested in *Owl* than in her. At any rate, she hadn't thought such attention was something that happened to fifties-something women.

While she ate, Sarah pulled her purse from the bottom of the canvas carryall and looked again at Myra's worn snapshots

The William Tell picture was on top.

Myra had probably heard them laughing and came out to investigate just as Marlee Sue posed herself against the big oak tree near the water's edge and held the stray arrow to her stomach, pretending to be skewered.

One of Marlee Sue's more delightful gifts in those days was the ability to roll one eyeball upward and the other one down while wiggling her eyebrows like Groucho Marks, and she performed this feat for the camera, draping her tongue out of the corner of her mouth in a hideous grimace. Myra captured the tableau with her Brownie camera, called them bloodthirsty brats, and stalked off. The photo didn't do credit to Marlee Sue's facial gymnastics.

Why did Myra send her these pictures? She must have had a reason. Myra had a reason for everything she did, though she usually expected you to figure out what it was. Sarah suspected this photo was saved because it showed the disputed oak tree on the Borofsky's property line. She still didn't understand why the old woman wanted her to have the photo, or the apparently worthless deed, for that matter. Why would Sarah need to know where Myra's property lines were? Cathy probably could have answered Sarah's questions if she hadn't died first. Is that what had gotten the girl killed? Sarah wondered if she was Myra's backup, in case something happened to Cathy. Not a comforting thought.

Sarah got out the Heathen Brats picture.

It had been taken the summer before the William Tell photo. Myra must have followed the two girls as they worked their way along the wooded shoreline. In any event, she came upon them just as Sarah discovered a tall splinter of rock set into the ground a few yards back from the shore. It was almost as high as she was.

"You two ain't got yourselves lost again, have you?" Myra never let them forget their first visit.

"We're just exploring," Marlee Sue replied defensively. Strictly speaking, they weren't supposed to go away from camp unsupervised, and Myra knew it.

"Don't mess with that monument," Myra snapped. Sarah was leaning against the stone pillar, and she decided this frowsty woman in the grimy cotton-print house dress wasn't so smart. Sarah had been to Bunker Hill many times, so she knew what a real monument looked like, and this little piece of rock wasn't even close. She willfully wrapped her arms around the stone in a bear hug and tried to wiggle it, but the granite post was too firmly buried.

Taking her cue from Sarah, Marlee Sue flopped to the ground, her head lolling to one side while she did the famous Eyeball Roll.

The camera angle made it look as though Sarah was about to topple the stone onto Marlee Sue.

Myra's glare sobered them. "Get back to camp, you heathen brats," she growled.

The two girls ran off through the woods laughing, flapping their arms, and yelling "heathen brats" at each other, oblivious to Myra's withering stare.

If the William Tell picture was meant to show Myra's property line with the Borofskys, the Heathen Brats picture must show the line on the other side. Grinshnell was the name Brian had mentioned. There was still the Missing Ring photo of Sarah digging potatoes. She had no idea what it meant.

A light breeze from the south began to ripple the glassy water, and *Owl*'s sail slowly filled.

Sarah set a course across the sound towards the Borofsky's pier.

Oliver found Pearly and Eldon seated in front of the boat shed on a pair of battered metal chairs liberated from the office. They had just finished lunch.

Eldon was feeling uncooperative.

"I've been telling the cops all that stuff for days," he grumbled. "Why should I go over it again for you?"

Oliver pulled up a sawhorse and sat on it, facing Eldon. "Because I think whoever killed Cathy is after Sarah too."

"Why's that?"

"That's what I'm trying to figure out," Oliver replied, more patiently than he felt. "Did Cathy and Myra talk about any of Myra's snapshots?"

Eldon looked perplexed, then intrigued. "The cops never asked me anything like that. But yeah, Myra had a big cardboard box full of them. She took a helluva lot of pictures. She and Cath used to look through them."

"What were they pictures of?"

"I don't know—the usual stuff," Eldon said, thinking. "She had a lot of shots of the place, the vegetable garden, a tree that blew down in some storm or other, a deer in the back yard, big snow storms, that kind of stuff. There were a bunch of pictures of Burnt Cove, and she had pictures of people too, but I don't know who they were."

The same south wind that was carrying Sarah to the far side of the sound caressed Oliver's cheek as he sat and wondered what any of this meant.

"When was the last time she had them out?" he asked, groping for some clue that would make sense of it all.

"Who knows?" Eldon grumbled, then thought for a moment. "Wait. Last fall, just before Thanksgiving. I remember because it was colder than hell, and I was filling up Myra's wood box. They had a bunch of pictures out on the kitchen table."

"Did you look at any of them?"

"Not much. She had so many, they kind of blurred together after a while. Anyhow, they're all burned up now."

"Not all," Oliver replied.

Eldon's eyes widened as understanding dawned. "Oh no, you mean Myra was blackmailing someone with them?"

"Mmm," Oliver said. Eldon was quick. Plus, he knew Myra altogether too well.

"And that's why someone killed her?" Eldon went on, "And they burned her house to get rid of the evidence?"

"Maybe, but I think there's more to it than that. I just don't know what," Oliver said.

Eldon scowled. "Why Cathy?"

"I'm not sure, except that Cathy knew where Myra had hidden some of the photos," Oliver said carefully. He wondered just how much it was safe to say.

Pearly groaned. "In the Herreshoff?"

Oliver nodded reluctantly.

"You mean we're going to have to cut open another *dern* flotation tank?"

"Flotation tank?" Eldon glared at them. "I don't like it when you guys go off like this."

"Cathy may have gotten into trouble over the headstone," Oliver said hurriedly.

"She had nothing to do with the headstone," Eldon said, leaning forward in his chair and looking stubborn. "Like I told the cops, Cath would never have dug up a gravestone. That's desecration."

"Eldon, Eldon," Pearly scolded, "we found it sealed up in Cathy's boat."

"So? Maybe I hid it in there."

Oliver turned on the young man. "For goshsake, if you really want to find out who killed Cathy, you've got to cut out the crap!"

"What about you? You guys have been giving me and the cops a load of crap, leaving that stone lying around the shop."

"I was just trying to keep you out of trouble," Pearly said. "Not that it did any good."

Like an enraged bull, Eldon exhaled a great blast of air that stirred the dust at his feet. "Well I sure as he. didn't put the d thing in Cathy's boat, and I don't know who did. I didn't even know there was a headstone until the cops started asking about it."

"Cathy never mentioned it?" Oliver said.

"I just said so, didn't I? What's so hard about all this, anyway? Find the other half of the stone and you'll find the killer."

"I don't know why that makes sense," Oliver said, "but I'm afraid you're right."

Chapter 27

Pearly's office was a small room, attached like an afterthought to the side of the boat shed. A computer and oversized printer took up most of the desk that filled one wall, while a torn Naugahyde sofa dominated the opposite wall. Oliver slouched in Pearly's gray metal swivel chair and pecked at the phone.

Brian didn't answer. Perhaps he was with a customer and had turned off his cell phone. Perhaps he was out in his boat, beyond range of his cell phone. Perhaps Sam was out shopping. Perhaps they were both innocent of murdering Myra and Cathy.

Or perhaps not. After all, Sam had killed Evan. Though, when Oliver thought about it, Kate hadn't actually said that in so many words.

He was getting nowhere. Even the photographs, the "blackmail stuff," was a dead end. What had he missed?

The chair creaked as Oliver turned to stare out the window. What made Myra tick, anyway? He had thought of her as a survivor, the last of her kind, a dying old woman clinging with ruthless stubbornness to a dying way of life. He had seen something noble in Myra's struggle, in spite of her curmudgeonly, even illicit, ways. Yes, she had extorted money from people in her effort to hang on, but that was a matter of survival.

Myra had extorted money from the Borofskys and the Merlews, and there could have been others for all he knew. Apparently, she persuaded Cathy to dig up a headstone. Had Myra gone too far with the headstone, and gotten herself killed?

What fatal mistake had she made in the last few weeks of her life? Despite her failing mind, Myra was still hard-headed enough to know the end was near, and she appeared to have been putting her affairs in order. Updating her will and getting rid of her car seemed to indicate that, even if there was an ulterior motive to her Yuletide generosity. What might she have done that turned out to be deadly?

Sarah had shown him another side of Myra, an unexpected altruism. *Owl* had been a generous gift to Migawoc's girls—an anonymous gift to a bunch of kids who treated her with scorn. Myra may have hated the wealth the camp represented, but she must have cared about the individual girls, a few of them at least. How had she resolved those conflicting emotions?

A flash of movement caught Oliver's eye as a red Porsche wheeled into Pearly's yard. A figure emerged from the vehicle. From Sarah's description, this must be her ex-husband. What was his name? Whatever he was called, the leisure-suited individual sauntering towards Pearly's shop looked too flashy and pleased with himself for Oliver's taste.

His mind drifted back to Sarah's conversation with Pearly that morning. He jerked himself upright in the chair, realizing what he'd missed before. Myra did have a weapon at her disposal, one that would appeal to her idiosyncratic view of justice. But what had gone wrong? Had she put her trust in the wrong person, a mistake that had cost her and Cathy their lives?

The morning's land-warmed, northerly breeze was a fond memory as a cool south wind sped *Owl* across the sound. A big yawl with all her sails spread, and a huge multicolored spinnaker pulling her along, crossed Sarah's bow. Five people in the cockpit waved as the yawl raced by. Close to shore, one of the ubiquitous fleet of lobsterboats was working a line of traps. Further out, a speedboat tossed spray as it bounced off the wave-tops. Ahead, the Borofsky's new pier jutted into the sound, reaching out to her, luring her in.

Sarah put on her windbreaker against the cool air. A light haze added a translucent glow to the sunlight, heralding fog. Fog was a fact of life along the Maine coast, especially in early summer when the seawater was still cold. Guessing that it would be thick in two or three hours, she decided to keep her excursion short.

Eventually, the Borofsky's pier would have a float on the end, but at the moment there was just the L-shaped structure, a row of pilings with decking on top. A ladder was bolted to one of the pilings and Sarah brought *Owl* up to the shelter inside the L. She made a clumsy landing, for she wasn't used to this manoeuver, and nearly scraped her precious shear plank. She tied *Owl* to a piling with the end of the anchor line, lowered and furled the sails.

Being Saturday, the Borofsky's nearly-finished house was de-serted as Sarah stepped onto the lawn. Most of the trees had been cleared between the house and the water, leaving only a few large, well-pruned specimens. The building was three stories high, with turrets and balconies in what Sarah could only describe as a Neo-Victorian-Castle style. To her left, the manicured, freshly sodded lawn abruptly collided with Myra's tangle of fir and spruce.

A huge oak tree stood at the edge of the lawn, up against Myra's scrubby woods. Sarah pulled out the William Tell picture that showed Marlee Sue pretending to be skewered against the tree. The shape of the branches appeared the same as the photograph, though bigger after forty years, and the curved limb that arched over the Borofsky's new lawn looked the same. Sarah moved until the other trees lined up with the picture. This was where Myra had stood, and the oak was the one where Marlee Sue had posed with the arrow.

Sarah walked to the tree and found a newly driven iron rod decorated with orange paint just beyond it. Along the shore, closer to the Borofsky's mansion, was another big oak. That must be the one Myra had claimed to be her property line, as there weren't any other possible candidates. The old woman had certainly laid claim to a hefty portion of her new neighbor's land.

But if Myra believed that she owned to the farther tree, then what was the purpose of the William Tell picture, which showed the actual property line? Was it her way of saying that she knew her claim was false and she had cynically blackmailed the Borofskys with her old deed?

Sarah wondered if she had guessed wrong about Myra's motives entirely, and the photo had nothing to do with the boundary line after all. Maybe these photos were simply a random assortment from Myra's collection and had no special significance, in which case Sarah was wasting her time.

She walked along Myra's shore front in search of the monument, site of the Heathen Brats picture. Surely that was a marker for the other property line.

She found the monument at the edge of an area of freshly cut brush and saplings. It was wrapped with orange tape. Okay, she thought to herself, the two snapshots showed on the ground what the old deed said on paper. But so what?

Of course, the Heathen Brats picture might be showing more than just a property line. She took the photo out of her pocket and studied it. A twin-trunked pine tree showed in the picture, just behind the monument, between it and the water's edge.

The same tree stood off to the left of the stone as Sarah faced the water. Had the monument been moved after all? If so, why move it to the right and give Myra another ten feet of land? Unless, she though bleakly, Brian had moved it so Myra's land would have enough frontage to split into two lots. But surely a surveyor would catch that kind of tampering.

It only took a moment for Sarah to realize her mistake. Myra must have stood off at an angle in order to get both girls into the picture. Sarah shifted over until monument and tree lined up, moving onto Grinshnell's land in the process. She looked around. If Myra stood here, then Marlee Sue must have been lying right in front of where Sarah was now standing.

Someone, probably Grinshnell, had been cutting saplings and young trees to open up a view of the water and had piled brush willy-nilly around the area in waist-high tangles. One of those tangles covered the spot where Marlee Sue had been lying, making her

Halloween face, when Myra clicked the shutter. Sarah tried to poke through the brush pile, but couldn't see anything through the maze of branches. She wondered if Oliver's radar device would work here.

Had Myra been trying to extort money from Grinshnell as well as Borovsky? If so, what did the Missing Ring picture mean? She would explore the vegetable garden next.

Sarah started towards Myra's burnt-out house, visualizing the Missing Ring photo in her mind's eye: The smell of freshly turned earth, Myra bemoaning her lost ring, Sarah digging in the sun-warmed dirt. A sudden realization came to her just as she tripped and fell over something hidden under the layer of pine needles, leaves, and twigs. She sat on the ground nursing her bruised shin and discovered that she had fallen over a headstone, or more accurately, half a headstone.

She kneeled and brushed away the debris. The stone's top edge had a break that looked like a match to the piece hidden in Cathy's boat.

That was why the location of Gerhard Burndt's grave had been kept a secret all those years—it was located on Squirrel Point in the middle of Huggard land, not on Oak Hill in Burndt territory. The grave site had probably been neglected and then forgotten after the Huggards bought up the land.

Sarah couldn't see any inscription. It must be on the other side. She heaved the stone upright and stared at the dead leaves and pine needles underneath where it had lain.

She had her proof. The freshness of the leaves and pine needles meant the stone must have been dug up this spring and moved well after Cathy took the top half away last fall.

A voice shot Sarah to her feet. "I was afraid you'd figure it out sooner or later."

Chapter 28

"The old woman where my wife is staying said she's here," Claude announced, indicating Sarah's Explorer with a casual wave of his hand.

"I didn't know you were still married," Oliver said from the doorway.

"Semantics." Claude did a double-take and stared, frowning, at the SUV's tortured bodywork. "Is she around?"

"She's out sailing her boat," Oliver replied. Pearly, still seated in his chair, watched the unfolding scene like a nightclub patron anticipating an especially lively floor show.

Claude tore his gaze from the battered Explorer, glared at Oliver, and advanced menacingly. "Are you the one who is messing around with that old wreck of hers?"

Oliver's dislike of Claude was growing fast.

"Nothing wrong with that boat," Pearly said stoutly. Claude stopped, glanced at Pearly and Eldon, and regained his composure.

"When's she coming back?" he demanded.

Eldon wandered over to the Porsche and stared down at it.

"She packed a lunch," Oliver said.

"But it's foggy out there. She could get lost," Claude protested.

"That's nothing," Pearly said from the comfort of his chair. "Wait 'til later."

"I think I saw her heading across the sound about an hour ago," Eldon said.

"Isn't she required to file a sail plan or something before she goes out?" Claude asked.

"This isn't an airport," Oliver pointed out.

Eldon circled Claude's car, peering at it as though the Porsche was a cherry bon-bon.

"But you don't even know where she is." Claude's head rotated back and forth as he tried to split his attention between Eldon, Oliver, and Pearly.

"We don't know where a lot of people are," Pearly said reasonably.

Eldon leaned over and peered through the driver-side window. His hand brushed the door handle and it looked for a second as though he was going to try and get inside. Oliver figured his curious young friend would need to tear the roof off to succeed.

"She never answers her cell," Claude complained distractedly as Eldon kneeled and looked underneath the vehicle.

"Maybe she keeps it turned off," Oliver said with approval.

Claude looked aghast. "Why would she do that?"

"To get some peace and quiet?" Pearly suggested.

The Porsche creaked faintly as Eldon lifted the back end off the ground to get a better view underneath.

"Hey—"

"You pay much for this?" Eldon inquired, putting the car back on all four wheels.

"She'll be back before dark," Oliver said.

"I can't wait here forever. I've got to get back to Freeport."

Eldon sauntered around to the Porsche's front end, leaned over, and rested his hand thoughtfully on the hood.

"Look," Claude said hurriedly, "just give her a message. She asked me to check on this Grinshnell character. Tell her the guy claims to be a financial adviser, but he's a phoney, strictly a small-time operator. He doesn't own that land any more than I do. He and a lawyer up here named Kincaid are fronting for somebody. I haven't found out who yet."

"How did you learn all that?" Oliver asked.

"I used to be a tax attorney for the IRS. I know how to get answers out of people."

Oliver stared out at the sound. "Clever," he murmured.

"Can you remember all that?" Claude said, anxious to leave.

"We certainly can," Pearly assured him.

"Darn ," Oliver said. "I should have seen it before. That's why Cathy was killed."

Eldon abandoned his study of Teutonic automotive design. "You think Kincaid killed Cathy?"

Pearly lurched to his feet. "Whoa—"

"No, I don't," Oliver said "But I suspect Kincaid is passing information to Grinshnell, and whoever does own the land." He turned to Eldon. "When was the last time Myra saw Kincaid?"

"Cathy took her over right after I got the car running, beginning of the year. I figured Myra was going after Borofsky some more."

"I think it was more than that," Oliver said.

"Like what?"

"We need to know who really owns that land."

"I bet Kincaid can tell us," Eldon said grimly. "Let's pay him a little visit."

"Not so fast, for gosh sake," Pearly protested.

Oliver, who had been looking preoccupied, turned to Claude. "You didn't mention Sarah to Grinshnell, did you?"

"Of course," he said proudly. "I told him to watch his step with my wife because I was keeping an eye on him."

"That's bad." Oliver said as he frowned at the haze creeping up the sound. "I knew she shouldn't be out there alone."

"Come on," Pearly said, "there are boats all over the place."

"She might have been heading towards Myra's place last time I saw her," Eldon said. "Could have landed at Borofsky's pier."

Oliver turned to Pearly. "Got a boat I can borrow?"

"You mean she's in *danger?*" Claude said, appalled. "Where are you going? I'll take my car."

• • •

"Why you scared me half to death," Sarah exclaimed.

"Sorry, but I couldn't resist watching you play detective. Once I saw those photos, I knew it was just a matter of time."

"You discovered the gravestone when Myra took the Heathen Brats picture. That's what you were lying on. That's why the Halloween face."

"I remembered the gravestone when I bought the land."

"So this really is your land," Sarah said, her heart pounding.

"I had Kincaid set it up so Grinshnell would look like the owner. Kincaid called him a straw man, or something like that."

"You didn't want Myra to know it was yours?"

"You always were her favorite," Marlee Sue complained. "She hated me, so I figured it would cause less trouble if she didn't know I was her new neighbor. You know how she plagued Borofsky. Just imagine what she would have done to me."

It was true. Myra would have taken special pleasure in thwarting Marlee Sue, just as Marlee Sue had taken pleasure in trying to put one over on Myra. It had been almost a game between the two of them. A game based on mutual dislike. She looked down at the broken piece of stone. "Is it really Gerhard Burndt?"

Marlee Sue gave a dismissive shrug. "Who cares? It was in the way, so I moved it onto Myra's land this spring before I had the brush cleared. The witch took the top half last fall."

"What did Myra and Cathy want?"

Marlee Sue glanced at the brush pile as though Gerhard Burndt might rise up out of the ground. "They told you about it?"

"I expect Cathy was going to, but she died first," Sarah said, trying to figure out how to talk her way out of the trap she had stumbled into.

"Myra and her darn pictures. She sent Grinshnell photos of the stone lying there last fall, and said she'd notify the town about the grave if he didn't pay her off. On top of that, the crazy old bat wanted him to make a 'proper graveyard' for Gerhard Burndt."

Marlee Sue waved at the brush pile. "Can you believe it? Nobody would pay good money for a piece of land with a graveyard on the front lawn. I had to move the stone. What else could I do?"

Sarah felt a surge of protectiveness towards Burnt Cove's founding father. "I can't believe you would—"

"For josh sake, Irish, I wouldn't kill her over that. She would have died in a few months anyhow, and I could have gotten a court order to move the grave. The trouble was, she wouldn't leave well enough alone. The gravestone wasn't enough for her. She wouldn't stop at that. The hag went too darn far."

"But she was just trying to protect Gerhard's—"

"You know perfectly well there was more to it than that. You must have wondered why Myra kept that wreck of a boat all those years, and why she decided to give it to you last fall."

"Myra kept *Owl* for sentimental reasons," Sarah said.

Marlee Sue gave a short, bitter laugh. "She didn't have a sentimental bone in her body. The only reason Myra would keep *Owl* is if it was worth more for her to hang onto the boat than to sell it. And the only thing that would make the boat valuable was if she hid something in there. Something she wanted you to have."

"How did you dream all that up?" Sarah said, trying to keep her voice light.

"I started to wonder as soon as you told me *Owl* belonged to Myra and not the Merlews. At first I thought she was just getting rid of it, like her car, but she gave *Owl* away before she redid the will. What made it so special? Why give it to you?"

Marlee Sue gave Sarah a triumphant look. "Then I realized nobody would go looking for something hidden in the boat, except maybe you, after you thought about those pictures."

It almost made sense, when Marlee Sue put it that way. *Owl* might seem like an ideal hiding place to an eccentric old woman who didn't believe in banks or safe-deposit boxes. Who would think to look there? Cathy probably knew, and would have told her if she had lived.

On the other hand, *Owl* had been in the Merlew's barn, and out of Myra's reach, for years. "What in the world would Myra hide?" Sarah said.

Marlee Sue eyed her suspiciously. "I bet Myra used the fool boat to hide all kinds of stuff. The question is where?"

"Maybe the flotation tank." It was one place Sarah hadn't taken apart in her repair work.

"Flotation tank?"

Sarah reminded herself that her companion thought of boats as though they were cars—something that one drove without understanding the innards. She had always ridden in the Whaler.

"The front end is sealed off to keep the boat afloat if it swamps," Sarah explained.

"How would you get into it?"

"There's a bronze cover on the deck. You can unscrew it to pump out the tank. The hole is pretty small though. I'm not sure you could even get your hand through."

"You never found any papers in there?"

"Papers? I never looked. Besides, they'd get wet."

"Nice try, Irish. If you didn't find anything, then why were you checking up on Grinshnell? What clued you in?"

Sarah swore under her breath. Claude was an idiot. No, she was an idiot for calling him and thinking her ex could be discrete.

"Your expression in the Heathen Brats picture for starters," Sarah replied. "The rest was guesswork, putting pieces together. Myra's snapshots and her old deed got me thinking about the property lines. She had plagued Borofsky, why not Grinshnell? And he supposedly bought the land about the same time you moved here.

"On top of that, it seemed like an awfully big coincidence to encounter you on the streets of Belfast like that," Sarah went on. "I began to wonder if you knew Kincaid, and he told you I was coming, so you arranged to bump into me and find out what I was up to. He handles a lot of real estate transactions around here, and you knew right where is office is."

"That's all it took? I suppose we could look around *Owl*." Marlee Sue said thoughtfully, fumbling under her sweatshirt. "On the other hand, it might be safer if you and *Owl* were lost at sea. Your boat-builder friend probably missed a bunch of rotten planks."

Sarah figured that it was just a .22, but the pistol in Marlee Sue's hand looked more than lethal enough.

"You don't need that. Let's just talk it over," Sarah said, knowing the gun had been inevitable as soon has her old friend appeared.

"Yes, I think we should have a little talk," Marlee Sue replied comfortably.

Chapter 29

"This is the craziest wild goose chase I've been on yet," Pearly bellowed above the earsplitting racket of *Roaring Whore*'s engine.

They had taken Hoot Howlett's lobsterboat. "I've been working on it," Eldon explained. "Chance to give her a test run. Besides, he borrowed my truck without telling me."

"You should have picked something faster," Oliver said. "What's-his-face will beat us yet."

"What are you talking about? It's thirty miles by car," Pearly said. "He'd have to go a hundred miles an hour."

"Maybe I should get one of those little buggies," Eldon said as he opened up the throttle some more.

"What would you do with it?" Pearly demanded.

"Why would someone go after Sarah today?" Eldon said.

"Because that fool in the little red car spilled the beans to Grinshnell," Pearly replied.

"It's also a chance to get Sarah alone with *Owl*," Oliver said, "and I think she knows where Gerhard Burndt is buried."

Marlee Sue grinned impishly. "Would you like a tour of Borofsky's palace? I did some spying and saw where Roy Tupper hides the key."

"I'd like to see you get rid of that gun."

Marlee Sue motioned with the weapon for Sarah to move.

They crossed in front of Myra's cellar hole, while Sarah tried to convince herself that this was really just her friend's idea of a joke. How could Marlee Sue wave a gun at her, and act as though they were out for an afternoon stroll?

As they came onto the Borofsky's lawn, Marlee Sue pointed up to the roof looming overhead.

"See the skylights? They have a full-size swimming pool up there on the third floor."

The landscaping was still in progress around the foundation, and Marlee Sue rummaged through a small pile of dirt beside the front door, all the while keeping the gun pointed at Sarah's chest. She picked out a rock, eyed Sarah, and made as though to throw it through a window.

"The old key-hidden-in-a-phony-rock trick? You're kidding," Sarah said, trying to sound as casual as Marlee Sue. What was it about keys and the Tupper clan? Eldon, with his trick shingle and his truck keys above the sun visor, and now Roy's plastic rock.

Sarah wished her companion wasn't having so much fun.

"Whatever works," Marlee Sue said. She swung open the front door with a flourish, and the aroma of fresh paint surged out. "Wait until you see the front hall."

The space soared to the third floor. A gigantic staircase swept up to a columned second-floor landing that circled the upper entryway, and a huge chandelier hung down from above. The place was like a vast, ante-bellum southern mansion. No wonder Marlee Sue was so enthusiastic.

"Just look at it." Marlee Sue's rapturous gaze circled the hall. "The guest wing is up there to the right, and the owner's living quarters are to the left."

Sarah thought about her granny flat up the road. Her entire apartment would fit in the cloak room here.

"Just imagine a formal ball, with everyone in their best. Or a wedding, with bride's maids tossing flowers from the balcony while the happy couple descends the staircase," Marlee Sue gushed.

The hall was still being painted, and a metal scaffold, with two extension ladders beside it, ran up past the second floor balcony, to the ceiling far above.

"My Word of God," Sarah said in awe.

"They're going to paint murals on the ceiling, like the Sistine Chapel, and floor is going to be imported Italian marble tile. Better shut the door, Irish, we don't want riff-raff wandering in. Wait until you see the upstairs."

Marlee Sue sashayed up the staircase behind Sarah like a southern belle in a formal gown. A well-armed southern belle. "Your going to love the master suite."

The upstairs balcony was littered with canvas drop cloths and assorted gallon-cans of paint. Babbling like a realtor on amphetamines, her captor ushered Sarah down a hallway.

The master bedroom had a picture window that looked over the lawn and down to the water. Sarah could see *Owl*, still tied up, waiting patiently. With a sinking feeling, she realized the boat, nestled inside the corner of the pier, would be virtually impossible to see from the water, especially with fog dimming the sound.

"It'll be pretty thick in a couple of hours," Marlee Sue said.

"How did you get here?" Sarah asked.

"You said this was launching day, so I brought my boat. Easier to follow you. The Vincents seemed to be away, so I tied up to their dock."

"You killed Evan, didn't you?"

The gun wavered slightly as Marlee Sue took a half-step back. "You knew all along? I was never sure if you did."

"It dawned on me a few minutes ago, just before you turned up. Remember when we were reminiscing over lunch in Belfast, and you saw the Missing Ring picture? You talked about how Myra told me she had lost her ring and fooled me into digging her potatoes. But that was my last summer, long after the chicken beheadings, and you never went over to Myra's after that. You must have been following me and eavesdropping, in order to know what Myra said."

"Those were the good old days, Irish. I used to play spy and follow you, see how close I could get without being spotted. You two never knew I was there."

"You've been spying on me almost since I got here," Sarah said. "I thought I caught a glimpse of somebody when I was at Myra's the other day. You must have followed me down from Belfast after we had lunch."

"I've burned up a bunch of vacation time playing spy, just like the old days at Migawoc," Marlee Sue said. "It's been a ball."

"And you were there spying on me when Evan—"

"I saw him jump you, so I snuck up behind him and crunched his head with a rock," Marlee Sue said. "Then I heard Myra and Sam coming, and took off.

"Myra never had the guts to kill him, even though I bet she wanted to a hundred times. She thought I was a wimp, but she couldn't even stop Evan from beating her up. I saved your life."

Marlee Sue seemed lost in her memories. Sarah wondered if she could grab the gun.

"But you never let on, not even the next day," Sarah said. "You never gave any sign that you—"

"—felt guilty? Why should I? I did the world a favor."

"Who paid Hoot to run me off the road?"

"Grinshnell. I figured nobody would know him. I didn't want to hurt you, Irish. I just wanted to make the boat disappear, scare you off, and get rid of the evidence that way."

"You painted my car to scare me off?"

"I thought 'slut' was a nice touch. I was giving you one last chance to get out of Dodge, but then you traced me through Grinshnell, and I knew you'd figure out the rest."

"But what did Myra—"

"Myra, Myra, Myra! Is that all you can say?" Sweat beaded Marlee Sue's forehead. The gun trembled in her fingers as she struggled for composure.

"I didn't actually kill her, if that makes you feel any better. I didn't have to. I got the fire going in the kitchen and she fell down the stairs all by herself, without my having to do anything at all. She was pretty much dead when I found her. Lord, that dump went up like a torch. I barely got out of there myself.

Marlee Sue's nose wrinkled. "*Phew*, that house was a pigsty. It stank to high heaven in there. The place was so filthy my feet kept sticking to the floor.

"The *hag* loved ruining people's lives. She just never let up. It's her fault I had to kill Cathy."

"Why leave her car at Pearly's place?"

"Eldon was her boyfriend, right? I figured if Cathy's car was left right in front of the door he'd move it and leave his prints on the wheel for the cops to play with."

"Talk about being an innocent." Marlee Sue did her Eyeball Roll. "I called Cathy up and told her I had some information about Myra's death and to meet me at the boatyard after dark. Over she came, fat dumb and happy. And she didn't even know me. I drove her over to Myra's and shot her. She was such a sap, never suspected a thing 'til we got there and I pulled the gun. Ker-splash, down the well she went."

Roaring Whore's engine sputtered, then resumed its din.

"Just a hiccup," Eldon assured them.

The engine stopped.

"*Dang*," Eldon and Pearly said in unison.

"Now what?" Oliver demanded.

"*Drat*," Eldon said, "Guess I didn't get all the crud out of the fuel line. Hoot doesn't take care of his boat worth a damn." He hauled open the engine hatch.

"So clean it out and let's go," Pearly said.

"Not that simple. This old pig won't self-prime. We'll have to bleed the air out once I clean the line."

"What the hell does that mean?" Pearly said.

"Diesels can be a hassle, and we're going to be here a while." Eldon opened a tool box and turned to Oliver. "Hit the starter when I tell you, and keep her cranking 'til I say stop."

"We could have sailed there quicker," Oliver grumbled.

"I hope the battery ain't flat," Eldon said.

Her jailer locked Sarah inside what looked like a big, walk-in storage closet. The room was completely bare.

Sarah guessed that Marlee Sue had gone to get her boat, so she could tow *Owl* out to deep water and sink the boat and its owner. It would take Marlee Sue a few minutes to bring her boat over from the Vincent's dock, and there was no rush, since she'd have to wait until it was dark, or foggy enough so they wouldn't be seen.

Sarah looked around her prison. A small window, up against the high ceiling, provided some light. Sarah chinned herself on the sill, but the window wasn't designed to open and besides, the drop was at least thirty feet to the ground.

The room hadn't been painted yet, and Sarah could see the seams between the panels of drywall. She remembered watching her father put up drywall once. The stuff was about a half-inch thick, plaster sandwiched between two layers of thin cardboard.

Marlee Sue hadn't noticed the new pen knife in the pocket of Sarah's jeans. The knife had a two-inch blade, and another about half that length. There was also a nail file, and an odd device with a screwdriver end and a serrated side.

She opened the bigger blade and cut a Sarah-sized rectangle in the drywall's cardboard surface, between the wall studs. The plaster underneath was harder stuff. She ran the knife around the rectangle again, pushing as hard as she dared. Round and round she went, up one side, across the top, down the other side, across the bottom, slowly working through the plaster.

She contemplated her unsavory predicament. If Marlee Sue's motive wasn't the headstone, then what was it?

Sarah had thought she knew the "why" of the murders, namely Gerhard's grave, but not the "who." Now that she knew the "who," she no longer knew the "why." It was irritating.

The knife broke.

Sarah swore as she opened the small blade. She would have to be more careful and go more slowly. The slowly part was hard when she could imagine her captor returning at any moment. It was tempting to just kick a hole in the wall, but that would be hard on her sneakered feet. It would also be noisy, and she wasn't sure that Marlee Sue was still out of the house.

The piece finally came loose, and she found herself staring at the back side of the wall to the adjoining room. How long had it taken to get this far, ten minutes?

Sarah went to work on the next piece of drywall. She hoped Marlee Sue wasn't trudging up the stairs for her. She hoped the room she was cutting into wasn't locked. She wondered if Marlee Sue had any idea how to sink *Owl*, though Sarah figured her childhood friend would kill her before starting to chop holes in the boat.

Chapter 30

A boat is seldom completely still in the water, even when it's not moving forward, and *Roaring Whore* rolled uncomfortably in the gentle swell. The starter ground away more and more slowly as Eldon ministered to the engine and the battery tired. The smell of diesel fuel was gradually masking the aroma of overripe bait.

A puff of smoke belched from the exhaust stack.

"She's blowing smoke," Pearly said, hopefully.

"Good sign," Eldon agreed. "We're getting there."

"Get there faster," Oliver said. A morbid fear gnawed at him, a fear that Sarah might die simply because she was in the wrong place at the wrong time. Like Arlene. If only he had figured out what Myra was up to sooner.

The rectangle of drywall fell away, and Sarah crawled through the opening on her hands and knees to find herself in total darkness. It must be a small closet—too small to warrant a window. She stood up, reached out her hand, and took a cautious step towards what she hoped would be the opposite wall, and, with luck, a door. The far wall was only an arm's length away, a tiny space by Borofsky standards. She groped along it and tripped over a pile of things that clattered loudly.

Sarah froze. Had Marlee Sue heard? She bent over, and her fingers located a group of metal objects that felt like pipe fittings. And also a propane torch.

Stepping around this assortment, she shuffled a bit further, found a door and opened it.

The Borofskys spared no expense when it came to the master bath. The room was still being painted, and the plumbing fixtures hadn't been installed yet, with the exception of a whirlpool bath that looked like a small swimming pool made of reddish marble. It sat regally in front of the window, and Sarah wondered if the Borofskys were planning on curtains. Glancing out, she could see *Owl* still tied to the pier, with a powerboat alongside. The far shore was barely a smudge. It wouldn't be long before Marlee Sue came for her. How could she get out of the house without her jailer spotting her?

Perhaps a distraction.

Sarah opened the windows and piled one of the canvas dropcloths that covered the floor into the whirlpool bath.

A portable kerosene heater, looking like a miniature jet engine on wheels, was parked against one wall. A five-gallon fuel can sat nearby. Sarah removed the can's top and dumped the container on top of the drop cloth in the tub, tossing in a can of paint for good measure. She hoped the drain was closed, but the controls, looking like something out of a NASA space shuttle, were beyond her.

The closet's propane torch had one of those nifty self-lighting clickers. In it went, blazing away.

A gratifying "Whump," and a cloud of black smoke erupted from the tub. There must be a fire alarm system, and with luck, it was already hooked up and calling for help. A passerby might even see smoke billowing out the windows and raise the alarm. At the very least, Marlee Sue, an orderly soul, might be sufficiently distracted by a flaming bathtub to give Sarah a chance to escape.

Sarah backed away from the growing flames and wondered briefly if she'd overdone it.

"What the HELL!"

Marlee Sue had turned up too soon. She stood frozen in the

closet doorway, the gun hanging at her side as she gaped in horror at the oily billows of smoke.

"Cassidy, you're dead."

Sarah darted through the nearest door into the hall.

To the left, the hall led towards the Grand Staircase. No place to hide there.

Sarah sprinted in the other direction. The hallway seemed to stretch on forever, a veritable shooting gallery with her as the target. An archway opened off to the right, and Sarah ducked through it as a whiplash crack echoed down the hall. A bit of wall exploded near her head. Marlee Sue had been good at archery in camp, and the skill had obviously carried over to firearms.

The room looked like a conservatory of some sort. The outside wall was all glass, stretching two stories up to the roof. The Borofskys obviously liked plenty of headroom.

"You're DEAD MEAT, Cassidy!" Marlee Sue bellowed.

There was a balcony half way up the inner wall, probably for the third-floor swimming pool.

Sarah ran towards another archway at the end of the room, darting under a ladder. She pulled it off balance as she went by.

The ladder fell with a crash as Sarah reached the archway. Perhaps it would slow down her pursuer.

The archway opened onto a stairwell, one flight leading up, the other down. Sarah headed down, taking the steps two at a time with a reckless abandon she hadn't displayed since she was a kid racing through the woods at Camp Migawoc. Of course, Marlee Sue hadn't been chasing her with a gun in those days.

Clouds of black smoke erupted from *Roaring Whore*'s exhaust stack, filling the air with a welcome din.

"See? That didn't take long," Eldon shouted happily above the engine's deafening noise.

Eldon's repair had taken ten minutes. Ten minutes that had

seemed like an eternity to Oliver. The shore was barely visible through the fog.

"Does the radar show anything?" Oliver bellowed. He wished Hoot had spent some money for a quieter muffler.

"Kind of," Eldon replied.

Oliver fumed as he stood on tiptoe, trying to see around Eldon's massive back. "Any other boats around?"

Eldon fiddled with the knobs. "Looks like a boat way out. Too much clutter to be sure about anything close to shore."

"Let's head for Borofsky's pier first," Oliver said.

The boat's stern squatted as she built up speed and began to climb her bow wave.

Sarah hit the landing and skidded to a stop, panting for breath. Above, she could hear the gun-toting Amazon in hot pursuit. To the right was a large open space—probably the dining room. No cover there, and no time to find a way outside.

Sarah darted through a door to the left and slammed it behind her. She was in a pantry of some sort, with a counter running along one wall. She heaved three heavy boxes off the counter and shoved them against the door. A pair of plaster buckets followed. Her impromptu barricade had only taken a few seconds to construct, but Marlee Sue was already thundering down the last steps.

A swinging door at the far end of the pantry led to a hotel-sized kitchen. Sarah tossed a saw horse at the door as it flopped shut behind her.

Marlee Sue grunted as she slammed into the outer door.

Across the kitchen was a doorway leading to the patio. Sarah sprinted to it, but the door was secured with a deadbolt lock that required a key, and there was no key hanging on a convenient nail. Darn these security-conscious Russians.

Her escape to the outside blocked, Sarah looked around. There were too many big, open spaces in this house, and they would be fatal if Marlee Sue caught up with her.

Sarah ran back across the kitchen to a pair of doors and opened the first. Cellar stairs. She grabbed one of the ubiquitous cans of paint and rolled it down the steps, leaving the door ajar.

"You're TOAST, Cassidy!" Marlee Sue yelled from the other room. She was hurling herself against Sarah's barricade, and it sounded as though she had almost worked her way through.

Sarah wished she had a floor plan of the place. The adjacent doorway opened into a room with a pair of laundry sinks that looked like they were being used by the workmen to wash up. Nearby was hookup for a clothes washer. She opened the valve and was greeted by a torrent of water. A utility cord was draped over the counter. Most unsafe. Sarah dropped the cord end into the growing puddle and ran to the far end of the room, where a short hallway led to more stairs. She headed up them as silently as possible.

"I know you're down there, Irish. Come on out and let's talk about this." Marlee Sue's voice was muffled as it reached Sarah. She must be aiming her blandishments down the cellar stairs. It wouldn't take long for her to realize that was a false trail.

This part of the house was the servant's quarters. A doorway led from the servant's wing to the main upstairs hall, and Sarah sprinted down the hall towards the Grand Staircase. With luck she could get out the front while Marlee Sue was sweet-talking the cellar. Gasping for breath from all the running, she reached the balcony and swerved towards the stairs.

It was the scaffold, reaching from the entrance hall past the balcony, that saved her life.

With a vicious whine, a bullet ricocheted off the scaffold's metal leg inches from her ear.

Sarah caught a glimpse of Marlee Sue, and ducked out of sight against the wall. Her pulse pounded in her ears, but fear gave way to fury. She was *not* going to be hunted down without a fight.

A pile of paint cans sat on a tarp against the wall. Sarah hurled one over the balcony towards the foot of the staircase. A second and a third can followed.

The trouble was, she couldn't see what effect they were having.

Sarah grabbed another can and ventured a peek. The missiles had burst as they hit, splattering the floor and Marlee Sue with a pale taupe color. Marlee Sue had swerved to the far side of the hallway to avoid the barrage and try to get a glimpse of Sarah. They spotted each other at the same instant, and Marlee Sue snapped off a shot as Sarah launched her paint can and ducked out of sight.

"YOU BITCH!" thundered through the hall.

Gathering up another paint can, Sarah risked quick look. Marlee Sue was swearing and holding her left leg. The last missile must have hit the floor just short, bounced, and struck her shin.

The next can ricocheted off Marlee Sue's right hip and sent her sprawling. The gun skittered across the floor.

Sarah reached for another can, realized there were none left. Marlee Sue had lurched to her feet, was hobbling towards the gun. There was no way Sarah could get to the weapon first.

A plank, extra flooring for the scaffold, lay against the wall. Sarah snatched it up and used it like a battering ram to charge one of the extension ladders leaning against the railing.

The ladder sprang away from the balcony, scythed towards Marlee Sue—and hung up on the chandelier with a clang. A hailstorm of glass pendants rattled to the floor.

Marlee Sue looked up at the wildly gyrating chandelier, slipped in a puddle of electric blue paint and fell headlong.

Sarah wondered what they were going to paint that color as she backed up with her trusty plank and charged the second ladder, sending it after the first.

She swore as it too hung up on the chandelier.

Marlee Sue was on her feet again and reaching for the gun, her face and front a startling shade of blue.

Sarah tried to throw the plank like a javelin, but it was too heavy and fell a few feet short with a crash that made Marlee Sue jump and skid in the wet paint. She recovered, picked up the gun.

The chandelier pulled from the ceiling with a groan.

Marlee Sue looked up again. She had just enough time to leap clear before the tangled ruin crashed down.

But she didn't move. Instead, she raised the pistol and fired.

Sarah ducked or fell, she wasn't sure which, as the wreckage hit the floor.

Sarah staggered to her feet as the Grand Entrance door crashed open, and Eldon Tupper, one of the few people who could make the Borofsky's front hall look cramped, hurtled onto the scene.

He spotted Marlee Sue under the wreckage and bent over her. Glass beads from the chandelier lay on and about the body like diamonds. Well " he said as he stood up.

Oliver sprinted through the door, nearly colliding with Eldon in his rush. "How is she?"

"Dead as a haddock," Eldon replied. His face was gray and he looked wobbly on his feet.

"Where's Sarah?" Oliver said.

Chapter 31

Sarah stumbled down the Grand Staircase, leaning on the bannister for support. The steps were steeper than she remembered, and she seemed to be having trouble controlling her feet.

Oliver looked at her worriedly. "Are you all right?"

"I think so." She couldn't stop shivering.

Eldon looked down at the body. "Was she the one?"

Sarah nodded, tore her eyes away from Marlee Sue, clambered around the wreckage.

Oliver held out a hand to steady her.

"What happened to your arm?" he said.

She looked and saw blood dribbling down her left hand onto the floor. "I must have scratched it."

Eldon came over. "Let me take a look. I trained as an EMT."

"I was a nurse," Sarah countered.

"Then you know I'm an expert at this," Eldon replied, gently lifting the arm. The blood-soaked sleeve of her sweatshirt had two holes in it. "Looks like you've been shot." He produced a large bandanna handkerchief and tied it expertly around her arm, sweatshirt and all. "That should stop the bleeding 'til the EMTs get here."

Eldon reached for his cell phone.

"It's just a scratch. Everything works fine," Sarah said.

There was a screech of tires on the cobbled driveway, and Claude appeared at the door.

"How the he. did you get here so fast?" Pearly said, still panting after his run up from the pier.

Claude's face was flushed with excitement. "There's a cop-car about a mile behind me."

"Good. Flag it down," Eldon said. "Tell them we need an ambulance."

But Claude stood frozen, spellbound by the scene of destruction. A trail of black smoke rolled like an oily serpent down the Grand Staircase.

He turned to his ex-wife with a look of awe and said, "*Dang*, this is way worse the dining room suite thing."

The wail of sirens echoed through the hall.

"For *Pete's* sake don't say anything about *Owl*," Oliver said urgently as a State Police cruiser pulled up to the door.

"May I ask why not, Mister Law-and-Order?" Sarah retorted.

"Because Sam—"

"Considering all this," Claude interrupted, waving his arm expansively, "you'd be well advised not to tell them *anything* without a good criminal lawyer present. They're going to think you're the queen of doom as it is."

The next few hours passed in a blur of police, firemen, EMT's, and technicians, all adding to Sarah's feeling of unreality.

The bullet had carved a deep furrow across her upper arm, and the EMT's grumbled disapprovingly when she refused a trip to the hospital.

"I'll come down later and have it stitched up," she insisted firmly. They applied a bandage, put her arm in a sling, and made her sign a form. They warned her about the potential dangers of her stubbornness, to no avail. Sarah was convinced Oliver knew something about this affair that she didn't—an unacceptable situation.

Sarah gave the police an abbreviated version of what had happened: she came across the other half of Gerhard Burndt's gravestone, found it had been moved illegally, and encountered Marlee

Sue, who took her at gun-point to the Borofsky's house, locked her in a room, and tried to shoot her when she escaped. Beyond that she pleaded shock, confusion, and ignorance—all of which were true.

Claude, no doubt mindful of his various traffic violations, behaved with uncharacteristic tact, assuring the police in his capacity as an attorney that Sarah was trustworthy and would be in the next morning to make a formal statement.

Pearly stepped in too. "She needs to have that arm patched up and get some rest. I'll see that she comes down tomorrow to make a statement." He had been sheriff in town for years, and his nephew, Charlie Howes, was sheriff now, so Pearly's words carried weight.

It was late afternoon before they were free to leave. With the excitement over, Claude suddenly remembered Lurlene, loose in Freeport with his credit cards. Burdened with a pricey assortment of traffic citations, he beat a retreat under the watchful eye of the law.

The remaining four walked slowly down to the dock through a cool, fog-laden mist.

"We'll tow *Owl* and what's-her-name's boat back," Pearly said. He looked at Sarah's pallor in a fatherly way. "Then you're going to the hospital, young lady."

"I need to look at something first," Sarah said.

"Maybe two things," Oliver said.

They peered into *Owl*'s flotation tank with the help of a flash-light from *Roaring Whore*.

"I don't see anything," Sarah said.

"Myra wouldn't just drop it into the bilge anyway," Oliver said. "Feel around under the deck."

"I can't quite get my hand in there. The hole is too small. Exactly what am I looking for anyway?" she demanded peevishly.

"Photographs," Eldon said.

"Shouldn't the police be doing this?"

"No," her three companions said in unison.

Sarah seethed. Was she the only one who didn't know what was going on? She ran her fingers as far as they could reach and felt a lump of plastic.

"Wait. There's something there. I can feel a thumb tack."

She removed a packet sealed in layers of plastic wrap.

"Is that all?" Oliver said.

Sarah glared at him venomously. "What the he, else did you expect me to find?"

"What is it?" Pearly said.

"They're Eldon's photographs," Sarah snarled as she began to unwrap the bundle.

"We can look at those later," Oliver said. The urgency in his voice made her pause and jam the package into her pocket.

"That's all there is," she repeated, glaring at Oliver again.

"That makes sense," Oliver said, in a way that further infuriated her. "We need to look in your car."

"Let's go then," Eldon replied, heading for *Roaring Whore.*

"Her Studebaker," Oliver said.

Sarah was exhausted and her arm was throbbing by the time they had walked the short distance to Myra's backyard.

Eldon jerked at the car door. "It's locked," he said.

"The keys are probably in there," Pearly said, cocking a thumb at the cellar hole. "Nobody has been in the car for years anyway. Look at the trees all grown up around it."

"Not on the passenger's side," Oliver pointed out.

He was right; the saplings on that side had been trimmed.

"There's a hatchet over the lintel inside the chicken-coop door," Sarah said. "Myra kept it there to encourage the hens."

They stared at her.

"It's my car, break the damn window," she commanded.

Eldon swatted the passenger-side glass with the hatchet and unlocked the door.

They were greeted with the smell of mold and rotting fabric. The headliner had come unglued at the front end, and it hung down from the dome-light like a malodorous curtain, blocking off the rear seat.

Sarah leaned in and pushed the headliner aside. The back seat was covered with a rotting assortment of men's clothing, while the floor area contained enough empty beer bottles to send Ziggy into an ecstatic fit. Evan's legacy, she supposed.

"Nothing back there," she said.

"Try the glove compartment," Oliver suggested.

The smell made her gag and the sling on her left arm kept Sarah from slipping into the seat. She gestured to Oliver, who got into the car.

The glove box was locked, but Eldon and the hatchet dealt with that problem.

Inside, was an envelope with Myra's name on it, with a return address of "C. Jamison Kincaid, Esq., Attorney at Law."

"That's why the Missing Ring picture," Sarah mused.

"The what?" Oliver said.

"One of Myra's pictures showed me digging potatoes, with a saucepan full of them on the hood of the Studebaker. At first I thought the photo was about Marlee Sue, but Myra was showing me where this was hidden—insurance in case Cathy wasn't around to tell me something was in here."

Oliver gave her a blank look, shrugged, and opened the envelope while Sarah looked over his shoulder.

"That's just another copy of Myra's will," she said. This was a total waste of time. She was tired and sore. And it was starting to rain.

"Kincaid already gave me one," she snapped as Oliver scanned through the document.

"Does your copy leave the house and land to Doctor Ziegfield Follies Breener? Or if he should predecease her, the Spruce Cone Camp? No wonder your friend killed Myra. Imagine what Ziggy's Zoo would do to the value of her land."

"What are you talking about?" Sarah demanded.

Oliver looked up at her, his face a mask of confusion. "I thought you knew. You found the key—the connection between Grinshnell, Kincaid, and what's-her-name—"

"Marlee Sue. And this—"

"Is the *real* will," Oliver said. "Kincaid must have told your friend about it."

"I bet she went ballistic," Sarah said. "She must have bribed Kincaid to make a phoney version with Cara as the beneficiary."

"Cara was probably the beneficiary in the original will anyway," Oliver replied.

Sarah nodded. "They must have planned to burn down Myra's house after she died to destroy the real will."

"Kincaid knew Myra didn't believe in banks," Oliver said, "so he probably figured she would keep her copy in a drawer somewhere, leaving him with the only other copy in the office safe."

"It helped that he was executer," Sarah added. "I suppose there was a chance that someone would discover the change, but not such a big one, considering Myra's secretiveness. A little fraud to protect the neighborhood."

"His civic duty, even," Eldon said sarcastically.

"So why kill anyone?" Pearly said.

"Marlee Sue had two worries," Oliver replied. "First was the possibility of the real will turning up. The bigger worry was that Myra might sign her house over to Ziggy, instead of selling it, if she had to go into a nursing home."

"There's no way Myra would have sold her place to pay for a nursing home," Eldon said.

"Exactly" Oliver replied. "You said Cathy took Myra to see Kincaid around New Year? My guess is that Myra went to have him transfer ownership to Ziggy before she had to go into a nursing home."

"Just like she gave her car to Cathy," Sarah said. "And Kincaid stalled her long enough to tell Marlee Sue."

"He'd have had an excuse," Oliver said, "since nobody knows where Ziggy spends the winter."

"I can see her killing Myra to keep the place from going to Ziggy, but why Cathy?" Eldon said.

"Killing Myra raised the ante," Sarah said. "If Kincaid had just been caught swapping the will, he could have blamed it on a clerical error—the wrong revision pulled out of the file. But things got a lot more serious once Marlee Sue killed Myra. Marlee Sue couldn't take a chance that Cathy knew Myra was about to sign her land over to Ziggy."

"Cathy might have gotten suspicious and had the cops look into Kincaid, Marlee Sue, and the fire," Oliver added.

"I suppose Ziggy would have been toast too if he wasn't away, " Pearly said.

"I talked to Ziggy," Sarah said, "and he had no idea about the will. He was assuming the place would be sold."

"It must have been a question of which was worse for Marlee Sue, anyway: Ziggy, or a camp for troubled teens," Oliver said.

"I bet Myra learned about the Spruce Cone Center from Cath," Eldon said, his eyes glittering.

Sarah rested her hand on Eldon's arm, partly in sympathy, and partly to prop herself up. "When I told Marlee Sue that *Owl* belonged to Myra, she started wondering if the old lady had hidden her copy of the will in the boat instead of the house, and had given *Owl* to me figuring I'd find it."

"I wondered about that too," Oliver said. "What threw me off was that Myra didn't have access to *Owl* and couldn't hide the new will in there. Then I realized Marlee Sue probably didn't know that *Owl* had been in the Merlew's barn for years, so to her the boat would seem like a logical hiding place."

"So she went to your place to steal *Owl*," Sarah added.

"What about the headstone?" Pearly asked.

"Your turn," Oliver said to Sarah.

"The location of Gerhard's grave was lost for all those years because it wasn't in the Oak Hill cemetery, but on Huggard land, and of course the two families didn't get along. Marlee Sue found the grave when we were kids, and remembered, but I didn't realize it until today when I thought about Myra's photos."

Sarah paused to collect her thoughts. "Myra knew where Gerhard was buried, but she was too secretive to tell anyone until Marlee Sue had her land surveyed. That's when Myra sent Cathy over to take pictures and get the headstone so they'd have proof they knew where the grave was, and they quarreled over what to do with it. I expect Cathy wanted to go to the town, but Myra wanted to blackmail Grinshnell."

Oliver turned to Eldon. "Remember the photos you saw Myra and Cathy looking at last November? I bet Myra was showing Cathy where to find the headstone, and she got the top half, but the ground had frozen and the bottom was buried too deep for her to dig up."

"Marlee Sue dug it up this spring and dumped it on Myra's land to get it out of the way," Sarah added.

Eldon beamed at Oliver. "See? I told you, 'Find the rest of the headstone and you'll find the killer.' Maybe I should be a detective."

Pearly replied, "Sam Spade, the rhinoceros."

Chapter 32

The sun slid below the rooftops of Burnt Cove, taking with it both the daylight, and the wind. *Owl* drifted across the glassy water towards her mooring where Oliver's Puffin, a graceful eight-foot dinghy dubbed *Puff* by Sarah, waited patiently.

The three figures were still as they watched the shrinking distance to the mooring. Wes scanned the water from his perch at the forward end of the cockpit, with Oliver beside him, and Sarah at the helm. The sling was gone, but she still needed help at times.

They crept up to the mooring at last and put everything away, performing their individual tasks in a well practiced routine that had become almost like a dance. Reluctant to go ashore, they sat in the cockpit in silence, as though afraid to shatter the evening quiet, and watched night descend.

Sarah had moved to Oliver's left, out of respect for her tender arm. Wes, sitting beside her, sniffed the bandage, more out of habit than concern, and lay down with his head on her leg. She absent-mindedly scratched his ears, careful of the partially bald spot on his neck.

They sat close in the cool air, and Oliver's arm, resting on the cockpit rail, felt warm across her shoulders.

"I just learned that the Borofskys have decided not to press charges after all," she said. "It was good of them, considering what I did to their house."

Oliver glanced at Sarah. This was the first time she had mentioned the subject since Marlee Sue's death.

"I think Claude threatened them somehow," she added.

"Are Cara and her son still contesting the will?"

Sarah nodded. "She's pretty upset. After all, the original will did leave the place to her."

"Are those Boston lawyers your ex came up with going to be able to uphold the new will?"

"They seem to think so, but it may take some time."

"Lucky for Myra you're here to protect her interests."

"I still don't see why she picked on me. She knew a teen-age girl for six summers."

"You and Myra shared more than you imagine. Think about all those visits with her. You kept going back when the other kids didn't bother. And there was Evan's murder."

"Yes, there was Evan's murder."

They sat in silence for a while, hearing only the occasional lap of water against *Owl's* hull.

"I hear they caught Kincaid trying to sneak out of the country with the firm's escrow account," Oliver said finally, "and he's singing like a bird."

"A vulture," she replied. "According to him, the plan was to produce the phony will if Marlee Sue's neighborhood improvement bonfire succeeded in destroying Myra's copy. Otherwise, he'd go with the real will."

"The cautious legal mind at work."

"Marlee Sue had promised him ten percent of the profit on her land for his services. He swears the plan was for Marlee Sue to burn the house *after* Myra was dead and gone, and he had no idea anybody would be killed, even after Myra asked him to sign the land over to Ziggy," she said.

"He's trying to plea-bargain his way out of a murder charge?"

"In return for admitting to the phony will." She turned to look at Oliver's profile as he surveyed the harbor. "Now it's your turn.

How did you know Myra had left her land to Ziggy?"

"I didn't know, exactly. I just couldn't see Myra leaving her place to Cara, who had left Burnt Cove years ago and obviously didn't care about the property. It didn't seem like something Myra would do—forty years ago, maybe, but not today. It didn't fit."

Oliver paused. "Remember when we were launching *Owl*, and you asked Pearly about Evan's boats? Something bothered me at the time, but I was so focused on the missing dory that it took a while to realize it wasn't the boats that were bothering me, but the will itself.

"If Cara was the beneficiary in the original will, then what did Myra actually change when she rewrote it last November? Leaving her boats, plural, to you must have been in the old will, because she'd already given you *Owl* and didn't have any boats. That meant the only real change was adding you and Cathy as beneficiaries."

Sarah nodded. "And why rewrite the whole thing just for that, when a codicil would have been enough. And if they did rewrite the whole thing, why not put in the correct number of boats?"

"Yes. And that got me wondering if Myra *had* made a bigger change, in addition to adding you and Cathy—like making someone else the beneficiary instead of Cara. All Kincaid had to do was a little cutting and pasting to add you and Cathy to the original will and pretend it was the new one."

Sarah nodded. "Myra wanted to save part of Squirrel Point the way she remembered it, and who better than Ziggy?"

"Holding onto the last of her roots."

Sarah sighed. "I suppose that's what the boundary-line photos and the old deed were really about—showing us what was important to her: her roots, the way of life she grew up with, that the place had originally been in her family. Burndt land."

"Her Home Place."

"Anyway, Myra won, as long as Ziggy can afford it," she said.

"He's going to lease part of the place to the Spruce Cone Center, and they'll pay the taxes. It's an ideal spot for them, and there's more land than he needs for his livestock, even after he gets a bunch more chickens and pigs."

"You like the idea of Ziggy's Zoo, and a horde of noisy teens moving into the middle of all those mansions, don't you?"

"I love it," he said placidly. "It's the Maine way."

"I'm sure Ziggy will be true to Myra's memory."

"He sees it as a crusade against the powers of darkness, a battle against Mammon and the evils of materialism, a chance to balance the space-time continuum, and an opportunity to bring harmony to the mists of Myra's karma."

"You're making fun of Ziggy," she said accusingly.

"Gosh no, I'm quoting him, and Ziggy is just the man for the job."

After a while, Oliver said, "What about the photos?"

"The moisture had gotten to them. There was nothing to see." Sarah felt his gaze on her. "I burned them."

"I don't think Myra cared about the photos anyway; she just wanted you to have the boat," he said. "Still, Sam was an accessory to murder, and I bet he knew that Marlee Sue killed Evan."

"Even so, I burned them. Kate and Sam were relieved."

"It might have been better if they hadn't protected her."

"She was only eighteen. Who could have guessed what was better?"

"It wasn't just about Myra's will, was it?" he said.

"Marlee Sue couldn't stand the idea that Myra looked down on her. It was a mutual hatred."

"So, Myra was both the victim and the villain," he said.

"Yes, and more." Sarah gave him a peck on the cheek. "She was a such a strong person, a force of nature. More than we realized, she left her mark on both Marlee Sue and me."

Shore-front windows sent out beams of light that lay on the still water like arthritic fingers reaching towards them.

"For better or worse, Myra was part of our lives," she added, "never far away. And in the end she drew us back."